ILLUSIONS OF PRESENCE

ILLUSIONS OF PRESENCE

Lost Christmas Ghost Stories

Edited by
JOHNNY MAINS

THE BRITISH LIBRARY

This collection first published in 2025 by
The British Library
96 Euston Road
London NW1 2DB
bl.uk

1 3 5 7 9 10 8 6 4 2

Selection, introduction and notes © 2025 Johnny Mains
Volume copyright © 2025 The British Library Board

'"The Malignant Thing"' reproduced by kind permission of the Estate of Vincent Cornier.

Every effort has been made to trace copyright holders and to obtain their permission for the use of copyright material. The publisher apologises for any errors or omissions and would be pleased to be notified of any corrections to be incorporated in reprints or future editions.

Represented in the EU by Authorised Rep Compliance Ltd., Ground Floor,
71 Lower Baggot Street, Dublin, D02 P593, Ireland. arccompliance.com

Cataloguing in Publication Data
A catalogue record for this publication is available from the British Library

ISBN 978 0 7123 5593 3
e-ISBN 978 0 7123 6894 0

Frontispiece illustration by Harry O'Connor from '"The Malignant Thing"', *The Mackay Daily Mercury*, 22 December 1928.
Illustration on page 235 from "The Haunted Vicarage", *Manilla Express*, 24 December 1903.
Cover design by Mauricio Villamayor with illustration by Mag Ruhig.
Text design and typesetting by Tetragon, London.
Printed in Scotland by Bell & Bain, Ltd.

CONTENTS

Introduction   vii
A Note from the Publisher   xix

In Deadly Peril
   John Pendleton   3

The Ghost at the Red Farm
   Mabel Collins   21

The Child Who Had Everything But
   John Kendrick Bangs   37

The Haunted Vicarage
   Emeric Hulme-Beaman   51

Nights of Terror
   E. J. Thomas   77

The Ghost of Moor Hall
   M. E. Murray   93

"The Malignant Thing"
   Vincent Cornier   103

The Spectre Bridegroom
   Mrs. Gordon Smythies   111

A Christmas Ghost Story
   Bessie May Tobin-Montague   129

The Ghost of Appledore Pool
   J. Y. T.   145

The Lady of the Mistletoe
   Mary Hall   161

The Ghost of Cheldon Court
    May Wynne   171

That Terrible Dentist
    Anonymous   183

Claus and Defect
    William J. Koen   201

Shadows of Evil
    Anonymous   213

Acknowledgements   233

INTRODUCTION
Christmas Ghosts and the Stories They've Told

> The children sit before the fire,
> And shout with glee as the sparks rise higher
> Up from the crackling wood;
> And half in pleasure, half in fear,
> They gather together of ghosts to hear
>
> "CHRISTMAS EVE"—ANONYMOUS (1893)

I'm not really a fan of Christmas. There, I said it. *Bah Humbug.*

But as much as I hate the tinsel and the expense and the insanity that goes with the season (always have done), there's one part of Christmas I *adore*. It's reading ghost stories at Christmas. Extra bonus points are given if the stories are about families coming together on Christmas Eve or Christmas Night, and a ghost proceeds to haunt them and scare them silly, or a Victorian granny has got the children round and then proceeds to tell the wee ones a tale that'll turn their hair as white as hers.

I've been reading all sorts of spooky stories on Christmas Eve and I've done so for the past twenty years. I normally start at 10PM (after I've done the last of the wrapping), maybe one year I'll re-read *A Christmas Carol* or, for non-Christmas-themed reading, I'll find some M. R. James, E. Nesbit or E. G. Swain and let the stories do their trick. By the time I next look at the clock, it's 1AM on Christmas morning. Relieved that I've not been kidnapped by festive wraiths, I'll take myself off to bed. And on Christmas Night, I'll do a little bit more reading, but I'll stick on a horror film to drone away in the background. For me, it's a great tradition which respects those

INTRODUCTION

authors who made Christmas so deliciously spooky.* And the best thing about ghost stories? They're a part of the season that anyone can enjoy, whether they celebrate the festival or not.

As this is a special book, you deserve a special introduction. I have mulled (but no wine, please, I don't drink) over how I should approach it. Should it be a history of the ghost story at Christmas, or should it be about the art of finding lost stories? I didn't really want to do the former as that's been done to death (and the ghosts are there to prove it!), and if you want to find that kind of thing, type the phrase "ghost stories at Christmas" into your preferred search-engine of choice and you'll see that a lot has been written on the subject. So, what I thought I'd do is put together some chronological observations about the Christmas ghost story—how it's been used by others in many interesting ways—and write about some bits that you might be familiar with, with some information that might be new to you; and then sprinkle in a little bit about finding these lost ghost stories at the end.

THE CHRISTMAS GHOST THROUGH THE YEARS

In Dick Merryman's *Round About Our Coal Fire: or, Christmas Entertainments* (J. Roberts, c.1730–1732),† we find a very early example of ghost stories that were explicitly told at Christmas by the buying public in a Christmas-themed book. The first is "Of a Terrible Ghost", where after a Lady is killed by a "Toad-shaped creature" (the ghost of the man to whom she was pledged), the narrator discovers "that a Ghost and a Fart are the same thing; for a Fart will make the candle burn blue as well as a Ghost". The second is "Another Story of a Ghost and How Much it Concerned a

---

* M. R. James famously wrote ghost stories to be told on Christmas Eve, so it's only fair that I read some of those stories on the night!

† This also contains the first printed version of "Jack and the Beanstalk", under the title "The Story of Jack Spriggins and the Enchanted Bean".

Bishop", which, quite frankly, isn't as fun as the first tale. A copy of *Coal Fire* (2nd edition) sold at auction in 2024 for £200–£300. Needless to say, if it was *you* who bought it, I'm extremely jealous.

Jean-Pierre Claris de Florian's "Valérie, nouvelle Italienne", the French premature burial story which has a gathering of people at Christmas telling strange and ghastly stories, was first published in *Nouvelles Nouvelles* in 1792. It was translated in the US as "Valeria" in *The Literary Museum* (March–May, 1797); and as "The Apparition" in *The Dessert to the True American* (March/April, 1799). The first UK printing of the story was under the name "Valeria; or The Ghost Alive", featured in John Bell's *La Belle Assemblée*, a magazine for women, in April 1906.* The story has become noted as an early short story that marks the transition between "apparition" tales and more corporeal-based supernatural ones.

In the 9 December 1818 edition of *Felix Farley's Bristol Journal*, there was a spirited review of *Fantasmagoriana, ou recueil d'histoires d'apparitions, de spectres, revenans, fantômes, etc.* (1812, Paris), a horror anthology originally translated from German to French, and partly to English in the 1818 edition. The reviewer explains that due to the recent work of physicians rationalising how ghost sightings may have various psychological or physiological explanations, one is now able to go out at "'the very witching time of night' [...] in a damp, gusty, gloomy December," without being afraid of spectral encounters (though still mindful of rheumatism). However, reflecting on what must be "sacrificed for the attainment of such beatitude," including "the very pleasure which in some uncomfortable manner mingles itself with [...] real terrors," and of course, "the thrilling delight of a ghost-story by a Christmas fireside," the reviewer concludes that the benefits of a life without the fear of ghosts "might be too dearly purchased."

Now for a real life tale. In 1823, watermen Philips and Gadd were sent to jail for causing the death of Baker, who was said to have fallen from a

---

* See E. W. Pitcher's "A Possible Source for Florian's 'Valérie, nouvelle Italienne' in *Nouvelles Nouvelles* (Paris 1792)" in *ANQ*, volume 1, issue 3, 1988.

INTRODUCTION

vessel on Christmas Eve at Hawkins Point, Patapsco River, Maryland, and drowned. The reason they were arrested is because once on dry land, they started telling people about Baker's ghost being on the vessel. They then tried to leave for Poplar Island but felt "compelled to put back" by the ghost as the wind was too strong. By the time they returned, the tale had gathered much notoriety, and when they tried to explain why they were back, they were taken before the Justice of the Peace who sent them to jail on the Saturday. They stuck with their story though: Philips swore that on the Sunday night in jail the ghost of Baker had laid next to him all night and when he left the jail on Monday, the ghost just sat and let him be. When he got back to the vessel, Baker was there, alive. The only explanation anyone could give was that Gadd's head was swollen at the time of the account due to pleurisy and Philips had been suffering from a head cold for three months.*

The *North Wales Chronicle* (12 November 1829), saw an author writing as "Omicron" finish part two of his *Essay on Ghosts*, following part one in October. He ended his list with "The Ecclesiastical Ghost":

> This apparition appears in a gown of doleful black, bearing an ebony rod in his right hand. Two of these apparitions haunt the cathedral of Bangor all the year round, but appear at the doors of respectable inhabitants during the Christmas Holidays, a domiciliary visit which those who dislike may easily prevent by placing a penny in the hand of one of these spectres on Christmas Day, the receipt whereof is acknowledged by grinning a *ghastly* smile.

Right, I know someone will message me if I don't mention the one work that cemented the Christmas ghost story forevermore! *A Christmas Carol* was published on 19 December 1843. Six thousand copies were sold on the first day alone and by the end of 1844, fifteen thousand copies had been sold. Dickens was already a household name and E. T. Jaques, in his 1914

---

* "Mysterious Affair", *Lexington Weekly Press*, 17 February 1823.

work *Charles Dickens in Chancery, Being an Account of His Proceedings In Respect of the "Christmas Carol" With Some Gossip In Relation to the Old Law Courts at Westminster* (Longmans, Green and Co.), came closest to capturing the zeitgeist of Dickens: "He is the only author to whom our great non-literary public has ever given the same attention which it always gives to politicians and notable criminals. Even Sir Walter [Scott] was not master of a spell so far-reaching as this."

If you were living in Lincoln in around 1858, you would have been bombarded by adverts from Page Woodcock, trying to sell his "wind pills". Headed "A Ghost! A Christmas Ghost!", the advert went on to say that "indigestion will not fail to haunt those who, at this festive season, indulge too freely in the good things. But this ghost can be *laid*, this sprite *destroyed* by Page Woodcock's Wind Pills."

There was a rather delightful tongue-in-cheek essay called "Christmas Ghosts and Scientific Ghosts" published in the *Teesdale Mercury* on 30 December 1863, that posed questions such as "why are ghosts always six foot away when they follow someone?" and "why should ghosts rise merely to make our hair rise?". My favourite: "why do they keep appearing *until something is found out!*" But of course, the writer had common sense when it came to writing about the Christmas Ghost: "it is a species of flat heresy to disparage ghosts at Christmas. There are tellers of supernatural stories who would as soon as die as give up the ghost; they grow cheerful at the prospect of a batch of horrors, and never seem so much in spirits as when they revel in the spirit land."

"Whenever five or six English-speaking people meet round a fire on Christmas Eve, they start telling each other ghost stories," Jerome K. Jerome wrote in *Told After Supper* (1891). "Nothing satisfies us on Christmas Eve but to hear each other tell authentic anecdotes about spectres. It is a genial, festive season, and we love to muse upon graves, and dead bodies, and murders, and blood."

The Times, on 7 December 1903, published a *Scooby Doo*-esque article titled "Real Ghost Story":

INTRODUCTION

A young woman, at a country house party one Christmas had been thrilled with delicious horrors by tales of ghosts told by her fellow-guests around a generous fire just before they separated at night. The next morning she appeared at the breakfast table, ready for departure, and, when pressed to explain her reason for going, explained that she was afraid to sleep under that roof another night. She said that about midnight she was awakened by a stealthy step and to her horror saw a spectre, all in white, at the foot of her bed and it raised its claw-like hand and actually drew the coverlid off the bed. There was no hallucination about it, for the coverlid was gone!

While the interest was at its height, a belated breakfaster appeared and remarked genially—

"How cold it was last night! Knowing the room next to mine was unoccupied, I took the liberty of helping myself to an extra covering from there!"

In 1904, *The Strange Visitation of Josiah McNason: A Christmas Ghost Story* was published by *The Strand Magazine*. A crueller and more gruesome spin on *A Christmas Carol*, it was written by Marie Corelli. It follows the nasty millionaire Josiah as a goblin creature from hell takes him on a voyage, in which he sees his fate as a goblin, watches a goblin preacher exhorting his congregation of fallen souls, travels to the bedside of a dying man he has refused to save, and faces the horrors of a fate that cares as little for him as he does for his fellow man.

In 1905 in America, you were actually given instructions on how to hold a "Ghost-Story Party", found in the December issue of *Woman's Home Companion*:

What can be more genuinely enjoyable than to be one of a congenial company gathered about an open fire to enjoy a feast of nuts and apples and to hear and tell ghost stories?

They are to be ushered in from the winter night to find the room lighted by a single-shaded lamp, and by the blue and lilac flames from the log of driftwood resting on its bed of glowing coals, while from piano or violincello in the semi-darkness comes the soft music of old and half-forgotten times.

Their exuberant spirits have been subdued by the half-light and low music [...] everyone has a story of the supernatural at his command [...] there is sure to be some clever raconteur with a mind of the weird to draw upon [...] There should also be a musician in the magic circle. If the songs are of a melancholy or sorrowful character, they will add much to the effect of the stories.

In Maurice Noel Hennessey's article "Why Christmas Ghosts?", published in the Southern England newspaper *Western Gazette* in 1938, he has this to say on "family ghosts":

... an excellent case for the appearance of the family ghost at Christmas can be made. Christmas is the great occasion for the gathering together all the members of a family. From far and near people come to spend the festive season in the bosom of their families. This fact itself constitutes a feature of the old Christmas that is fast dying out, but nevertheless presents an interesting point of view. Isn't it quite natural that in this family reunion, the members who have passed on should come back to the fold in order to be present at the family gathering? Perhaps the force of memory and the reminiscences of the past have such psychological effect that imagination runs riot and ghosts are "seen".

*

I'm the latest in a long line of literary gravediggers. I often think about those early authors, sending their stories off into the great unknown, not knowing if they would ever be published or not. It gives me a visceral thrill. They never were to know if their story or book would be "the one" to find fame beyond their death. And as we all know, apart from the lucky few, time and

INTRODUCTION

obscurity—not just six feet of soil—buries us all. That's why I've spent the last ten years researching "lost" stories. It's not always about being the first to find something (although knowing you're the first to read something in perhaps 150–200 years is more than its own reward). It's about finding yet another piece of this never-ending jigsaw. It's about who those people were and why they wrote ghost stories or horror yarns. Why authors tried to scare their readers when times were scary enough as they were. What the trends were, what worked, what failed. And, once found, does it still strike a chord? For me it's about that moment, when you read these long-lost stories from authors who long ago turned into unsettled dust, where you go, *oh*. And the space around you no longer feels safe, your mind is playing tricks on you, and you're left with that little bit of unease.

That's my *raison d'être* with "lost" genre fiction, and that's why I spend all of my time in the archives. And it feels like much more of a triumph when I find a great story written in a newspaper that came from a member of the public; someone who just tried their hand at writing a ghost story because they wanted to see if they could. And with this dive into the literary history of festive frights, I think I've been able to do that. It's my job to bring you stories you've never read before. There have been quite a lot of Victorian-era Christmas anthologies published in the last decade or so that have made the job of finding quality stories all the more difficult—so I've cast my net further afield, scouring the Australian and American newspaper archives as well as those of British journals and papers.

I'm so proud of the stories I've found; it makes this volume all the more precious and something to be treasured, to be passed down so your children and your grandchildren are reading the tales in the well-worn book to *their* children and grandchildren. From stand-out stories like the anonymously written "Shadows of Evil", "The Haunted Vicarage", the Devon-set "The Ghost of Appledore Pool" and the incredibly weird and off-kilter "That Terrible Dentist", I truly believe there's a story in here for you whether you like your hauntings delicate, tremblesome or, dare I say it, satirical. And if there are tales in here where the ghostly happenings are unravelled with a

INTRODUCTION

rational explanation, fear not—the way these authors use their "real life" horrors is enough to outdo some of their supernatural peers.

Now, how best to end this festive essay? After all, you have many treats awaiting you, but *everyone* needs a stocking filler to open before the main event. I would like to present to you "A Terrible Tale Told Round the Christmas Fire", published in the *Bury Free Press* in January 1857. It's not a ghost story, it's not even a *story*, but an account of a man haunted by a deed, confessed on Christmas Day, and as soon as I read it, I *knew* that I had to squeeze it into this book somehow as it encapsulates the very spirit of "telling tales" at Christmas…

A TERRIBLE TALE TOLD ROUND THE CHRISTMAS FIRE

A sickly-looking young man, who gave the name of Walter Booth, aged 19, at present an inmate of the Islington workhouse, London, but who was formerly a butcher, was placed at the bar of the Clerkenwell Police court, charged by James Arnault, a pauper in the same establishment, with committing a murder under the following extraordinary circumstances:

It appeared from the evidence, that on Christmas Day, several of the men in the Islington workhouse were sitting round the fire, and for the purpose of amusement agreed to tell tales or relate wonderful events. Some told ghost stories, and others murders, and it was observed that while the first murder was being related the prisoner became very uneasy, groaned loudly, seemed very much troubled in his mind, and ultimately left the room. On his return one of the men was telling a laughable story, and although it caused a great deal of laughter, the prisoner seemed duller than usual. The prisoner, when asked what was the matter with him, said he had committed "a most horrible and atrocious crime," that it very much troubled him; that he could get no rest night or day, and wherever he went, and whatever he was about, the thoughts of the deed he had committed were always uppermost in his mind. Everybody now became anxious to hear the particulars, and the prisoner was advised to "repent" and make a "full confession" of his misdeeds. The prisoner, after some hesitation, then said, that two years ago he was walking along the banks of the Regent's Canal, the afternoon being very dark, and a slight fog prevailing at the time, when being short of money, and having promised to go out with some friends, he was determined to rob the first person he met. He had not proceeded very far before he met an elderly gentleman, very respectably attired, and he demanded his money or his life. A struggle ensued between them, they fell to the ground together, but he being young, was quickly on his feet, and he took out a butcher's knife (he produced the knife from his pocket and drew their attention to marks of blood that were still upon it), and plunged it deep into his victim's body; he drew it out reeking only to replunge it deeper; he saw the blood flow beneath the oft-repeated strokes, and when his victim was quite dead, he coolly rifled his pockets, taking from them a quantity of loose gold, a purse containing several notes, and a gold watch and chain, and then threw the body into the canal, and having watched it disappear he proceeded to meet his friends. He had not proceeded far, however, before he began to reflect, being still on the bank of the canal, and could almost with the same knife have stabbed himself and died, consoled with the idea that no one would ever find him out, as he intended to jump into the water after using the knife. But he thought afterwards that he had better not take his own life, but would go and have a spree with his friends, intending afterwards to repent. He went out that evening, got drunk, and was robbed of the whole of the money of which he had become so foully possessed, and the image of the slaughtered man always haunting him, caused his illness, in consequence of which he was then an inmate of the workhouse. Arnault gave information to the police of what he had heard, and they, upon an examination of their books, found that about the time the prisoner stated he had committed the crime, and near the spot indicated by the prisoner, a body of an old man was taken out of the canal, but he was proved never to have been possessed of much

INTRODUCTION

money, and there were no marks of violence or stabs found on the body. The body then found was that of the father of a policeman who happened to be in court on other business. The prisoner, who is very ill, and in consumption, said, in defence, that it was only a terrible tale which he had told round the Christmas fire, for the amusement of his companions, and he never thought he should be given in custody and locked up for it. He was entirely innocent of the charge of murder.

Mr. Tyrwhitt said, after a long and patient examination, that there was no foundation whatever for the charge. It was evidently a Christmas story, and he should discharge the prisoner.

The prisoner then left the Court with his friends.

Now, gather your family together, even that one over there who doesn't like joining in. Get them to turn their phones off, or put down their presents and sit by the fire, or at the table, in the dark, with a single candle flickering away. Choose a story. No, not that one, it's too long—keep that one to yourself for later. Speak in a hushed tone. Dangle that hook, wait for them to bite, then scare them *deliciously*. The greatest gift you can give anyone this year is *pleasing terror*.

Oh.

Seasons Scarings,
JOHNNY MAINS
Winter, 2025

A NOTE FROM THE PUBLISHER

The original short stories reprinted in the British Library Gilded Nightmares series were written and published in a period ranging across the nineteenth and twentieth centuries. There are many elements of these stories which continue to entertain modern readers; however, in some cases there are also uses of language, instances of stereotyping and some attitudes expressed by narrators or characters which may not be endorsed by the publishing standards of today. We acknowledge therefore that some elements in the stories selected for reprinting may continue to make uncomfortable reading for some of our audience. With this series British Library Publishing aims to offer a new readership a chance to read some of the rare material of the British Library's collections in an affordable format, to enjoy their merits and to look back into the worlds of the past two centuries as portrayed by their writers. It is not possible to separate these stories from the history of their writing and therefore the following stories are presented as they were originally published with one edit to the text, and minor edits made for consistency of style and sense. We welcome feedback from our readers, which can be sent to the following address:

British Library Publishing
The British Library
96 Euston Road
London, NW1 2DB
United Kingdom

ILLUSIONS OF PRESENCE

Tell ghost stories, weird and bold—
The very same our fathers told
To make their youthful blood run cold!

"CHRISTMAS EVE"—DWIGHT ANDERSON (1900)

IN DEADLY PERIL
A STRANGE CHRISTMAS STORY OF MINING LIFE

John Pendleton

Published in The Belfast Weekly News, *24 December 1887*

John Pendleton (c.1853–5 September 1914) was a Chesterfield-born author and journalist. His childhood was spent at the bookshop of Mr. John Walton reading everything he could get his hands on, and in his obituary it was stated that he embarked on a career in journalism "quite by accident". He began at the *Derbyshire Advertiser* and moved to Wakefield, Sheffield, Leeds and Manchester, holding sub-editor posts at the *Yorkshire Post* and the *Manchester Guardian*. On retiring, he stayed in Manchester and dedicated himself to literary endeavours. He wrote the two-volume *The Romance of Our Railways* and the quasi-memoir, *A History of Newspaper Reporting*.

"In Deadly Peril" is a great, unexpected place to start this anthology off, and this is its first appearance since 1887. This isn't John's only mining related horror tale. His next was *The Underground Witch: A Thrilling Story of Mining Life* which I believe is a novel that only appears to have been serialised in 1888. What I've read of it so far, I really like.

Apropos of nothing, a "John Pendleton" has a hand grow out of his side in R. Anthony's "The Parasitic Hand", a suitably weird tale found in Christine Campbell Thomson's classic anthology *You'll Need a Night Light* (Selwyn & Blount, 1927).

"Y ou will not dream of going down to the pit today, sir?" said the banksman, touching his cap.

"Why not?" I replied, rather chagrined.

"Well, you see," he said, rubbing his chin reflectively, "we always try to dissuade gents like you from going down. We can never tell what may happen; and it will be awkward" (he called it "orkard") "if you're killed."

I thought the man might be joking. But the forefinger of his right hand kept moving, slowly and seriously, across his chin. There was not the faintest indication of fun, either at the deeply-lined corners of his mouth or in his eyes. His face was earnest, solemn, and, though I do not profess to be easily upset, the man's manner impressed me more than I cared to own. I had left the lamp-room bravely enough a minute or two previously, anxious to get down the mine. Now fear seemed to be creeping round my heart.

"The gent will be all right, Dick," said a short, thick-set miner, black as Erebus, by my side. This miner had "the exquisite gift of humour." His eyes twinkled with merriment, and his fat face expanded into a great smile, as he added, thoroughly enjoying the discomfiture I tried in vain to conceal: "The gent will be all right, Dick. The manager says I have to see him down the shaft, and give him into the care of Big Tom."

The banksman muttered to himself. Perhaps he did so to distract attention from the startled look that came into his eyes.

"Are you ready, sir?" asked the merry miner, turning towards me and speaking, I thought, a little too abruptly.

"Yes," I replied desperately.

Up the shaft glided the cage, and stopped with a clang at the pit bank.

"Now, sir. Quick," said the short, fat miner.

I was hurried on to the iron foot-plate of the cage. With my right hand I clutched the crossbar; with my left I gripped the safety lamp.

"Hold fast, sir," said the miner, grinning, as he stepped blithely after me.

The bell rang. There was a whirr of machinery. A noise as if a band of Siberian exiles were clanking above me in fetters. The floor of the cage seemed to be leaping away from me—plunging wildly into a terrible abyss. The daylight faded. I felt as though I was flying through a dark, damp, clammy sky. The darkness increased—decreased as rapidly, and the cage dropping steadily through a glimmering light, reached the bottom of the shaft.

I was thankful that I had come so far alive; yet had a wild yearning to go back.

I was dazed—bewildered. In the lamp-lit corridor the greatest confusion seemed to prevail. Everything about me looked uncanny—weird. Half a dozen creatures, with hoarse voices and black faces, looking more like imps than men, were running corves to and fro. The shouting, the din, was brain cracking. The echoes made my flesh creep. They died away, and sprang into life again in the most surprising manner. I imagined that these echoes, spreading to every working place in the mine, crept slowly behind the collier at his toil, and whispered mysteriously in his ears: "There's a stranger in the pit!"

Nor shall I forget the noiseless slouch of the miners, as they penetrated, safety lamp and teacan in hand, into the recesses of this subterranean workshop. It filled me with awe.

A door was suddenly thrown open, and I was conducted into a well-lighted room—a room bricked, arched, and whitewashed.

The walls were covered with plans of the workings, and instructions to the men in case the mine should be flooded, or fire be found in the pit.

A miner's kitten, shaking itself out of sleep, came slowly towards me, and rubbed its back against my ankles, possibly in sympathy.

At a little table sat a man with his face to the light. It was the deputy who had charge of the workings. He had a fine face, though it was covered with coal dust; a firm mouth, half hidden by a dark drooping moustache; a firm chin, a Grecian nose, and a broad forehead, beneath which his bright black eyes gleamed with a kindly light. The man, I knew, was of gigantic stature, though he was seated. His great, broad shoulders stretched half the length of the table; his hands were large, strong, sinewy. There was a look of power about him that strangely attracted me. I hoped he was to be my guide through the pit.

"Good day, sir," he said, rising, and grasping my right hand. "I suppose you are the gentleman who wishes to see through the mine?"

"Yes," I remarked, gazing with admiration at his tall form. "Are you Big Tom?" I hazarded.

"That is my name in the pit. You are," he continued, referring to a letter on the table, "Sidney Wild, dramatist, in search of a strong situation for your new play."

"Yes, that is my object in coming here."

"Well, I think we can oblige you," he said, laughing. "But I hope you have a strong nerve?"

"I'm not easily frightened," I replied, trying to laugh as heartily as he had done, but failing in the effort, and having (I am thoroughly ashamed to own it) rather an inclination to sob.

The air was grave-like. I was rendered sickly by the vitiated atmosphere. I was altogether ill at ease, and half demented by the noise. The steel track might have been laid on my brain, and the loaded corves running through my head, so acutely did I feel the rush and crunch of every wagon as it was propelled to the shaft. I would have given a fortune, and abandoned all hope of fame, if at that moment of hyper-sensitiveness I could have stood in God's sunshine on the pit bank.

"You have chosen a strange day for your adventure," said Big Tom gravely, having no doubt a shrewd idea of my mental perturbation.

"What do you mean?" I asked, in some surprise.

Big Tom, who was making an entry in the report book on the table, put aside his pen, looked at me searchingly, and ignoring my question, said, "It's not too late to go back—to go up the shaft again if you like."

"No," I retorted, my pride overcoming my fear, "I would rather go forward. I am not afraid."

Yet I could not help wondering what he meant by saying that I had chosen a strange day for my adventure.

"Don't you know it's Christmas Eve?" he said, with what I considered quite unnecessary amazement.

"Yes," I retorted, a little brusquely. "But there's nothing alarming in that—is there?"

"Well," he remarked, twirling the left end of his moustache between his forefinger and thumb, "perhaps I ought not to tell you."

"Oh, don't hesitate," I said, nettled at these Cassandra-like attempts to get me up the shaft again.

"The fact is, then," he continued, watching me intently, "Christmas Eve is an unlucky day in this pit. I have been here twenty years now, and have noticed, to my dismay, that the mine always claims a victim on Christmas Eve. I cannot understand it. The ventilation may be never so good. The greatest care may be taken. But before the bells ring in a merry Christmas at the old church yonder" (pointing upward with his great blackened hand in the direction of the village church, some half mile from the pit bank) "there is sure to be at least one lifeless form in the workings."

"You don't mean that—never!" I said, aghast, and my heart palpitated with a strange, though it might be a groundless, fear.

"It's true," he answered, sadly. "There is a curse on the pit on this day—the day that should be the brightest in all the year to the miner. Above ground, as you know, there will be festivity. Kindly greetings, meetings of old friends, the father's heart will be gladdened at his daughter's safe return from her bread-winning in some great city, the mother's eyes will fill with tears of joy as she welcomes her lad home again after his first tussle with the world. Happy faces will encircle many a fireside that we make bright with our perilous toil; but here there will be calamity."

Tears stood in the deputy's eyes, and his lips quivered.

I was labouring under a strong emotion now—I had almost forgotten my own terror in pity for this mining Sisyphus, who had been striving year after year to roll disaster out of the mine.

"Cannot you account for it in any way?" I asked.

"No," he replied, in a serious tone, "without it is to be accounted for in this way—She's always about at this time!"

"She?" I exclaimed, surprised. "Who's she?" imagining vaguely that he must be referring to the heroine in a recent novel.

"The Weight!" he replied, with a sigh.

"The Weight? What on earth do you mean?" I asked.

"This is what I mean," he went on. "There are three things the miner dreads—fire, water, and the Weight! If he has a safety lamp the collier may escape the explosion's blasting breath. If water breaks into the pit he can run for his life. But if 'the Weight' comes on—if She's about," Big Tom added suddenly, seizing my right wrist, and paling with excitement, "there is no escape! In a moment the earth itself moves. The props break as if they were matchwood. The roof gives way like a house of cards. The stone and coal fall with a mighty thud. There is a shout of despair—a startled cry—a moan; and the collier, who had been thinking of his wife and little ones, of the tidied hearth, the Christmas tree, the feasting and jollity of the next two days during which the pit will be idle and the men at play, is crushed out of all semblance of life. It's horrible," he continued, wiping his eyes with a piece of greasy cotton waste. "Little Punch, the pony driver, was crushed to death last year; Ranting Charley (he was a local preacher) was buried alive the year before; and the master's son was found dead beneath a heap of bind and broken posts two years back. Somebody is sure to be killed in the mine today—it might be you, sir," he said, with sudden intensity.

"Nonsense," I retorted, thinking after all that the big deputy was not as brave as he looked, and that he was giving way to superstitious cowardice.

"There's no nonsense about it," he said severely. "It's retribution. It's grim justice. The earth is only claiming a recompense—a cruel recompense for Christ's crucifixion."

"What?" I exclaimed, staring at Big Tom, startled at the wild originality of this thought, and beginning to question the man's sanity.

"I'm all right here," he said, drawing his right hand across his brow. "I'm sane enough," he observed, guessing my thoughts, and indulging in a peculiar smile. "A fire trier went mad in the pit the other day, and we found him singing hymns and playing with a naked light in the return air way. The wonder is we were not all blown to Jericho. But there's no madness about me. I'm as sane as any statesman. Still, going about the pit on our lonely tramps to see that all is safe, we fellows get singular fancies. This is mine. I look upon the earth not as a senseless mass, but as a being. I feel certain that it is alive! Anyhow it is never still, never silent, and it is the most restless on Christmas Eve. Then it speaks in the strangest voices. It moves hideously; the gas hisses and seethes in the heading; supernatural lights gleam on the coal face, which indulges in frightful grimaces—'makes faces' at you. The roof is shattered by gas, and crashes down without warning, in most unexpected places. The dangers of the pit on this day are legion. There is disaster in the air. You had better go up the shaft, sir—and come another day."

"Not if you will take me now," I replied. "Having got thus far, I should like to see the pit, whatever the peril."

I had an idea that Big Tom was playing some prank with me—that it would afford him a rare laugh if I went up the shaft again.

"Then you insist on going through the workings," he asked.

"No, I don't insist," was my reply; "but I really should like to see how the miners get the coal. And, candidly, I don't place much faith in your Christmas Eve forebodings."

"Very well, then," he remarked, with what I thought was a rather sinister smile. "Now we perfectly understand each other. Perhaps, after all, my forebodings are childish. But I have been strangely unnerved today."

Big Tom did not say what had arisen to disturb his imperturbability. He looked at his watch—went to the telephone, and asked, "Is there any fire in the far bank?" (really "benk" or working place, in which the miners hew the coal.)

By-and-bye a voice answered from a distant part of the pit. "No trace of fire now, sir, ventilation good."

"That's lucky," muttered Big Tom, giving a keen look at the safety lamp I carried, and placing a collier's cudgel, a short alpenstock, in my hand.

"The road is very rough, and the roof low," he said; "keep at my heels, and take care to bend your head when I shout."

"Thank you," I said, clutching my safety lamp, and wildly keeping on his track as he treaded his way through the maze of corves that were being hurried to the pit bottom.

Now, we were in the main road. The floor, as Big Tom had said, was uneven. Across it were fixed wooden sleepers, such as one sees on a railroad track. On the sleepers ran the steel rails, over which the loaded corves came from the distant workings. Between the sleepers were slimy pools, made of coal dust, and the water that dripped continuously from the roof. The subterranean pathway along which I stumbled was awful in its darkness. The glimmering light of the safety lamps only intensified the gloom. Dimly it shone on the greatest wooden pillars that propped up the roof, on the gleaming face of the coal, on the refuge holes into which we had to dash to let the corves go by. The hauling wire hissed and creaked as it went to and fro drawing its train of wagons. Now a miner passed us with black face and teeth glistening white. He seemed to be bounding, with bent back, into chaos. A trapper would pop his head out of the cavernous hole in which in darkness and solitude he earned his daily bread. A pit pony, surprised at my blundering tread, so different from the miner's footfall, lifted its head from the sodden hay by the damp wall side, and pushing its nose almost into my cheek, evidently wondered "Who are you?" For two miles this went on; lights ever glimmering in the distance. All around us awe-inspiring noises, mingled with strange echoes that now resembled the shrieks of bodies in pain, and then demoniac laughter. At one part of the road the heat was so intense that the perspiration trickled down my face; in another the atmosphere was so icy that I shivered and could scarcely hold the lamp. Collier after collier had passed us by the time we reached the level. They had gone by, like a phantom procession, with bent knees, bent backs, bent heads, almost without uttering a word. Big Tom had not spoken, except to say "Head, sir," as we passed along the road where the roof was the lowest. I likened him to a human will-o'-the-wisp that might lead me treacherously to death; and yet, though my heart went pit-a-pat and fluttered at the terrifying noises and darkness about me, I felt some confidence that the man with the giant form would bring me safely out of the pit.

Suddenly Big Tom halted opposite a broad heavy door.

"This is the way to the far bank," he said. "Have you had enough of the pit, or will you go on?"

"I will go forward," I replied.

He pulled open the door.

Through it came a great gust of wind that made me stagger—that nearly threw me off my feet.

"Close the door after you," shouted Big Tom.

I did so. It went to with an angry, menacing bang. On it was painted in red letters: "No miner must pass here with a defective safety lamp; dangerous ground."

The air as soon as the door was closed became nauseous.

A dull, aching pain took possession of my temples. I thought, in a hopeless sort of way, that I was stronger than Atlas. He carried the world on his shoulders. I seemed to be carrying it on my eyebrows. And my nostrils rebelled at the foul atmosphere that had the odour of the charnel-house and the dissecting-room. At least to nothing else can I compare it.

The light in my safety lamp seemed to shrink; then to flare in a blue halo.

It was very pretty. The flame leapt eagerly to this delicate ring of colour that might have been compassed by fairy fingers. Yet it made me shudder. It reminded me of a night at sea years ago, when the moon looked out of its beauteous film of blue and grey, and shone with a mocking cruel light on the white face of the drowning skipper, in his last wild struggle with the storm-tossed waves.

"Are you asleep, man? For God's sake make haste!" said Big Tom, dragging me unceremoniously along the dark way. "There's fire here!" he whispered with unsteady voice. "How silent it is too—follow me!" he added nervously.

There were black cloths that felt like shrouds hung across the narrow road. He lifted these so that I might pass beneath them. Then, reaching another broad heavy door, he opened it, and through the doorway we crept cautiously on our hand and knees—our safety lamps hooked to our belts.

We had reached the far bank.

It was in darkness.

There was not the faintest ray of light except that cast by our own lamps on the threshold.

Not a sound of toil could be heard.

Only the drip, drip of water.

The bank was deserted!

"My God! The men have gone!" said Big Tom, in a sort of wail, and breathing heavily.

And a gust of wind, hurrying rudely past us, took up his words, and flung them against the bank-side, from which they rebounded in new phrase. "What fools you are—the wise men have gone!" were the words dashed in our teeth by the boisterous wind.

But there was not a soul about except Big Tom and myself; unless the bank was haunted by a ghost, that like Galatea was endowed with the gift of speech, the words were never uttered, were simply the feverish creation of my own fancy.

"It's not three o'clock yet," said Big Tom, breaking in abruptly on my foolish reverie, "but all the men have cleared out. I was afraid of this. We are lost—we shall never leave the bank alive!"

"Why?" I asked in dread. "Is there not time to escape?"

"No; the Weight is coming on," he replied nervously. "She's been here already—can't you taste the vixen's poisonous breath in the air?"

The atmosphere certainly was vile. It was hot, parching, choking, as if mixed with sulphur; and yet there was moisture everywhere. Water trickled and steamed down the wooded props that kept up the face of the coal. It slowly accumulated in great black drops on the jagged ledges of the seam. It gathered in a thick slimy stream on the rocky floor of the bank. And in the far corner of the ebony-like cave from which the miners had evidently hurried with fear, the coal seemed to be frizzling. It crackled, and split, and fell crashing in great slabs on the ground. It hissed, as if every pore in the black surface was a serpent's tongue. I was terrified—dismayed, and I turned wildly, intending to rush from the bank.

"Not quite so fast, sir," said Big Tom, in a strangely altered tone, seizing me roughly, grasping my white neckerchief and coat collar with his left hand. "You are a dramatist," he went on with a sneer; "a dramatist in search of a strong situation. You shall not be disappointed. You shall have a situation strong enough for any stage—a situation with a splendid climax that will bring down the house!"

The bank echoed with strange wild laughter, that died away in a merciless chuckle.

Big Tom had gone mad!

There was no doubt about it.

The deserted mine, and his superstitious dread of "the Weight," had turned his brain.

"What a pity you can't put the next act in your new play," he said, mockingly, never relaxing his hold. "It would make your fortune, good sir—the people like something sensational nowadays, don't they?" he added, with sneering persuasiveness.

The man's crafty leer and cunning look, and stealthy, panther-like movement, told me intuitively that I had to struggle with a maniac.

Down the bank, over great pieces of rock, and jagged lumps of coal, he dragged me, laughing sardonically meanwhile.

I was like a child in his grasp.

The dew of death seemed already to be gathering on my forehead.

What hope of escape was there from this madman?

None!

My head and my heart ached with hopelessness: my limbs trembled, and would not support me.

"You're a nice dramatist," hissed Big Tom. "Why, the situation is altogether too strong for you!" and he laughed fiendishly, revelling in my terror.

Resting against one of the packs that had been built to hold up the roof was a pick—a patent steel hoop pick, with points almost as sharp as needles.

I saw it gleaming in the fitful light cast by my safety lamp.

Now, as he dragged me towards it, I realised his merciless intention.

The madman meant to kill me—to slay me, to send his pick crashing through my heart.

The awfulness of the place had no terror for him, now his mind was unhinged.

He had no pity for me.

Big Tom had been transformed into a fiend.

"It's realistic, isn't it," he said, mockingly, grasping the pick with his right hand, and grinding his teeth in maniac rage.

"Oh, horror," I gasped. "Have mercy!"

But the baleful light grew fiercer in his eyes.

"This—is—the—climax," he said, jerking out the words venomously, and raising the pick swiftly above his head.

Oh, God! I could not die like this. I must make one frantic struggle for life. Desperation gave me courage. Nay, I think I went mad too with dread. I wrenched myself, somehow, from Big Tom's grasp; and the pick-point, crashing downward, buried itself in the coal face instead of my heart.

"Curse you—I will kill you yet!" screamed the madman, as I crawled dazed to my feet, and scrambled in terror out of his reach, while he strove to tear the pick out of the coal.

He tugged at it in vain. The pick would not move. He abandoned it with an oath. Then he crept towards me, with a devilish light in his eyes, and his big hands strangely working.

Big Tom meant to strangle me.

I cowered in the far corner of the bank, limp and helpless—heartsick. There was no escape now. The adventurous dramatist would soon be lifeless. The curtain would speedily go down on the terrible play—the realistic tragedy. The situation was—how bitterly I acknowledged it—"altogether too strong for me."

Nevertheless, so closely does a man's profession permeate his nature, that I could not avoid thinking what a grand hit this dramatic scene would make on the stage. The gloomy bank, my cowering form and terror-stricken face, the madman creeping towards me in a paroxysm of rage—the flash of limelight, the crowded house in a thrill of suspense—

Ugh! Why did I shudder? Dramatic art and possible fame had gone like a flash out of my brain. My mind was in the pit again. I thought I could feel Big Tom's relentless grasp about my throat.

The light in the safety lamp (which still hung from his belt) changed colour—it turned pink, and then to the tint of blood, and suffused the bank with a ghastly light, through which a demon's face was peering.

It was Big Tom's face, working with hate, as he thirsted for my life!

Craftily he crept towards me, past a half-loaded corve, and over a great slab of coal that was lying ready for the wedger. He crouched to spring. I felt his hot breath—was dismayed at the look in his eyes. Death was very near now, and yet how terrible it was to die!

Perhaps you will not believe it, seeing that I am a dramatist, but I prayed!

And Big Tom, catching a word of supplication, laughed defiantly, and mimicked me with a sardonic glee.

But his glee, mad though he was, soon turned to terror.

The earth trembled. There was a noise louder than thunder. The bank cracked, and reeled on the thick props.

"She's here again," gasped Big Tom, a great fear, as well as the madman's light, in his eyes.

"The Weight" had come! The vixen was flying savagely about the pit. Had she, I wondered, like Medusa, her hair entwined with serpents? For I had never heard such hissing on the earth or in the earth before.

Never, in my wildest imagery, had I conjectured anything so terrifying.

The heat was intense. The coal broke out, as it were, into a hot sweat. The bank filled with vapour. My heart felt as though it were between a Gorgon's teeth. I clutched madly at my throat. I could not breathe—was this suffocation—death?

The madman, crouching in front of me, passed his right hand across his forehead, and great beads of perspiration trickled through this fingers.

"It's rather warm," he said, sarcastically, gasping for breath; "hotter than on a summer night in the theatre—hot enough to roast all the chestnuts" (old jokes) "in your play," he added maliciously, with a smile that lost some of its scornful venom as it struggled for expression through the froth—the maniac froth—that encircled his lips.

I strove to reply to his taunt, but in vain. I was speechless, well-nigh asphyxiated.

"You shall not escape!" Big Tom muttered feebly, crawling a little nearer. "I will kill you! A collier's life is no sop for our Lord's death. You shall be the victim. It should count something to offer a dramatist up as a sacrifice, as some slight recompense for Christ's crucifixion!" and he laughed again, a heartless, bloodthirsty laugh that made me quail.

The light from his lamp glimmered to the left of the bank.

Oh, God! I was not hemmed in, then!

There, just beyond me, was a cave, dark, dreadful, full of weird shadows; but it might lead to safety, to freedom!

How sickening was the carbonic acid in the air; would it poison me on the threshold of escape?

I rose with difficulty. But hope—a wild longing for life—dashed aside my fear. I staggered towards the cave.

Big Tom, scrambling to his feet, reeled after me, with a curse on his lips, in pursuit.

With my teeth set, and my hands clenched, I took six or seven steps onward into the cave. My lamp had darkened—gone out.

But there was a faint gleam of light behind me—it was from Big Tom's lamp. And I could hear his heavy breathing, low down, near the floor of the cave. The madman's strength had failed him; but HE WAS CRAWLING AFTER ME ON HIS HANDS AND KNEES!

Suddenly the ground shook as if it were on stilts. There was an awe-inspiring rumbling—a mighty crash! The earth seemed to open, and I was hurled down into chaos!

"Bring a light here, Ned," shouted a little fat miner (the man—I recognised him by his voice—who had taken me down the shaft). "Here's that play-writing chap as come to see through t' pit lying i't Devil's Gorge wi' his head cut open."

"Thah niver says," replied Ned, incredulously, holding his lamp over the ravine. "Howiver's he getten here?"

"Thah moant ax me," said the fat pitman, lowering himself dexterously by a rope to the bed of the gorge, and climbing over the grey, slimy boulders to where I lay. "He's had a narrer squeak, Ned," continued the stout miner. "Cut away wi' thi to t' telephone—signal for a drop o' brandy, and t' wide ladder from t' lamp room."

Ned's retreating footsteps made sweet music in my ears.

The fat miner's tenderness, as he gently raised my head, and pillowed it on his flannel jacket, brought the tears to my eyes.

It seemed years since I had staggered into the dark cavern, pursued by Big Tom. I had wandered (perhaps in delirium) through every part of the pit. I remembered now I had recovered consciousness (just as you remember a dream on awakening) how I had prowled, hopeless and in despair, through the mine—crying aloud for help that came not, wandering desperately in unutterable darkness—alone in the deserted pit.

I had, God knows, been "In Deadly Peril."

Now I should soon be rescued.

The dread scene in the bank surged up vividly before me.

"Where's the madman—Big Tom?" I asked opening my eyes, and speaking faintly from loss of blood.

"The madman?" asked the fat miner wonderingly; and then he whispered aside to Ned (who had returned with the ladder), "poor chap, he must a hurt hissen—he's wanderin.'"

"No, I'm not," I replied to his amazement. "In God's mercy, where's Big Tom, the deputy?"

"Oh, he's all right, lad," said Ned, the fire trier, tying a handkerchief round my bleeding forehead; "he's havin' his Christmas dinner wi' t' manager ar reckon; plenty of roast beef and plum pudding."

"No, he's not," I replied, solemnly. "He's dead!"

"Gammon," burst out the fire trier, laughing.

But when the pitmen had half-lifted, half-hauled me out of the Devil's Gorge, and went, on my entreaty, to the far bank, they found it a wreck, and crushed beneath a huge piece of rock was Big Tom's lifeless form!

The pit had claimed its victim on Christmas Eve.

THE GHOST AT THE RED FARM
Mabel Collins

Published in Gravesend & Northfleet Standard
(Christmas Supplement), 17 December 1892

Mabel Collins (1851–1927) was "a great and true mystic" and anti-vivisectionist, best known for her treatise on Eastern wisdom *Light on the Path* (1885). Other works include *Morial the Mahatma* (1892), *Fragments of Thought and Life* (1908) and *The Locked Room: A True Story of Experiences in Spiritualism* (1920). Mabel joined the Theosophical Society in the 1880s and helped Helena Blavatsky with editing its *Lucifer* magazine. Mabel then became a vocal critic of the Society after she was expelled from it. She went on to co-found the British Union for the Abolition of Vivisection and gave her time to the Animal Defence Society and slaughter reform. Mabel Collins knew (and lived with) one of the suspects in the Jack the Ripper case, Robert Donston Stephenson, who was a fellow author. Her apocryphal last words were: "the whole creation groaneth and travaileth in pain together". She died at Cintra Lawn, Cheltenham, and was buried in the cemetery there. This story appears here for the first time since 1892.

THE Red Farm is a quiet old house standing in a solitary spot in Berkshire. It is a very long drive from the nearest market town; but that market town, when reached, is but a brief journey from London.

To Lucy Fielding, the light and life of the Red Farm a few short years ago, London was but a name. She had spent all her bright, brief, girlish life in the woods and meadows of her father's land, living with nature, and learning nothing about men and women. She knew nobody, as a matter of fact, but her father, Luke Fielding and George Hayward, who owned the next farm. She was left motherless when a mere child; her father's sister had kept house for him after his wife's death, and reared Lucy, but she, too, had long since joined the majority. And Lucy was left alone with her father and two old servants. She scarcely spoke to anyone else, social life being conducted on the arbitrary principles common in English country places. The Squire's daughters nodded to Lucy when they met her in the lanes; the clergyman's wife stopped and spoke to her for two or three minutes. And that was all Lucy saw of the world. There was George Hayward, of course, stout and red-faced at twenty-five years of age; he had an admirable character, but no conversation. But Lucy need not be pitied. She was infinitely happy with her pets and her flowers, and her many useful occupations. She had not yet learned the meaning of the word unhappiness. But it was to come.

The Red Farm was a small house, but solid and full of comfort. The name came to it simply because it was built of substantial warm-coloured red brick, while most of the houses in the neighbourhood were of a cold grey cement. Luke Fielding had been wild, so it was said, when he was young; but when his father died and left him the broad farm and the comfortable house he came home, he settled down and married. It was late in life for a countryman to marry, but he made his young wife happy, and when she died Lucy became his idol. He was a grave man now, saddened and hardened by his experience of the world, and stern sometimes to others; to Lucy always gentle. But he was never demonstrative. If there was a want in Lucy's young life it was that of expressed love. It was certainly a want, but as yet she did not realise it.

Her fate came one day, as it arrives to most of us, in a very simple manner; the fate which was to teach her life and turn the light-hearted girl into a woman.

She was loitering about the garden one afternoon, admiring her rose-trees, when a stranger came to the gate, and looked at the house, then at Lucy. Then he opened the gate a little, raised his hat, and addressed her.

"Mr. Luke Fielding lives here, does he not?"

"Yes," answered Lucy. "Do you wish to see him? I think he is in the house."

At that moment her father came to the door. It was summer, and all the doors and windows stood open; hearing her voice he imagined she was addressing him. He came out, his after-dinner pipe in his mouth. When he saw the visitor who asked for him, he slowly took the pipe from his mouth and held it in his hand. His colour changed; a grey shade stole over his face.

"Frank Desmond!" he exclaimed, "I thought you were dead!"

"What a cheerful sort of welcome," said Desmond with a laugh. He entered, closed the gate behind him, and sauntered up to the house-door. "I look pretty well for a revived corpse, don't I!"

There was certainly nothing ghostly about him. It was twenty years since these men had been friends, but Desmond was not much changed. He had a fine figure, well carried; at a glance you saw he was a soldier. His long moustache was half grey, and his black hair was grizzled, but his bold black eyes were just the same as ever, and rested on Lucy with the insolent admiration he offered to every pretty girl he had met in the course of an adventurous life. Lucy thought him very handsome, and no wonder; Frank Desmond had the gift of fascinating women.

With an uneasy glance at Lucy, Luke Fielding led the way into the house. He shut the window of the sitting-room into which he took Desmond. Lucy lingered in the garden, wondering how long the visitor would stay, and secretly wishing for another glance at him as he went out. She was immensely astonished when she found he did not go away; he was at the tea-table, and at the supper-table, and ate like a man who had been famished, with an eager, ravenous hunger which soon passed. Luke Fielding regarded him constantly with cold eyes, saying but little. Desmond, on the contrary, made himself very agreeable. He was a practised *raconteur* and could amuse most companies. He watched Lucy's face to see what kind of talked pleased her most, and so kept her in a state of delight and interest such as she had never known before. But her surprise was unlimited when her father told her to have a room made ready for Desmond, as he was going to stay the night. Such a thing had never happened before as the arrival of an unexpected visitor to stay in the house.

Desmond stayed all night and many nights afterwards. Luke Fielding was manifestly uneasy, but he seemed to be powerless. Lucy could not understand the position at all, but she was entering upon a new world of feeling, which soon occupied all her mind and thoughts. She was not much alone with Desmond, for her father prevented it; but when chance gave them a few minutes together he made the most of them. It was in the evening, and at the dinner-table, that Desmond flung his spell upon her. He talked to her father, but for her. To Lucy, it seemed that she had been asleep always till he came. She never thought of love; she looked on Frank Desmond as her father's contemporary, though, as a matter of fact, he was much younger. But when, not long after Desmond's arrival, George Hayward asked her to marry him, in his simple, straightforward way, she was startled at her own feelings. She shrank passionately from the idea of the dull companionship of the young farmer. And yet. She had sense enough to ask herself, What could she expect that would be more agreeable?

Desmond would soon go (for he was always talking about going), and then she would have no one to speak to but her father, who seemed to her colder and sterner than ever. So he was; but not from want of love. A silent fear of the consequences of his own acts, of his own early follies, chilled him. He could not shake off Frank Desmond, and the thought of his helplessness maddened him.

Lucy refused George Hayward as gently as she knew how, for she had long felt that he really cared for her. And when he told her he must go away for a time, to get over it, she felt she should miss his continued good nature, and the many kind little offices he found occasion to do for her. But not as she would miss Desmond when *he* went! Oh, no; that was strangely different. Desmond fascinated her, and she was beginning to have a kind of awestruck admiration for him as for a being of another world. For he told her—when they were alone, not when Luke Fielding was present—how he was a nobleman's son, who had been cast from the lofty sphere to which he was born to undeserved misfortune. She felt profoundly sorry for him; and that, with women of Lucy's stamp, is fatal.

At last, one day when he thought he had prepared the way sufficiently, he filled Lucy's cup of amazement to the brim by asking her to marry him. Such a thought had never entered her head; she forgot that he was much older than herself, forgot that his hair was turning grey while she was in the first freshness of her girlhood; forgot to wonder whether her father would approve of such a marriage, and whether Desmond was in a position to ask for her. All these things were as nothing. She only felt the honour done her by this man who had lived among noble and beautiful women, and that to yield to the fascination he exercised over her would be a wonderful joy. She felt dimly uneasy when she thought of her father, that was all.

After she had gone to her room that night, Desmond told her father what had happened. They were sitting smoking—Desmond, as always, helping himself out of his host's tobacco jar.

"I suppose, Fielding," he said, in his most urbane manner, "you have noticed how I admire your daughter?"

"Leave my little girl alone, Frank," said Luke Fielding, sternly, "or it will be the worse for you."

"Oh, I will not do her any harm!" replied Frank Desmond, complacently. "I want to marry her." Luke Fielding took the pipe from his mouth, as if to regard Desmond the better, just as he had done when he saw the visitor at the gate; but this time his hand trembled so that the pipe fell to the ground and was smashed into little pieces. Desmond looked at him with cool contempt. "Don't get angry, Luke," he said, "it's a waste of energy. I mean to marry her."

"I will kill you with my own hands, as I would a mad dog, before you shall marry my innocent girl, and make her life miserable. You scoundrel! You ought not to be under the same roof with her; you ought not to sit at the same table. Marry her! Never! The very thought is like blasphemy. You blighted my life; you shall not blight hers."

So saying he strode out of the house. He was too angry to stay near Desmond; his hands longed to clutch the throat of this man he so hated and feared, and crush the life out of him. The cool air refreshed him a little. He put his quivering hand to his forehead, damp with the dew of passion.

"There will be murder done if he stays here long!" he said to himself. "Marry my Lucy! that black villain, turned out by his own father, turned out of the army, turned out of every honest place! Why does he want to marry her? Oh, I see it—I see it, fool that I am. He knows my Lucy is all I have, and that I shall leave her in comfort. He is getting on in life, and hates work. He will steal her heart that he may have a table to sit at when I am dead. Oh, my poor child, what a fate for you! I must save you, come what will. How can I do it? While I live you shall be safe—but afterwards!"

Lucy had heard the raised voices, had heard the front door opened and shut again. Had her lover been sent away? With a beating heart she crept downstairs, and softly approached the half-open door of the parlour. Frank Desmond sat there alone, a curious smile on his face. At his feet lay the broken fragments of Luke Fielding's pipe. Lucy, entering, glanced at these fragments, and guessed there had been a scene. She flew to her lover like a frightened bird, and he took her in his arms. He altered his expression for her the instant he heard her step; he was a consummate actor. Lucy only saw in him a passionate, earnest lover. She hid her face on his shoulder, for she was crying a little with terror. Luke Fielding, entering, saw this picture, and saw the smile of triumph on Desmond's face, ill-concealed.

"Lucy," he said, sternly, "go to your room. This man is a scoundrel, not worthy to touch your hand. He is deceiving you if he has told you he loves you. He is incapable of such a feeling. I have decided what to do. You refused George Hayward the other day. He is faithful. He told me that if you altered your mind he would ask you again. You will marry him. I will see that you do. I will provide against accidents. I give this information for the benefit of this man who pretends he cares for you. Tomorrow I shall ride into town and make a new will. I shall leave you penniless unless you marry George Hayward. Go to your room now, and do not leave it in the morning."

Lucy went silently away and crept upstairs, terrified. She had never seen her father like this before. She dared not speak to him, or plead for herself. The motherless, friendless girl was naturally timid and quite unable to take her own part.

Luke Fielding went away to his own room without another word to Desmond, who sat for some time thinking. Desmond knew Fielding well, and knew he would carry out all he said. Before he went to bed he went out of the house again and round to the stables.

When he came down to breakfast in the morning Fielding had gone out. His good bay mare had been saddled early; he had his farm to attend to, and intended to ride into the town, see his lawyer, and ride back in time for the work of the day. He had the key of Lucy's room in his pocket, and felt safe about her. He was sure Desmond would go in search of better game when he knew the will had really been made. So he went off, fairly contented with his extreme measures.

Desmond discussed an excellent breakfast in solitary state. He had been living so temperate a life of late in order to carry out his scheme, that his health was comparatively good. But he was full of hungry longing to go back to his accustomed ways.

Before he rose from the table some men came hurriedly to the door. They were men on the farm, and knew the house well. The door was only latched; they opened it and came into the large kitchen.

"Where's Miss Lucy?" asked one of them.

"Upstairs," answered the old cook, who was busy by the fire. "Why? And what are ye in here for with your muddy boots?"

"The master's been thrown," said the man; "the doctor's with him and says he's dying. They are carrying him home."

"Thrown—by Bess?" said the cook, staring in astonishment.

"Can't make it out," was the answer, "but it's true. Here they are."

In another moment a dismal procession had reached the door, and softly entered the house. Luke Fielding was laid on a wide old settee that stood under the window, which was gay with Lucy's flowers.

"I don't think he'll recover consciousness," said the village doctor, who had just been starting on his rounds in his old-fashioned gig when summoned to Luke Fielding, who lay in the road like one already dead.

But he did recover consciousness. He opened his eyes, and said faintly, "Where's Lucy?"

The old cook, who knew all that had happened, took the key of Lucy's room from his coat pocket. She ran upstairs, her dim eyes blinded with tears, for Fielding had been a good master, and all his dependents loved, though they feared, him. In a few minutes she returned with Lucy, who was white as death herself.

"Here's Miss Lucy, master," said the old woman gently. Luke Fielding heard, and, opening his eyes, fixed them on his daughter. "This is his work, Lucy," he said in a strange voice. "I know it; he is the Devil. I said I would kill him sooner than he should marry you, and I will if I have to come back from the grave to do it." He spoke so low it was hard to hear him. Desmond, who was close by, leaned forward, and Fielding caught sight of him. He stopped speaking, and with a terrible effort, suddenly raised himself and clutched with his two hands at Desmond's throat. In that effort spirit and body parted; he fell back dead. It was awful; and all those who surrounded him drew away in silence saying no word the one to the other.

Lucy was left mistress of the Red Farm, and with a comfortable fortune. This she soon learned from the lawyer, who came over to the funeral and read the will. Annuities were left to the old servants, and everything else to Lucy. She took no interest in what happened; she seemed prostrated by the sudden blow. She crept quietly about the house in her deep mourning, looking pale and wan.

 Desmond had removed himself to the village inn before the funeral took place, and stayed there. He was unpopular, all the rustics believing that he had played some trick with the mare, though for what reason they knew not. But he stayed on in the dull village; sometimes visiting Lucy for half an hour in the afternoon. This was all, but it was enough—she could not free herself from the spell he had cast on her. At the end of three months their banns were published.

 They were married very quietly one morning in the village church. Desmond paid his bill at the inn and returned to his old quarters at the Red Farm.

 And then Lucy began to understand what she had done.

 Directly they were married he threw off the mask he had worn so long; for he was very tired of playing a part. He had won his prize, and now he meant to enjoy it.

It was Christmas time; a year and a month after Lucy's marriage. She stood in the old parlour, among the old surroundings; but how changed herself! It was late; she was listening for the creak of the gate, for a step on the path.

 Frank Desmond was one of those expert and practised drunkards who can walk with a soldierly gait when other men would fall helplessly by the way; who retain their cunning until the final moment when drowsiness clouds all the faculties. He had been drinking steadily now for a year, and he cleverly changed the scene of action during the twenty-four hours from the house to the inn, and sometimes to the market town. He did what he liked, almost; Lucy was like a terrified child in his hands. For the first month, or perhaps not so long, he had kept up the show of a certain feeling for her, but he soon got tired of that. He spent money like water, asking for it in the early days with the manner of a lover. But that quickly passed; he demanded it defiantly, sometimes threateningly, and at last began to assume an air of injured pride at having to recognise that it was hers and not his. He had earned a name of dread in the neighbourhood. Rumours of his evil reputation had come from London through the Squire, and everyone looked pityingly on Lucy. But no one could help her, no one wished to approach her. She was quite alone. She had chosen this man, and must stay by him. He made love to the village girls; he lay in his bed half the day, sleeping off the effects of drink; he expected to be waited on like a prince, and he had not a kind word for anyone, even for Lucy—indeed less for her than for anyone. She passed her life in shame and fear. And now she was frightened at a new aspect of things. She saw that the farm was going to ruin for want of a master; she saw her little fortune melting, without anything being put by to replace it. She dreaded the disgrace of debt, which seemed close at hand, to her amazement, and she found courage enough in her trembling heart to wait up this night and speak to Desmond earnestly. She had been looking over the accounts, and she was frightened. She knew from bitter experience that it was useless to speak to Desmond in the morning, that, like most habitual drunkards when in their swing, he had no sense till he had taken enough to make an ordinary man foolish. So she determined to speak to him tonight. The account books all lay on the table; she had just risen from her seat, and stood listening. Yes, that was the creak of the gate and the familiar step on the path. He was coming through the garden where she had first seen him. There was snow now where there were roses then— as there was ice in her heart now which had once been full of love.

He came in and flung himself into a chair. Heavens! Was this dull sot the man she had loved? Love had not made a woman of Lucy; she was too gentle and timid for it to effect the great transformation. But indignation and righteous anger changed her. The bitter consciousness that this evil creature was wasting her whole life gave her a new strength. She spoke to him; for the first time she told him her mind. His glazed eyes followed her as she moved restlessly about the room speaking out all her injured heart.

But at last he roused himself. He got up from his chair and walked to the mantelpiece with a true soldier's swagger, where he proceeded to fill a pipe and light it.

"You poor, pale, useless piece of goods," he said. "Can you ever have been so foolish as to think I liked you? I that have had the prettiest women in Europe at my feet? Bah! When I've finished your money—and according to your story it will soon be at end—I shall have finished you, never fear. I'd quite enough of you and your white, whimpering ways long ago. I like a fine woman. Don't be afraid, when the money's done you'll have seen the last of me. Put that in your pipe and smoke it, and don't bother me any more! Good God, what's that!" He staggered back like a man struck. Lucy, who stood silent, turned to stone by the words she had heard, thought it was only some drunken fancy. But to her amazement he dropped his pipe and began to fight desperately as if for dear life. His hands passed wildly to and fro before his throat; he bent himself backwards; then he violently turned aside as if he had wrenched himself free from some unseen adversary. But a moment after the same dreadful struggle began again. Then he began to stagger about the room as if trying to escape from someone or something. He passed close to Lucy, apparently not seeing her, but wildly struggling with some imaginary thing that fastened at his throat. Lucy, petrified with the horror of the scene, stood perfectly still, without the strength even to leave the room or call for help. But presently she heard a panting voice beside her: "Ma'am, what is it!" and she knew the old cook was at her side. In his desperate struggles Desmond had knocked against the tables and chairs, and made a noise loud enough to alarm the old servant, who had hurried downstairs expecting to have to protect Lucy from some attack from her drunken husband. What she saw astonished her as it astonished

Lucy, and both stood in perfect silence, watching the extraordinary scene. Desmond went on fighting, without uttering a sound after the first cry of alarm; it seemed as if he could not, as if something prevented him. All round the room, once, twice, three times, he passed—knocking against the wall and the furniture with the desperate indifference of a man fighting for his life and losing the battle. At last he fell on one knee as if forced down—his head fell back—how dark and bloated his face looked! "He's mad, I think," whispered the old cook; "come out of the room, ma'am. I'll run for the doctor."

"Oh, don't leave me alone!" cried Lucy, as the woman drew her into the passage.

"Come with me, then," said the servant, as she opened the door and ran out into the cold night air. The snow lay on the ground; but the doctor's house was not far distant. Lucy, her teeth chattering from fear and cold, ran with old Hannah over the snowy ground rather than stay in the house. The doctor had not gone to bed, and came quickly out of his warm parlour, where he had been comfortably drinking a final glass of grog. He was a pleasant, rough, good-natured man; like everyone else he was very sorry for Lucy. He drew her hand under his arm to help her back to the Red Farm, for she tottered as she walked. They were soon back in the large kitchen of the farm. Desmond lay stretched on the ground. The doctor bent over him, examined him quickly, then suddenly fetched a lamp and placed it on the ground by his side to see the better. After a moment or two he looked up with a strange expression at the two women; his brown face looked pale.

"He is dead," he said. "He has been strangled! Let me look at your hands— No—they are too small—you could not have done it."

The doctor gave a certificate of death, writing down the cause as heart disease. He had known Lucy all her life, and had been good friends with Luke Fielding. It seemed to him that no good could come of an inquest and of public inquiry into an occurrence so strange. There was no way of accounting for those great black marks on Desmond's throat.

But in spite of this attempt to hush the matter up there was talk. For the very night after Desmond's death Lucy and the two women-servants rushed out into the snowy garden in the night, roused from their beds by the sound of the same awful struggle as that of the night before in the farm kitchen! They were too terrified to stay within doors. At last the sounds died away, after they heard the heavy thud of a body falling on the floor. All was still; there was nowhere else to go; so, holding tightly each to the other they re-entered the house and crept upstairs, to sit trembling together till daylight came.

This happened every night for a week, and at last all three women were so completely unnerved and worn out that they could bear it no longer. Directly the funeral was over Lucy left the house and went to some small lodgings in the village. She could live quietly, like this, without any anxiety, in spite of the bad condition the farm had fallen into; and she determined to do so, and to try and find a capable bailiff to get the land into good order again.

One day the clergyman of the parish called on her, wearing a very grave face.

"Is it true, Mrs. Desmond," he said, "the extraordinary story I hear, that you could not live at the Red Farm after your husband's death, because it is haunted?"

"Yes," said Lucy, very much agitated by the question.

"Will you let me have the key for a night?" he asked, "I should like to hear these sounds."

"Willingly," said Lucy, "but do not go alone!"

He smiled at her warning. But there was no smile on his face when he brought the key back two days afterwards.

"I have spent two nights at the farm," he said, "and I cannot account for what happens there. It is as if a devil was in the place! The first night I heard the struggle so distinctly I could not believe my own eyes, which told me the room was empty. The second night I took my man-servant with me, and I doubt if I should have escaped with my life otherwise, for I was myself attacked. Never have I felt anything so horrible as that clutch at my throat! He dragged me out of the room, and I got over it. But I shall never forget it. Mrs. Desmond, you should have that house pulled down!"

Two years later Lucy changed the unlucky name she had taken, and became Mrs. George Hayward, for the quiet farmer was faithful. George Hayward was a simple man in society, but he was an excellent farmer, and under his management Lucy's property soon became valuable again. She had found a good bailiff.

The Red Farm still stands, locked up, and the windows barred; it is half covered with ivy, and Lucy's old garden is a riot of long grass and wild flowers. For no one will live in the house. Sometimes a party is made up to go and stand in the garden and listen to the awful struggle which nightly takes place in the old kitchen.

But since the clergyman's experience no one has been found daring enough to spend a night in the kitchen itself.

THE CHILD WHO HAD EVERYTHING BUT
A CHRISTMAS GHOST STORY

John Kendrick Bangs

First published in Lippincott's Monthly Magazine, *volume 88, issue 528, December 1911*

John Kendrick Bangs (1862–1922) was an American author and humorist, best remembered for the first volume of his "Styx" sequence, *A House-Boat on the Styx: Being Some Account of the Divers Doings of the Associated Shades* (1896), which imagined the ghosts of historical figures sharing a house-boat, with Charon as Janitor. Born in Yonkers, New York, he was educated at Columbia College, taking a course in Classical Philosophy and graduating with a Ph. B in 1883. He studied law for a year, but his love of literature tore him away from it. He became an associate editor of *Life* in 1884, and from there moved to the humour department of *Harper's Magazine* before becoming the editor of *Harper's Weekly* and *Puck* magazine. In 1894 he tried his luck in becoming the Democratic Mayor of Yonkers, but was defeated. In 1899 he wrote *The Enchanted Typewriter*, followed by another well-loved book in 1900, *The Idiot*. He died after several operations to remove "a malignant intestinal growth".

"The Child Who Had Everything But" is one of the gentler stories in this anthology, but it's written so beautifully that it more than deserves its place here. One to mesmerise the very young and perhaps introduce them to their very first ghost! It appears here for the first time since 1911.

I

I KNEW it was coming long before it got there. Every symptom was in sight. I had grown fidgety, and sat fearful of something overpoweringly impending. Strange noises filled the house. Things generally, according to their nature, severally creaked, soughed, and moaned. There was a ghost on the way. That was perfectly clear to an expert in uncanny visitations of my wide experience, and I heartily wished it were not. There was a time when I welcomed such visitors with open arms, because there was a decided demand for them in the literary market, and I had been able to turn a great variety of spooks into anywhere from three thousand to five thousand words apiece at five cents a word, but now the age had grown too sceptical to swallow ghostly reminiscence with any degree of satisfaction. People had grown tired of hearing about Visions, and desired that their tales should reek with the scent of gasoline, quiver with the superfervid fever of tangential loves, and crash with moral thunderbolts aimed against malefactors of great achievement and high social and commercial standing. Wherefore it seemed an egregious waste of time for me to dally with a spook, or with anything else, for that matter, that had no strictly utilitarian value to one so professionally pressed as I was, and especially at a moment like that—it was Christmas morning and the hour was twenty-eight minutes after two—when I was so busy preparing my Ode to June, and trying to work out the details of a midsummer romance in time for the market for such productions early in the coming January.

And right in the midst of all this pressure there rose up these beastly symptoms of an impending visitation. At first I strove to fight them off, but as the minutes passed they became so obsessively intrusive that I could not concentrate upon the work in hand, and I resolved to have it over with.

"Oh, well," said I, striking a few impatient chords upon my typewriting machine, "if you insist upon coming, come, and let's have done with it."

I roared this out, addressing the dim depths of the adjoining apartment, whence had risen the first dank apprehension of the uncanny something that had come to pester me.

"This is my busy night," I went on, when nothing happened in response to my summons, "and I give you fair warning that, however psychic I may be now, I've got too much to do to stay so much longer. If you're going to haunt, haunt!"

It was in response to this appeal that the thing first manifested itself to the eye. It took the shape first of a very slight veil of green fog, which shortly began to swirl slowly from the darkness of the other room through the intervening portières into my den. Once within, it increased the vigour of its swirl, until almost before I knew it there was spinning immediately before my desk something in the nature of a misty maelstrom, buzzing around like a pin-wheel in action.

"Very pretty—very pretty indeed," said I, a trifle sarcastically, refusing to be impressed, "but I don't care for pyrotechnics. I suppose," I added flippantly, "that you are what might be called a mince-pyrotechnic, eh?"

Whether it was the quality of my jest, or some other inward pang due to its gyratory behaviour, that caused it I know not, but as I spoke a deep groan issued from the centre of the whirling mist, and then out of its indeterminateness there was resolved the hazy figure of an angel—only, she was an intensely modern angel. She wore a hobble-skirt instead of the usual flowing robes of ladies of the supernal order, and her halo, instead of hovering over her head as used to be the correct manner of wearing these hard-won adornments, had perforce become a mere golden fillet binding together the great mass of finger-curls and other distinctly yellow capillary attractions that stretched out from the back of her cerebellum for two or three feet, like a monumental psyche-knot. I could hardly restrain a shudder as I realised the theatric quality of the lady's appearance, and I honestly dreaded the possible consequences of her visit. We live in a tolerably censorious age, and I did not care to be seen in the company of such a peroxidised vision as she appeared to be.

"I am afraid, madam," said I, shrinking back against the wall as she approached—"I am very much afraid that you have got into the wrong house. Mr. Slatherberry, the theatrical manager, lives next door."

She paid no attention to this observation, but, holding out a compelling hand, bade me come along with her, her voice having about it all the musical charm of an oboe suffering from bronchitis.

"Not in a year of Sundays I won't!" I retorted. "I am a respectable man, a steady church-goer, a trustee for several philanthropic institutions, and a Sunday-School teacher. I don't wish to be impolite, but really, madam, rich as I am in reputation, I am too poor to be seen in public with you."

"I am a spirit," she began.

"I'll take your word for it," I interjected, and I could see that she told the truth, for she was entirely diaphanous, so much so indeed that one could perceive the piano in the other room with perfect clarity through her intervening shadiness. "It is, however, the unfortunate fact that I have sworn off spirits."

"None the less," she returned, her eye flashing and her hand held forth peremptorily, "you must come. It is your predestined doom."

My next remark I am not wholly clear about, but, as I remember it, it sounded something like "I'll be doomed if I do!" whereupon she threatened me.

"It is useless to resist," she said. "If you decline to come voluntarily, I shall hypnotise you and force you to follow me. We have need of you."

"But, my dear lady," I pleaded, "please have some regard for my position. I never did any of you spirits any harm. I've treated every visitor from the spirit-land with the most distinguished consideration, and I feel that you owe it to me to be regardful of my good name. Suppose you take a look at yourself in yonder looking-glass, and then say if you think it fair to compel a decent, law-abiding man, of domestic inclinations like myself, to be seen in public with—well, with such a looking head of hair as that of yours."

My visitor laughed heartily.

"Oh, if that's all" she said, most amiably, "we can arrange matters in a jiffy. Your wife possesses a hooded mackintosh, does she not? I think I saw something of the kind hanging on the hat-rack as I floated in. I will wear that if it will make you feel any easier."

"It certainly would," said I; "but see here—can't you scare up some other cavalier to escort you to the haven of your desires?"

She fixed a sternly steady eye upon me for a moment.

"Aren't you the man who wrote the lines,

> The World's a green and gladsome ball,
> And Love's the Ruler of it all,
> And Life's the chance vouchsafed to me
> For Deeds and Gifts of sympathy?

Didn't you write that?" she demanded.

"I did, madam," said I, "and I meant every word of it, but what of it? Is that any reason why I should be seen on a public highway with a lady-ghost of your especial kind?"

"Enough of your objections," she retorted firmly. "You are the person for whom I have been sent. We have a case needing your immediate attention. The only question is, will you come pleasantly and of your own free will, or must I resort to extreme measures?"

These words were spoken with such determination that I realised that further resistance was useless, and I yielded.

"All right," said I. "On your way. I'll follow."

"Good!" she cried, her face wreathing with a pleasant little Nile-green smile. "Get the mackintosh, and we'll be off. There's no time to lose," she added, as the clock in the tower on the square boomed out the hour of three.

"What is this anyhow?" I demanded, as I helped her on with the mackintosh and saw that the hood covered every vestige of that awful coiffure. "Another case of Scrooge?"

"Sort of," she replied as, hooking her arm in mine, she led me forth into the night.

II

We passed over to Fifth Avenue, and proceeded uptown at a pace which reminded me of the active gait of my youth. My footsteps had grown unwontedly light, and we covered the first ten blocks in about three minutes.

"We don't seem to be headed for the slums," I panted.

"Indeed, we are not," she retorted. "There is no need of carrying coals to Newcastle on this occasion. This isn't a slum case. It's far more acute than that."

A tear came forth from her eye and trickled down over the mackintosh.

"It is a peculiarity of modern effort on behalf of suffering humanity," she went on, "that it is concentrated upon the relief of the misery of the so-called *sub*merged, to the utter neglect of the often more poignant needs of the emerged. We have workers by the thousand in the slums, doing all that can be done, and successfully too, to relieve the unhappy condition of the poor, but nobody ever seems to think of the sorrows of the starving hundreds on upper Fifth Avenue."

"See here, madam," said I, stopping suddenly short under a lamp-post in front of the Public Library, "I want to tell you right now that if you think you are going to take me into any of the homes of the hopelessly rich at this time of the morning, you are the most mightily mistaken creature that ever wore a psyche-knot. Why, great heavens, my dear lady, suppose the owner of the house were to wake up and demand to know what I was doing there at this time of night? What could I say?"

"You have gone on slumming parties, haven't you?" she demanded coldly.

"Often," said I. "But that's different."

"Why?" she asked, with a simplicity that baffled me. "Is it any worse for you to intrude upon the home of a Fifth Avenue millionaire than it is to go unasked into the small, squalid tenement of some poor sweat-shop worker on the East Side?"

"Oh, but it's different," I protested. "I go there to see if there is anything I can do to relieve the unhappy condition of the persons who live in the slums."

"No doubt," said she. "I'll take your word for it, but is that any reason why you should neglect the sufferers who live in these marble palaces?"

As she spoke, she hooked hold of my arm once more, and in a moment we were climbing the front door steps of a palatial residence. The house showed a dark and forbidding front at that hour in the morning despite its marble splendours, and I was glad to note that the massive grille doors of wrought-iron were heavily barred.

"It's useless, you see. We're locked out," I ventured.

"Indeed?" she retorted, with a sarcastic smile, as she seized my hand in her icy grip and literally pulled me after her through the marble front of the dwelling. "What have we to do with bolts and bars?"

"I don't know," said I ruefully, "but I have a notion that if I don't bolt I'll get the bars all right."

I could see them coming, and they were headed straight for me.

"All you have to do is to follow me," she went on, as we floated upward for two flights, paying but little attention to the treasures of art that lined the walls, and finally passed into a superbly lighted salon, more daintily beautiful than anything of the kind I had ever seen before.

"Jove!" I ejaculated, standing amazed in the presence of such luxury and beauty. "I did not realise that with all her treasures New York held anything quite so fine as this. What is it, a music-room?"

"It is the nursery," said my companion. "Look about you and see for yourself."

I did as I was bade, and such an array of toys as that inspection revealed! Truly it looked as if the toy-market in all sections of the world had been levied upon for tribute. Had all the famous toy emporiums of Nuremburg itself been transported thither bodily, there could not have been playthings in greater variety than there greeted my eye. From the most insignificant of tin-soldiers to the most intricate of mechanical toys for the delectation of the youthful mind, nothing that I could think of was missing.

The tin-soldiers as ever had a fascination for me, and in an instant I was down upon the floor, ranging them in their serried ranks, while the face of my companion wreathed with an indulgent smile.

"You'll do," said she, as I loaded a little spring-cannon with a stub of a lead-pencil and bowled over half a regiment with one well-directed shot.

"These are the finest tin-soldiers I ever saw!" I cried with enthusiasm.

"Only they're not tin," said she. "Solid silver, every man-jack of them—except the officers—they're made of platinum."

"And will you look at that little electric railroad!" I cried, my eye ranging to the other end of the salon. "Stations, switches, danger-signals, cars of all kinds, and even miniature Pullmans, with real little berths that can be let up and down—who is the lucky kid who's getting all these beautiful things?"

"Sh!" she whispered, putting her finger to her lips. "He is coming—go on and play. Pretend you don't see him until he speaks to you."

As she spoke, a door at the far end of the apartment swung gently open, and a little boy tiptoed softly in. He was a golden-haired little chap, and I fell in love with his soft, dreamy eyes the moment my own rested upon them. I could not help glancing up furtively to see his joy over the discovery of all these wondrous possessions, but alas, to my surprise, there was only an unemotional stare in his eyes as they swept the aggregation of childish treasures. Then, on a sudden, he saw me, squatting on the floor, setting up again the army of silver warriors.

"How do you do?" he said gently, but with just a touch of weariness in his sad little voice.

"Good morning, and a Merry Christmas to you, sir," I replied.

"What are you doing?" he asked, drawing near, and watching me with a good deal of seeming curiosity.

"I am playing with your soldiers," said I. "I hope you don't mind?"

"Oh, indeed," he replied; "but what do you mean by that? What is playing?"

I could hardly believe my ears.

"What is what?" said I.

"You said you were playing, sir," said he, "and I don't know exactly what you mean."

"Why," said I, scratching my head hard in a mad quest for a definition, for I couldn't for the life of me think of the answer to his question offhand, any more than I could define one of the elements. "Playing is—why, it's playing, laddy. Don't you know what it is to play?"

"Oh, yes," said he. "It's what you do on the piano—I've been taught to play on the piano, sir."

"Oh, but this is different," said I. "This kind is fun—it's what most little boys do with their toys."

"You mean—breaking them?" said he.

"No, indeed," said I. "It's getting all the fun there is out of them."

"I think I should like to do that," said he, with a fixed gaze upon the soldiers. "Can a little fellow like me learn to play that way?"

"Well, rather, kiddie," said I, reaching out and taking him by the hand. "Sit down here on the floor alongside of me, and I'll show you."

"Oh, no," said he, drawing back; "I—I can't sit on the floor. I'd catch cold."

"Now, who under the canopy told you that?" I demanded, somewhat impatiently, I fear.

"My governesses and both my nurses, sir," said he. "You see, there are draughts—"

"Well, there won't be any draughts this time," said I. "Just you sit down here, and we'll have a game of marbles—ever play marbles with your father?"

"No, sir," he replied. "He's always too busy, and neither of my nurses has ever known how."

"But your mother comes up here and plays games with you sometimes, doesn't she?" I asked.

"Mother is busy, too," said the child. "Besides, she wouldn't care for a game which you had to sit on the floor to—"

I sprang to my feet and lifted him bodily in my arms, and, after squatting him over by the fireplace where if there were any draughts at all they would be as harmless as a summer breeze, I took up a similar position on the other side of the room, and initiated him into the mystery of miggles as well as I could, considering that all his marbles were real agates.

"You don't happen to have a china-alley anywhere, do you?" I asked.

"No, sir," he answered. "We only have china plates—"

"Never mind," I interrupted. "We can get along very nicely with these."

And then for half an hour, despite the rich quality of our paraphernalia, that little boy and I indulged in a glorious game of real plebeian miggs, and it was a joy to see how quickly his stiff little fingers relaxed and adapted themselves to the uses of his eye, which was as accurate as it was deeply blue. So expert did he become that in a short while he had completely cleaned me out, giving joyous little cries of delight with every hit, and then we turned our attention to the soldiers.

"I want some playing now," he said gleefully, as I informed me that he had beaten me out of my boots at one of my best games. "Show me what you were doing with those soldiers when I came in."

"All right," said I, obeying with alacrity. "First, we'll have a parade."

I started a great talking-machine standing in one corner of the room off on a spirited military march, and inside of ten minutes, with his assistance, I had all the troops out and to all intents and purposes bravely swinging by to the martial music of Sousa.

"How's that?" said I, when we had got the whole corps arranged to our satisfaction.

"Fine!" he cried, jumping up and down upon the floor and clapping his hands with glee. "I've got lots more of these stored away in my toy-closet," he went on, "but I never knew that you could do such things as this with them."

"But what did you think they were for?" I asked.

"Why—just to—to keep," he said hesitatingly.

"Wait a minute," said I, wheeling a couple of cannon off to a distance of a yard from the passing troops. "I'll show you something else you can do with them."

I loaded both cannon to the muzzle with dried pease, and showed him how to shoot.

"Now," said I, *"fire!"*

He snapped the spring, and the dried pease flew out like death-dealing shells in war. In a moment the platinum commander of the forces, and about thirty-seven solid silver warriors, lay flat on their backs. It needed only a little red ink on the carpet to reproduce in miniature a scene of great carnage, but I shall never forget the expression of mingled joy and regret on his countenance as those creatures went down.

"Don't you like it, son?" I asked.

"I don't know," he said, with an anxious glance at the prostrate warriors. "They aren't deaded, are they?"

"Of course not," said I, restoring the presumably defunct troopers to life by setting them up again. "The only thing that'll dead a soldier like these is to step on him. Try the other gun."

Thus reassured, he did as I bade him, and again the proud paraders went down, this time amid shouts of glee. And so we passed an all too fleeting two hours, that little boy and I. Through the whole list of his famous toys we went, and as well as I could I taught him the delicious uses of each and all of them, until finally he seemed to grow weary, and so, drawing up a big armchair before the fire and taking his tired little body into my lap, with his tousled head cuddled up close over the spot where my heart is alleged to be, I started to read a story to him out of one of the many beautiful books that had been provided for him by his generous parents. But I had not gone far when I saw that his attention was wandering.

"Perhaps you'd rather have me tell you a story instead of reading it," said I.

"What's to tell a story?" he asked, fixing his blue eyes gravely upon mine.

"Great Scott, kiddie!" said I, "didn't anybody ever tell you a story?"

"No, sir," he replied sleepily; "I get read to every afternoon by my governess, but nobody ever told me a story."

"Well, just you listen to this," said I, giving him a hearty squeeze. "Once upon a time there was a little boy," I began, "and he lived in a beautiful house not far from the Park, and his daddy—"

"What's a daddy?" asked the child, looking up into my face.

"Why, a daddy is a little boy's father," I explained. "You've got a daddy—"

"Oh, yes," he said. "If a daddy is a father, I've got one. I saw him yesterday," he added.

"Oh, did you?" said I. "And what did he say to you?"

"He said he was glad to see me and hoped I was a good boy," said the child. "He seemed very glad when I told him I hoped so, too, and he gave me all these things here—he and my mother."

"That was very nice of them," said I huskily.

"And they're both coming up some time today or tomorrow to see if I like them," said the lad.

"And what are you going to say?" I asked, with difficulty getting the words out over a most unaccountable lump that had arisen in my throat.

"I'm going to tell them," he began, as his eyes closed sleepily, "that I like them all very, very much."

"And which one of them all do you like the best?" said I.

He snuggled up closer in my arms, and, raising his little head a trifle higher, he kissed me on the tip end of my chin, and murmured softly as he dropped off to sleep,

"You!"

III

"Good night," said my spectral visitor as she left me, once more bending over my desk, whither I had been retransported without my knowledge, for I must have fallen asleep, too, with that little boy in my arms. "You have done a good night's work."

"Have I?" said I, rubbing my eyes to see if I were really awake. "But tell me—who was that little kiddie anyhow?"

"He?" she answered with a smile. "Why, he is the Child Who Has Everything But."

And then she vanished from my sight.

"Everything but what?" I cried, starting up and peering into the darkness into which she had disappeared.

But there was no response, and I was left alone to guess the answer to my question.

THE HAUNTED VICARAGE

Emeric Hulme-Beaman

Published in Manilla Express, *Christmas supplement, 24 December 1903*

Emeric Hulme Beaman (1864–1937) was an Indian-born British author, singer, composer and music critic. Moving back to England in his youth, he attended Bedford Grammar School and then entered the Royal Academy of Music. At twenty, he went to Egypt, where he took up literature and wrote articles alongside his brother for *The Times of Egypt*. On his return to Britain he moved to Eastbourne and co-wrote four mystery novels with William Senior Ellis under the pen name of "Ben Strong", including *The Secret of Gnome Head* (1928). Under his own name (hyphenated as Hulme-Beaman) he also wrote books of genre interest, such as *Ozmar the Mystic* (1896) and *The Experiment of Doctor Nevill* (1900). Beaman was blind for the last ten years of his life (as was another of his brothers, similarly afflicted), but was still attending Winter Garden concerts in Eastbourne until two months before he passed away. His older brother Sydney George Hulme Beaman is known as the author of *Tales of Toytown*, which spawned the popular children's radio play series *Toytown*, and as the illustrator of the 1930 John Lane edition of *The Strange Case of Dr. Jekyll and Mr. Hyde*. "The Haunted Vicarage" appears here for the first time since 1903.

I HAD a letter one morning from my old college friend, Alfred Marsden, in which he pressed me to travel down and spend a few days with him in his new vicarage at Walford.

"I am here, installed," he wrote, "in a singularly commodious and substantial house. The size of it and the grounds attached seem, indeed, ridiculously disproportionate to the needs of a solitary tenant. None the less I like the place, and I think when you see it you will agree that a poor parson could scarcely be better lodged. The fen country, as you know, is somewhat inhospitable—flat and bleak to a degree when the winter is on it—yet I am told it is not unattractive in summer time; and as for my Walford parishioners, I should be truly a churl were I insensible to the cordiality of the reception I have met with at their hands. Absolve me from vanity, I beg, when I state (with all proper modesty) that I believe the new vicar to be already quite a popular person in the town. I have been here now nearly a month, and the numberless duties that demand the almost continuous attention of a newly-inducted incumbent have prevented me from writing to you earlier. Come down and spend a week with me here, if your leisure permits, and I will promise you some good wine and roomy, if not luxurious, quarters. Indeed, I am most particularly anxious for you to see my vicarage. There are some points of interest about the house—'tis an old-fashioned enough one!—upon which I should be glad to hear your criticism."

As I have already said, the Rev. Alfred Marsden was an old friend of mine. At college, and before his ordination, he had been something of a wild fellow, and had distinguished himself not a little in the field of Athletics. He had sobered down considerably since those days, and while still retaining all the splendid vigour of intellect and body that had characterised his early manhood, he had developed an earnest and thoughtful cast of mind which peculiarly fitted him for the high office he now so conscientiously filled. He was a man of exceptionally clear and practical judgment, and I know no other to whom I would have more readily gone for advice upon any matter that required for its solution the strongest common sense, combined with the keenest appreciation of logical subtleties. He never permitted his judgment to be led astray by prejudice or passion; nor to be influenced by emotional considerations or the appeals of the imagination. In a word, he was what is commonly described as a "strong-minded" man; and I may add that he was an excellent companion and a very staunch friend.

It was early in December when I took advantage of the invitation conveyed to me by Marsden's letter, and arrived at the little town of Walford, which is situated on the outskirts of Lincolnshire in a somewhat dreary tract of country that looked drearier still under the dull snow-laden sky of a winter afternoon. The vicar met me at the station in his dog-cart.

"I am very glad you have been able to come, my dear fellow," said he, grasping my hand in his strong muscular grip. "To tell you the truth I have been feeling the want, lately, of company—the company of an intimate—of a friend with whom I may chat unreservedly as a man, and not as a clergyman, you understand!"

"In the old college fashion!" I laughed.

"Ah—the old college fashion!" he repeated, with a smile and a sigh. "Jump in. We have a mile's drive to the town, and the air bites a little shrewdly. You must be cool after your journey."

In ten minutes we rattled in through the large gates of the vicarage garden, and driving along a wide gravel path, pulled up at the front door of the house.

"By Jove, you have a nice place here!" I exclaimed, descending from the dog-cart and casting a glance at the solid building in front of me, and the extensive grounds surrounding it.

"Too large—for one man," he replied. "It was built by a predecessor of mine. It is a substantial mansion, truly—but come in and get warm."

I followed him into the hall, where we divested ourselves of our coats and wraps and stamped the snow from our boots; and here again I was struck by the vastness and odd architectural design of my friend's house. The hall was spacious, and stretched nearly the whole length of the side wing of the building, reaching upwards to the full height of the roof. On the right was a broad staircase that led by two flights (along the length of the walls on the right of the wing) to the upper storey, round which a rectangular gallery ran, looking down upon the hall beneath. The gallery and the staircase and the hall formed thus a kind of oblong well. There was but one storey to the house, but the rooms on the ground floor were not only commodious but remarkably lofty; and each room communicated with the rooms at either end of it, as well as with the hall on its right, by doors. Spacious indeed was the first impression produced upon the mind by the aspect of the interior of the house. The outer walls were built in a treble thickness, and the windows ran the full length of the wall from ceiling to floor, and could be slid open to half their width. The floor was nearly level with the ground, and from the windows you could step out on to the gravel path that bounded the lawn. Though the house was certainly large for the needs of a single occupant—so large, in truth, as to emphasise a certain feeling of solitude—it contained capacities for comfort that might be regarded as a more than counterbalancing advantage to its possible suggestion of dreariness.

I was shown to my room (which, like most of the others, opened into the corridor formed by the gallery of the stairway), and, after unpacking my portmanteau and changing my clothes, rejoined my friend Marsden, and sat down with him presently to a very excellently prepared dinner. After dinner parochial duties engaged his attention during the earlier part of the evening, and it was not till nearly ten o'clock that he announced himself free to settle down to a quiet uninterrupted cigar and a glass of hot whisky and water. He led the way to the study (which, of the three rooms on the ground floor, was the one nearest to the hall door) and there motioned me to an easy chair before a blazing fire. The room, lofty and well lined with book cases, heavily curtained and lit by a shaded lamp, presented a singularly snug and comfortable appearance. The vicar handed me his cigar case.

"This habit of smoking," he observed with a smile, "grows upon one with years—and solitude! You are looking well, Addison. Dear me, to think that we are both bachelors still—and I forty next birthday!"

"My dear fellow," I smiled, "what sensible man ever thinks of marrying before he is forty? But for a clergyman it must be difficult—" I paused.

The vicar laughed.

"To escape the inevitable? Well, well, perhaps it is—and perhaps it is best not to try and escape it," he added, thoughtfully.

"What!" I exclaimed, looking up; "are you tired, then, of your bachelor joys—do you meditate the fatal and irrevocable step?"

He shook his head.

"I believe it's the best thing—the only thing for a man to do," he replied; "at any rate, for a man in my position, for a clergyman. He has greater need for a helpmate (I use the word in its good old-fashioned sense) than other men. And consider, my dear friend, the solitude of my position. Look, for instance, at this house!"

He waved his cigar round him.

"It imperatively demands the presence of a mistress!" I agreed. "But are you seriously thinking of marrying?"

"I am. But—oddly enough, I am a little disturbed about this house. I am not sure that it would be entirely suitable for—for a young bride."

"Why on earth not?" I asked in surprise. "It seems to me to carry recommendations for domestic comfort?"

"Materially it conveys that impression," he replied. "By-the-bye, do you remember our psychological experiments at Oxford?" asked the vicar, with sudden irrelevance.

"Do I not! Ah, scoffer that you were!"

"No—no," he replied, "not scoffer. I was always open, as you know, to reasonable conviction—but," he smiled, "I must confess that I was never reasonably convinced!"

I glanced at Marsden's strong calm face, with its firm mouth and deep thoughtful eyes, upon which the flickering firelight cast fugitive shadows, and I thought how difficult it would be to "reasonably convince" my friend, the vicar.

"You were in those days," he pursued, "almost inclined to be a believer, Addison. Have your opinions changed since then?"

"I still retain an agnostic attitude." I laughed. "And you?"

He shrugged his shoulders slightly, and for a few moments puffed his cigar in silence.

"I think," he observed presently, "that every man who concedes immortality, must at the same time be prepared to concede the possibility of spiritual appearance. The difficulty is to discriminate accurately between subjective and objective phenomena; to know where optical illusion ceases, and actual manifestation begins."

He had hardly spoken the words when, to my astonishment, I perceived the door of the study, opposite to which I sat, slowly, very slowly open, upon noiseless hinges; and a draught swept across my face. The vicar noticed my look of surprise, and turning his head slightly, smiled.

"Here is an illustration to my hand!" he remarked. "Watch that door! Observe, it is opening to its widest extent. Now, we are able to satisfy ourselves by examination and physical contact, that the door is open, and that, therefore, we have not been the victims of an optical illusion." He got up from his chair and closed the door. "That, you see, is an instance that you can be made subject to the test of proofs," he laughed.

"What a very odd circumstance," I exclaimed. "The door must have blown open from outside."

"Quite possibly," agreed the vicar, blandly. "It very frequently behaves in that independent manner. Throw your cigar away and light another. Now, tell me your news!"

For the next half hour we talked on—of many an old association—past memories, college friends, our early ambitions, and how in some cases they have been destroyed, in others fulfilled—the half regretful, half tender talk of men who drag back the curtains of the past and look again upon the fading pictures of their youth altogether, sometimes with a laugh, sometimes perhaps with something very like a tear. It was in a pause in our conversation that I became suddenly conscious of a low but clear and distinct sound. The vicar was staring at the fire, and did not move his head. I looked up.

"What's that?" I asked.

"What's what?" said he.

"Do you not hear that odd tapping at the window? There must be somebody standing on the gravel outside."

"I heard it," said the vicar, "but I wished to satisfy myself that the sound was not an aural delusion of mine—so I waited to see whether you, too, would remark the noise. It is certainly a distinct tapping on the window pane, as you say."

I rose from my chair. "Had we not better open the window, and see who's there?" I suggested.

The vicar laid his hand on my arm.

"I don't think I should trouble," he said with a queer smile. "There's nobody there, Addison."

"Why, how do you know?"

"Because I have heard that tapping every evening those three weeks past," he replied calmly, "and have thrown open the window over and over again—aye, and thoroughly searched the garden walks all round the house, too—but to no purpose. There's never anybody there—not even a tramp," he concluded humorously.

"It must be the wind, then," was my lame rejoinder.

"Very likely," agreed the vicar again. "This is a rambling, great lonely house," he added, "for one man to live in alone. I say alone, for I scarcely count my two servants, who sleep in a contiguous wing. Often going up to bed by myself at one or two in the morning, I am conscious of odd thrills of uneasiness, as I ascend the creaking staircase, and traverse the deserted corridors with my candle in my hand. You are aware how the noises of the night will swell and gather confidence, as it were, in an empty house. Happily I am not a nervous man. Nor are you."

He spoke the last three words pointedly—almost as an interrogation. I laughed a negative.

"I have not your iron nerves," I replied; "but mine are pretty strong, too, I believe."

"If they were not, I should not have asked you to come here," said the vicar, enigmatically.

"And why not?" I asked.

"To be plain," said the vicar, "for a fanciful name such a house as this is full of disconcerting possibilities."

"Oh, indeed! Haunted, eh?" I smiled.

"I will not go as far as that," said Marsden. "Neither you nor I are fanciful men. But an empty house is an admirable field for the operations of the imagination, you know!"

We chatted a few minutes longer and then I expressed my intention of going to bed, for I felt sleepy after my journey. The vicar attended me to my room.

"I have a little writing to do," he said, as he wished me good night, "and shall return to my study for an hour. I hope you will sleep well. My room is next to yours." He closed the door, and I heard his firm footsteps echoing down the corridor outside. Suddenly they paused, then went on again and descended the stairs.

I turned up the gas, took off my boots and threw myself into an easy chair before undressing before the fire. I stretched my slippered feet towards it, and leaned back luxuriously. In this attitude of easy repose I became the next instant conscious of an odd sensation. I felt a soft touch on my shoulder, and looking round, thought I discovered the outline of a hand resting on my arm. As my eye fell upon it the hand disappeared. The touch, however, was repeated twice, and an involuntary shiver ran through me. I rose and paced the room, looking to the right and left of me. Then persuading myself I had been the victim of my own fancy, I undressed, and turning out the light, got into bed. I soon fell asleep, but my dreams became gradually assimilated with the suggestion of some external noise, which slowly dominating them at length awoke me to consciousness. The sound of which I had been dimly and uncertainly conscious in my sleep now assumed a distinct and definite character. I heard a low knocking at my bedroom door—as of someone demanding admittance. My first instinctive impression was that it was the vicar, and, still scarcely awake, I called out:

"Come in, is that you, Marsden?"

There was no answer, but after an instant's silence the tapping was resumed. I jumped out of bed, and lit the gas. Then I stepped rapidly to the door and threw it open. The corridor outside was in darkness. At first I could see nothing; but peering down the length of the passage I seemed to descry a tall amorphous figure, faintly discernible, in the act of turning the corner. I rubbed my eyes and looked again. But there was nothing. The yawning space below was also plunged in darkness. Marsden had evidently retired to bed. I returned to my room, shut the door and looked at my watch. It was past one o'clock.

"Fancy," I laughed, "mere fancy! Yet the tapping was clear enough!"

I closed my eyes, but in ten minutes opened them again with an exclamation of impatience. I now distinctly heard something tapping on the outside of the window pane. I lay still for some moments and listened. The tapping continued, regular and firm, a succession of rapid little knocks as though delivered by a man's knuckles, with pauses in between. I sprang from bed, struck a light, and ran to the window, which I flung open. A cold gust of air swept into the room, the night was black and damp. I thrust out my head, but the darkness was too thick for the eye to penetrate; I was nevertheless easily able to satisfy myself that at least no physical object was there which could be answerable for the tapping on the pane. It might, I reflected, have been a bird, and instinctively with a grim humour my thoughts reverted to Poe's Raven, and I got into bed chuckling. I was not, however, destined to remain long undisturbed. I lay with my right arm outside the coverlet of the bed; and in this position I became presently aware of a strange sensation, the sensation of a cold, light touch on my wrist. I opened my eyes with a start. Resting on my half-open palm, I perceived the luminous outline of another hand, its long sinewy fingers closing round my own.

With an odd fascination I fixed my eyes upon this hand, and as I stared upon it for the second time it faded gradually away; but in place of the light, cold touch, I now felt an invisible grip tightening upon my wrist. I withdrew my hand from the unearthly clasp, and to my relief I felt it yield to my resistance, though without relaxing its hold. On the contrary, directly I permitted my arm to rest impassive, the pressure on my wrist increased with a kind of gentle insistence, drawing me towards it. A strange idea struck me, and yielding entirely to the unseen pressure, I allowed myself gently but firmly to be raised from my recumbent position, till, in obedience to this guiding impulse, I stood on the floor. Still the pressure on my wrist continued, the unseen hand led me unresisting to the door, and there laid my fingers on the handle. The suggestion was obvious: I opened the door; the hand took mine, and conducted me along the dark passage outside. A few paces brought me to the door of the vicar's bedroom, and here my invisible guide stopped, the cold touch fell from my wrist, and as I stood shivering in the passage, I heard a low knocking on the panel beside me, the knocking that I had previously heard on the door of my own bedroom.

"Who is there?" called the clear, strong voice of the vicar from within.

The knocking stopped. An irresistible impulse made me answer—

"It is I, Marsden!"

And then the falseness of my position burst upon me with a keen sense of the ridiculous. The invisible presence had tricked me into performing lackey service for it!

"Well—come in!" said the vicar.

I opened the door, and entered the room. Marsden had sprung from his bed and lit a match.

"What's the matter?" he asked, turning on the gas and surveying me in my scant attire with a certain anxiety. "Not ill, I hope?"

"No," I said, a little shamefacedly; "but I seem to be the dupe of some very extraordinary agency, my dear fellow!" and then, as briefly as I could, I recounted to him the incidents of the last few hours.

The vicar listened to me, silently and without interruption, till I had quite finished. Then he knitted his brows.

"I have now, at least," he said, "the confirmation of your independent testimony, my dear Addison—and you are neither a hysterical nor an imaginative man. I carefully refrained from preparing your mind beforehand to receive impressions by relating experiences; for it is my opinion that if you inform a man that a room, or a house is haunted, his imagination is at once on the alert to detect—or even invent—phenomena to suit his preconceived ideas of what he is to expect. I may, however admit to you that I, too, have been confronted with the most remarkable occurrences, ever since I took up my residence in this house. I wished to convince myself that these occurrences were not due to subjective hallucinations. Tonight you have relieved my doubts on that head—for you yourself have also been a witness to some portion of them. May I ask if you experienced any sensation of fear?" inquired the vicar, a little anxiously.

It was not without a feeling of surprise that I was able to reply that I had not. It now struck me for the first time that the sentiment of fear had been strangely absent from me throughout the entire succession of incidents that had just culminated in my arrival at the vicar's bedroom. I had felt a certain degree of excitement—nothing more.

"There remains the fact," mused Marsden, "that this invisible hand led you to my room, and then knocked at the door. Why did it lead you to my room? What does this suggest to you?"

"Well," pursued the vicar, "to me it suggests that this unseen agency—whatever it is or however actuated—has for some inconceivable reason, identified me directly or indirectly with the accomplishment of its purpose. I may be wrong."

"That is rather difficult to determine," I replied.

The vicar looked at me curiously.

"Are you quite sure that your nerves are proof against any further manifestations?" he asked.

"I think so."

"Would you, for example, be afraid to take this candle, and go down to my study?"

"Certainly not," I answered.

"Then," said the vicar, "I should feel rather relieved if you would do so, Addison. I will not promise you that you will encounter anything on your journey to repay you for your trouble," he added with a smile. "None the less, I should feel more satisfied if you were to go."

"By all means," I said, "if you will permit me to put on my dressing gown first. It's precious cold."

I walked back to my room, whence I emerged in dressing gown and slippers a couple of minutes later, and took the candle from Marsden's hand.

"I will leave my door ajar," said he. "If you want me, call—and I will be with you in less than a moment."

"All right," I said, and proceeded slowly down the first angle of the corridor, the flame of the candle throwing fitful shadows on either side of me as I walked, and seeming to accentuate rather than to relieve the gloom before and behind. I traversed both sections of the gallery and reached the head of the staircase. Holding the candle high above me, I commenced to descend the stairs—as I advanced I fancied I heard the light fall of a footstep behind me, echoing my own; I stopped, and the footstep stopped, too—there was no sound. Again I advanced, and again, directly following me, as it were, I was sensible of a distinct footfall. I continued my progress, however, reached the abysmal hall, peered round into the darkness, saw nothing, and crossed to the study door. This I opened and entered the study. I remained nearly a minute in the room—it was still, silent, and empty, and—with the exception of the fact that the footstep which had followed me to the study door, ceased at that point—nothing at least worthy of notice appeared.

I left the study, closing the door behind me, and proceeded again to cross the hall towards the foot of the staircase. In the middle of the hall, however,

I paused; and in obedience to some sudden unaccountable impulse, looked up to the gallery above me. Then for the first time, a thrill of superstitious fear shot through my heart, for there above me, leaning on the balcony and gazing down upon me with a calm inscrutable countenance, I beheld the figure of a man. In the surrounding darkness the figure stood out luminous and distinct—even its very features shone with a singular phosphorescent transparency, as its eyes held mine for one brief moment. Then in the silence we remained for the space of a few seconds, contemplating each other—I below, the Apparition above, its arms folded, its attitude motionless. Then slowly it rose, straightened itself, and moving along the corridor began to descend the staircase towards me. A sudden inexpressible horror seized upon me, my knees shook. As, stair by stair, the phantom (for phantom I felt it to be) approached nearer and nearer to me, with an inexorable steadiness of progress, the sense of this mysterious advancing Presence froze my blood with the insidious impotence of some deadly nightmare. I could not stir; but in a sudden frenzy of fear I gathered up my energies for one despairing shout:

"Marsden!"

The cry rang out and echoed through the empty hall and along the corridors, and was in an instant answered from above.

"All right, Addison!" called the vicar, and a moment later, with candle in hand, my friend dashed from his room, and ran towards the stairs. At the same instant the Apparition disappeared.

"Hull—what's the matter?" asked the vicar. "Why, man, you are trembling all over!"

He took my arm and led me to his room. By the time we reached it I had recovered my nerve and self-possession.

"Funk—sheer funk, nothing else!" I laughed. Then I told him what I had seen.

"Ah," said Marsden, "that gentleman again!"

"That gentleman? What do you mean?"

"Merely, my dear Addison, that I, too, have seen the apparition of a man—a dozen times at least; sometimes I have met him (I did this evening—after I had said good night to you!) on the stairs—sometimes he has visited me in my study; once he visited me in this bedroom: but I was never quite persuaded that I was not the victim of some persistent optical illusion, and that is why I said nothing about the Apparition to you. I wished first to ascertain whether it were merely a creation of my own fancy, or whether it were really an apparition, that would present itself equally to the vision of another besides myself. Again you have satisfied me on this point. Two men acting independently, could not thus be afflicted with an exactly identical hallucination—the suspicion is absurd. There can be no doubt, therefore, that the Apparition is an apparition of some kind or other. But what is its motive in appearing? That is what I want to find out! And, if you have no objection—the night is already tolerably far spent, and I fear your night's rest is irretrievably spoiled—I should like to devote the remainder of the hours of darkness to a joint vigil. I should like if possible to try and solve this mystery at once. Are you agreeable?"

"Perfectly—though I will not trust my resolution to face any more solitary encounters!"

"No, no—we will go through it together: two heads are proverbially better than one. Put on your clothes and we will go down to the study, I can soon light a fire to keep us warm."

I repaired to my room and did the same. It was past two o'clock when at length we descended the stairs together. Arrived at the hall I again, with an involuntary shudder, cast my eyes to the gallery, but no figure leaned over the balcony this time, and I followed Marsden to the study, where with the help of a few sticks, a newspaper, and some dry legs of wood, we speedily had a bright fire blazing in the hearth. Two candles burned on the table beside us. The vicar did not light the lamp—the semi-gloom seemed better suited to the purpose in hand.

"Had you, then, no suspicion that this house was haunted," I asked, "when you entered into possession of it?"

"I had heard vague rumours only," answered Marsden, "but paid little attention to them. The late vicar lived here nearly thirty years—the last seven or eight years (after the death of his wife) alone. Apparently the manifestations were not sufficient to disturb his peace of mind—at any rate he made but slight allusion to them, and fulfilled his duties here quite tranquilly to the end. Now, there seems to me to be something oddly significant about the methods adopted by this Apparition—if apparition it is, something not devoid of intelligent motive and design. I am much struck by the circumstance of the hand leading you to my room, for instance. This is a feature foreign to my own experiences. Let us, my dear Addison, suppose then that this apparition is an intelligent Being—a spiritual appearance actuated by an intelligent motive—and see if we cannot contrive to fathom its object. For if I go so far as to admit that it is a Spiritual Appearance, I am unwilling to believe that such an Appearance can be the result of an absolutely purposeless and irresponsible caprice. We have both seen it independently; it now remains to be learnt whether we shall both see it together. Ha—!"

He paused abruptly. As once before early in the evening, the door of the study began slowly to open, and a gust of air fanned the flames of the candles. The door opened to its widest extent, showing the gaping blackness of the hall beyond. We saw nothing, but an extraordinary sensation assailed me that something had entered the room and was standing beside my chair. The next instant I felt a touch on my shoulder.

"Somebody is touching me," I said without moving.

"Keep still," said the vicar.

We neither of us spoke for some moments. Then I felt again the touch of a hand on my arm. The touch strengthened into a grasp and seemed striving to draw me from my seat.

"Something is dragging at my arm," I said.

"Obey it," said the vicar, calmly.

I rose to my feet, the grasp still on my arm, and then was conscious of an unseen force drawing me towards the open door. The vicar rose, too, and seized one of the candles from the table. I stepped to the door, the vicar close at my heels. I felt myself pulled with a sudden roughness into the hall, and at the same moment the door of the study closed with a bang behind us.

"That's curious!" muttered the vicar, peering into the darkness all round us. Suddenly he gave a little start. The candle spluttered.

"I, too," he said in a low voice, "felt something pull at my sleeve—ha, there it is again!" He turned round sharply.

I also turned and simultaneously we uttered an ejaculation. A few paces to our right was the front door, opening into the main approach to the house; a small flight of shallow steps led down from the hall to the door; and at the head of these steps was another door—a glass one, designed presumably to cut off the draught. Our eyes were directed towards this glass door; on the other side of it, and shadowed against the glass, we beheld a tall figure standing; it was the same figure I had seen leaning over the gallery; the same figure that had commenced to descend the stairs and had suddenly vanished at the approach of the vicar; the figure of a man—pale and luminous, shining out of the darkness with a remarkable transparency. For a moment we gazed upon this figure without speaking, and the eyes of the figure were fixed upon ours, strange sad eyes, oddly mesmeric in their glance, and of an unearthly brightness. The figure was dressed in a long grey cloak, the folds of which muffled the lower part of its face, leaving only the mouth and eyes exposed. It stood motionless surveying us.

"Well," whispered Marsden, "do you see it?"

"Yes, I see it."

Hardly had we exchanged the words, when the figure deliberately raised its right hand and beckoned to us.

"Come!" said the vicar, in a curious voice, and stepped firmly towards the door. I kept by his side. Before we had taken three paces the Apparition turned, laid its hand upon the knob of the front door handle with a significant gesture—and vanished. The vicar paused and looked at me in some bewilderment.

"What are we to do now?" he asked.

"Open the front door," I suggested.

"True, true!" replied the vicar.

We passed through the glass door down the steps, and Marsden, unlocking the main door, drew back the chain, and turning the handle flung it open. In front of the main entrance was a wide gravel space narrowing into the carriage drive. The grounds of the vicarage were bounded by a high wall, separating it on the one side from the old churchyard beyond; while some distance to the right was the new cemetery, into which access could be obtained from one end of the vicarage garden through a wicket gate.

The night was cold and dark. A frosty wind set the distant trees creaking dismally. A gust through the open door extinguished the flame of the candle in the vicar's hand. I shivered and turned up the collar of my coat. While we still gazed uncertainly into the gloom in front of us, we became aware of an odd indistinct light on the carriage drive—not unlike the faint glimmering of a glow worm across the gravel. The light grew and expanded as we looked, and the next moment there seemed to shoot up from the ground a luminous shadow, which gradually took the shape of a man's figure clad in a long grey cloak.

"There it is!" said the vicar, touching my arm.

"Yes—the Apparition!"

Now, out of the darkness, we could again plainly see it. For a moment it stood there, in the centre of the drive, facing us. Then a second time it raised its arm and beckoned: a second time we obeyed the summons and stepped into the darkness of the night. As we advanced the figure turned too, and glided onwards in front of us. We followed, walking as rapidly as we could in the dark, and with blundering steps.

"There seems purpose in this!" remarked the vicar. "I shall see it through—but if you would prefer to go back, Addison—"

"I'll see you hanged first!" I retorted.

"Ha!" muttered Marsden, "that is singular."

The Apparition had turned sharply to the right into a narrow path leading to the extreme end of the garden through a shrubbery, as he uttered the words. The vicar quickened his steps. I strode at his heels. In front of us the grey figure glided on, and presently plunged into the shrubbery. The wind moaned drearily through the trees on either side of us: the gloom was intensified—nothing was visible but the anthropomorphous shape, moving luminously before us. It traversed the shrubbery and reached the wicket gate at the other end; there for a moment it paused and looked towards us.

"It's the cemetery," said the vicar.

"The deuce! We must follow!"

"Yes, certainly, we must follow."

With a strange eerie feeling we unlatched the little wicket gate, and passed into the burial ground—the Apparition had continued its progress after that one brief glance backward, and was flitting now amongst the gravestones.

"Walk carefully," warned Marsden.

While he spoke my foot caught in a mound and I stumbled and fell on the frosty grass. I rose with a shudder.

"We must pick our way," said the vicar. "What mystery is this?"

Suddenly in the distance the Apparition stopped, and stood erect as though waiting for us. A few minutes more of stumbling brought us to the spot. As we reached it the Apparition raised both its arms with the strangest appealing gesture, pointed rapidly to the ground at its feet, and disappeared.

Marsden stooped down, then he uttered a curious exclamation.

"Have you a match?" he asked.

I felt in my pocket and produced a matchbox.

The vicar again stooped low and struck a light. The faint flame flickered in his hand, as he carefully shaded it. The match went out.

"It's a grave," said Marsden, on his knees. "There is a small headstone—here it is," and he struck another match, and placing it close to the ground, examined the stone, while I stood by.

"Can you make it out?" I asked.

"No. Bend down and strike a match, too."

I did so, and together we stooped over the stone, and tried to decipher the faded inscription upon it. It was no easy task; but at length, with infinite patience and by dint of striking match after match, we contrived to make out one by one the letters of the name—

JAMES BANNISTER.

Then the vicar rose to his feet.

"James Bannister!" he repeated. "James Bannister. I will consult the registry clerk tomorrow. Who was James Bannister—and why," he added slowly, "was he buried in unconsecrated ground?"

"Unconsecrated ground?" I exclaimed.

"Yes; this plot of ground is outside the consecrated portion of the cemetery," replied the vicar, and for some moments remained silent, as we groped our way back to the wicket gate.

"I am convinced," he said at last, "that this Apparition is in some way connected with the circumstances of the death of the unhappy man, James Bannister. My business now is to find out what those circumstances were, and then I think we shall be able to place a finger on the clue."

The church clock chimed a quarter past three as we re-entered the front door of the vicarage, and Marsden locked and bolted it behind us. In the candle-light the vicar's face looked strangely pale, but its expression was calm and determined as usual. I confess that my own nerves were not a little shaken by the singular experience we had just gone through, and I was glad enough to get back to my bedroom. No further noises, no fresh appearances disturbed me that night. I slept till late the following morning. When I descended to breakfast I found the vicar already at work. With his ordinary indefatigable energy, and in spite of the sleepless night he had spent, Marsden had already been down some hours, and with a smile he informed me that he had also interviewed the parish clerk.

"And what have you learnt about—James Bannister?" I asked.

"I have learnt," the vicar said gravely, "that James Bannister was once a respected resident of this town; that under somewhat remarkable circumstances he committed suicide, and that, in consequence of this act, my predecessor had refused his body Christian burial—and, in short, that he was interred in an unconsecrated plot of ground just beyond the cemetery, and that the burial service was not read over the grave."

"By Jove!" I exclaimed, "and you think—?"

The vicar smiled a trifle sadly.

"That bigotry can sometimes be carried a trifle too far!" he replied. "Oh, I know what you mean! Yes, I am inclined to think that, too!" he concluded, enigmatically.

"Was it long ago?"

"The clerk—an old man—remembers the event distinctly. Fifteen years or more ago. There was some scandal at the time, but it was hushed up. The late vicar had the reputation of being obstinately bigoted in some of his views, and opposition, it seems, only increased his obstinacy. He was a man that would have his own way."

"What do you intend to do?" I asked.

"I shall think the matter over," he answered, "and let you know as soon as I have come to a decision. Meantime, let me ring for breakfast."

It was not till dinner that evening that I had another opportunity of an uninterrupted conversation with my friend. He had been busy all day with parochial and other affairs, but his business had contrived to embrace the consideration of the subject which had been uppermost in both our minds for the last few hours.

"I wish to avoid all publicity and scandal in this matter," he said by way of preface.

"I think you are quite right," I agreed. "But with regard to the ghost, how is it that the servants in the house have never complained?"

"That is not the least odd part about it!" rejoined the vicar. "Neither the servants nor, it would seem, anybody else except myself, has ever (till you came) seen the apparition or heard the tappings. They were obviously intended for my sole edification! It is this which led me to suspect that I might be the victim of some optical illusion, and which made me anxious to secure the corroboration of some other witness like yourself. My dear

Addison, I have come to the conclusion that the Apparition (or Ghost, as you choose to call it) has manifested itself solely to me and to you for one purpose. To me, because I am the vicar; to you, in order to dispel my doubt by the corroboration of independent testimony as to its actuality."

"But why to you, because you are the vicar?"

"If a Vision is permitted to appear to us at all," replied the vicar, "my religious principles inflexibly persuade me that it can only be with some definite purpose—some intelligent moral reason for its appearance. Therefore this Apparition has appeared to me continuously for the past few weeks for some purpose. What purpose? Until last night I confess I was puzzled to assign any. My natural incredulity and scepticism acted no doubt as a bar to the establishment of any communicative sympathy between the vision and myself. You supplied (if I may use the term something too suggestive of charlatanry) the 'medium' necessary for more complete mutual understanding. I seem very clearly now to comprehend the motive of this Apparition."

"I, too, can guess it," said I, sipping my wine.

"That constant knocking, for instance—what could it signify except a clumsy attempt to impress upon me the notion of a summons? A request, I should say, to respond to some dimly expressed appeal? The Vision itself—I remember, now, it always eyed me with a strange and wistful invitation which puzzled me to interpret—what could it be but the spiritual presentment of some physical need? First, the leading you to my room (the room of the vicar); then the beckoning—it all pieces with one theory, of which the subsequent conducting us to the unhallowed grave provides, to my mind, a complete confirmation. It seems easy now to assign the true purpose for these manifestations."

"And that purpose?"

"A demand for Christian burial," replied the vicar slowly.

I nodded; the same thought had already occurred to me.

"You will give it?" I said.

"Unquestionably," was the firm rejoinder. "But as I just told you, I desire to avoid publicity and scandal. I have thought of a plan—not perhaps a pleasant one, but I fear inevitable—and wish you to assist me in carrying it out."

"What is it?" I said.

"I intend to exhume and re-bury the man—at night—and by myself," replied the vicar, solemnly.

"By Gad!" I exclaimed, "that sounds cheerful! But my dear Marsden, there is the difficulty of the grave to be opened—the new one dug!"

"Not a great one," he rejoined. "Two of us can dig a grave in a couple of hours; the disinterment will not be easy, but we are both strong men, and a stout rope, a spade, and a pickaxe are all that is required."

I was a little flabbergasted at the vicar's proposal, but knowing him to be a man of invincible determination, did not seek to dissuade him from his purpose; on the contrary I agreed to assist him in it to the best of my ability; and we set about our self-imposed task that very evening.

At nine o'clock, wrapped in thick overcoats, and carrying a lantern, rope, and a spade and a pickaxe each, we repaired again to the cemetery. The ground was shut out from the town by a wall and a thick hedge, so that there existed no probability of detection in our employment. The spot was private and secluded; our only witnesses were the silent gravestones round us, as we worked. Rain had fallen through the day and the ground was soft, which rendered our labour easier; but, even so, the coats and undercoats had long been discarded, and our shirt sleeves turned up, before our united efforts had succeeded in excavating a grave sufficiently deep for the purpose. The lantern burned dim beside us as at length we scrambled again to the level turf, our hands, arms, boots, and clothes spattered with clay and mud.

"Now," said the vicar, "there is the worst half to be accomplished," and he turned his steps with a little shiver of repugnance to the spot a dozen paces off, and just beyond the consecrated boundary, where the body of the unfortunate James Bannister reposed.

"Come, Addison," he cried, raising his pickaxe, "with a will!" and the dull thud of the implement fell crunching into earth, with a piston-like regularity, once more. At length we took to our shovels and heaped the clay deep on either side of us, pausing a moment now and again to take breath and give our weary muscles a rest. Suddenly my spade struck something hard. A few more shovelsful of earth revealed to us by the dull light of the lantern the outline of a coffin; and the neighbouring church clock struck twelve as we fastened the rope round each end of the oblong ark, and prepared to hoist it to the ground. The coincidence—grim though it was—raised a smile to Marsden's lips—"When churchyards yawn"—he quoted, and laughed a little oddly; then seized the rope with both hands. "Carefully, Addison," he said.

In five minutes the coffin rested on the level sward, and we wiped our foreheads and looked at each other.

"This is the strangest night's work I ever did in my life," observed the vicar, "but I believe it is not the worst!"

"You are violating the canons of the church!" I smiled.

"Not according to the interpretation of my conscience!" he replied quickly. "I prefer the spirit always to the letter; and the repose of a soul is of more consequence than the dogma of an arbitrary ritual. At least it seems so to my limited understanding. I have received an appeal—I should be neglecting my duty both as a clergyman and a Christian, were I to disregard it. Let us, however, not waste time; will you lift that end?"

We both stooped, and raising the heavy coffin bore it somewhat unsteadily to the newly dug grave. Here we again noosed the rope round each end of it, and gradually, with considerable difficulty, lowered it once more into the earth and for the first time for twenty years, the mortal remains of James Bannister rested at length in consecrated ground.

"Whatever his faults," murmured the vicar, "who are we to judge him? He was a good man, too, I am told—a religious man. The rest is with God," and he took off his hat.

On each side of the grave we stood, and then, slowly and with a singularly impressive solemnity, Marsden began to recite the sublime Burial Service of the Church. I have thought often of that scene since—the dark chill air of a December night, the glimmering lantern at our feet, the unbroken stillness of the cemetery round us, the vicar opposite me in his shirt sleeves, and beneath us the yawning grave!—and, even as I write, the deep earnest tones of my friend's voice seem sounding in my ears—"In the sure and certain hope of a glorious Resurrection!"

Nobody discovered the unassuming mound of earth that marked the fresh resting place of James Bannister; nor that the turf had been disturbed round the spot where the original grave had been—for, as I have said, this latter was quite in an out-of-the way corner of the cemetery and scarce ever visited even by the sexton himself, whose failing eyesight and rusting powers of observation may have caused him to overlook the newly, and it must be admitted, somewhat clumsily, constructed grave on the outskirts of the burial ground.

But never again from that day to this has the Apparition revisited the vicarage of Walford; and as for the vicar—he is no longer a bachelor.

NIGHTS OF TERROR
E. J. Thomas

Published in The Express and Telegraph
(Adelaide), 28 July 1913

"E. J. Thomas" presents a problem. As the story is based in Ohio, USA, if we assume that the author is American, then there are thousands of "hits" for that name in the American periodicals. As this tale was discovered in an Adelaide newspaper and no other printings of it have been found, we might look to a Mr. E. J. Thomas, also from Adelaide, who was the Vice President of the Unley Literary and Music Union in 1907. Two religious books published in 1913 in Australia called *The Time of the End, but the End Not Yet* and *Death and Beyond: A Christian's Answer to Rationalistic Teachings* (1917) were written by a Mr. E. J. Thomas. In the UK there was a scholar, Edward J. Thomas (1869–1958), who was also writing in this timeframe—however his work was only concerned with Buddhism. Typing "Nights of Terror" into archives with a precise date of 1910–1913 to see if the story was published (earlier) in any UK newspapers brings up hits on riots, scarlet fever epidemics, weeping eczema and the burning of the giant liner *Carmania*.

From the framing of the first line, the story is presented as a factual report, which makes it all the more entertaining. "Nights of Terror" has never before been reprinted.

Mr. August Schill, of Cleveland, Ohio, sat (writes E. J. Thomas) in his front room reading the paper, as he always did on Sunday evenings, while his wife cleared away the supper dishes and prepared the youngsters for bed.

As he glanced over the coloured comic pages he laughed, for the pictures were really funny. Suddenly, however, the laugh died from his lips and the paper slipped to the floor, for Schill felt a cold, clammy hand upon his cheek. He turned to see who had stolen in upon him so quietly, for he had heard no sound, but to his surprise he saw that he was alone.

Schill raised his hand to his forehead, and found that it was covered with a cold perspiration. Rising, he went into the kitchen, where his wife was engaged in her work, while children laughed and played.

"Who was it came into the front room?" he asked.

"Why, no one," answered his wife. "The children have not left the kitchen, and I certainly have not. Why?"

"Oh, nothing," said the mystified Mr. Schill, and he returned to his paper, but he found himself unable to read. He kept thinking of that clammy touch upon his cheek, and the more he thought of it the more convinced he became that he had dozed off and had been dreaming.

He said nothing to his wife of what had happened, however, and the family went to bed as usual. Nothing further happened until about two o'clock on the following morning, at a time when everyone was asleep and the house dark and still.

Suddenly the whole family was aroused by a heavy step on the stairs as of a big man ascending, wearing heavy boots. Schill, armed with a revolver, ran to the landing and looked down, but could see nothing. Filled with wonder, he turned to still the fears of the rest of the household, and even as he did so there came the sound of the front door banging. Bearing a lighted lamp in one hand and his revolver in the other, Schill rushed to the lower floor and tried the front door. It was locked, just as he had left it when retiring to rest. He went to the back door, but that, too, was not only locked but bolted. The windows were all closed and fastened, and there was no way by which a person could have either entered or left.

Thoroughly mystified, and half inclined to believe that they had all been dreaming, various members of the family retired to their rooms, but not to sleep, for the mysterious visitant had by no means finished with them.

All through the night, until shortly before daybreak, the sound of someone stamping about the house continued. The children, covering their heads with the bed-clothes, trembled with fright, and the puzzled Schill, in order to reassure them as much as possible, remained outside their door with the revolver.

From below stairs there came sounds of someone moving about, and a cold draught seemed to run through the house, causing the gas to flicker so violently that it often threatened to go out completely.

Finally, as though to properly finish the night's reign of terror, the mysterious visitant uttered a terrible shriek, which was followed by the shrill scream of a woman. The cry was that of a person in mortal agony and continued for several moments, finally dying away in a dismal moan.

When dawn came Schill and the other members of the family made a tour of the whole house, but could find nothing that would serve to explain the strange noises of the night.

A few nights following this hair-raising experience Viola Lozynska, a young woman who boarded with the Schills at their home in Leading-road, Cleveland, sat in the parlour reading. She was suddenly aroused by someone knocking at the front door, and rising, she went to answer the summons. What was her surprise, on opening the door, to find no one there. She heard a heavy step in the porch, however, and craned her head forward to see who it was. The porch was untenanted, and there was no sign of a footprint in the heavy blanket of snow which covered the boards.

Being alone in the house, the young woman was thoroughly alarmed, and hastily retreating, she double-locked the door and hurried around to all the windows, to make sure that they, too, were fastened. Then she lit every gas-jet in the house and returned to the parlour to await the arrival of the rest of the household.

Unable to read any more, she just sat still and listened, too terrified to stir. Presently there reached her ears a low, moaning sound, which appeared to come from the attic rooms above. Then it seemed to her that she heard a woman whispering, and later there came a terrible scream, followed by the thud of a heavy body upon the floor, which made the whole house quiver. Hastily rising, the girl rushed to the door leading from the parlour to the dinning-room and locked it. She even stood with her back braced against it, fearful that some terrible shape would force itself in upon her.

Meanwhile the shrieking and moaning had died away, only to be followed by the tramping of heavy feet, which seemed to wander about the upstairs rooms and then descend the stairs into the rear rooms.

Presently this sound, too, died away, and Viola, nerving herself, decided to open the door just a trifle and peep into the room beyond. She made to turn the key and open the door, but to her horror she found that the door was not locked at all! And yet she was positive that it had been locked, for she had taken the precaution to try it.

Carefully turning the knob, she opened the door a mere fraction of an inch and placed her eye to the opening.

The rooms beyond were dark! The lights had been turned out!

With a shriek the now thoroughly frightened young woman slammed to the door and turned the key in the lock. As she recoiled in horror to the front of the room she distinctly heard the sound of mocking laughter in the room above her head.

When the other members of the household returned shortly after, they found the unfortunate girl on the verge of fainting. Into their wondering ears she poured the story of her terrifying experience, and Schill, accompanied by his wife and two or three others, made a complete tour of the house, but could find nothing that would serve to explain away the mystery.

Every night thereafter, despite the careful watch kept by Schill and several of his friends, the ghostly visitations continued. The ghost, if such it chanced to be, seemed to have no regular hours for visiting its haunts. Sometimes its nightly visit commenced at eight o'clock; at other times it did not materialise until after midnight. On a couple of occasions it was heard as late as four o'clock in the morning.

Mrs. Anna Svoboda, Schill's mother-in-law, had perhaps the most terrifying experience of all. The old lady had been accustomed to sleep in a room by herself, her apartment being on the second floor at the rear of the house.

Like other members of the family, she had scoffed at the idea of a ghost haunting the house, but she could not deny having heard the heavy footfalls and the unearthly screams and groans.

One night, about a week after the ghost made its first appearance, Mrs. Svoboda found that she could not sleep. Her nerves seemed to be on edge—due, no doubt, to the experience of the preceding week.

A light was burning dimly in the room and the entire house was as silent as the grave. Suddenly, without any apparent cause, the light spluttered and went out just as it does in all properly-written ghost stories.

Mrs. Svoboda had no time to speculate, however, for next moment she felt a cold, rough hand pressing down upon her face. It closed relentlessly about the horrified woman's mouth, and she realised that she was slowly being smothered. She tried to free herself of the clammy clutch, but the hand was immovable and her struggles were in vain.

Next moment, however, the pressure on the woman's mouth was released, and for a moment she saw the hand poised above her face, surrounded by a strange, bluish light. Then the hand vanished completely in a puff of vapour. No sooner had it vanished than Mrs. Svoboda heard the heavy thump of a foot on the floor. The sound proceeded out into the hall and down the stairs, as though someone was walking away. When the noise had completely ceased Mrs. Svoboda sat up in bed and screamed at the top of her voice. In response the whole household came rushing to the door, which, strange to say, they found locked. The frightened woman had to open it herself to admit the others.

No more manifestations of the ghostly presence were heard that night, but again on the following night the spook showed up on schedule time. This time the ghost contented itself with rattling all the windows and setting up such an unearthly shrieking and groaning that people living in adjacent houses were awakened from their sleep.

The house was shaken so severely that Mr. Steve Mondock, who lives next door to the Schill home, was aroused. Mondock stated that he had often heard strange sounds in the adjoining house, and other neighbours confirmed the story, declaring they had suspected the place was haunted long before the Schills moved in.

On occasions when the windows and doors were rattled by an invisible hand Schill would hurry about with his revolver, intent on shooting anything or anyone he saw prowling about. But never did he see anything to fire at.

One night Schill remained downstairs on guard while the rest of the household slept. Taking up his vigil in the kitchen, the master of the house waited, his finger toying with the trigger of his heavy revolver.

Shortly after midnight he felt a chill draught strike his face. Next moment he felt a hand upon his shoulder. Swinging around, he raised his revolver, but, as usual, there was nothing to shoot at. Before Schill had recovered from his surprise he heard a slight click, and, turning again, he saw the kitchen door, which had been locked, slowly open! It opened to a width of two feet or more, then slowly closed again, and as it clicked shut Schill heard a weird laugh just outside. Rushing to the door, the master of the house frantically tried to open it, but it was locked!

So unpleasant did the ghost make it for everybody concerned, especially in the upper part of the house, that all the furniture was removed to the lower floor, and the attic was turned over to the uncanny nocturnal visitor.

John Svoboda, a brother-in-law of Schill, heard the stories of the ghost, and being a firm disbeliever in anything supernatural, he volunteered to come over one night and "lay" the ghost once and for ever.

"Take my word for it," said he, "there are no such things as ghosts. You people have been imagining things. How is a spirit going to come back and lock doors and bang windows? Answer me that."

Being vouchsafed no reply, John continued to ridicule the idea, and finally, when bedtime drew near, he advised everyone to go to bed, forget all about their troubles, and trust to him.

"I'm going upstairs," he said, "and I'm going to lay that ghost person by the heels."

And upstairs he went.

For ten minutes no sound came from the upper regions of the house. John had evidently cowed the ghost. Presently, however, a terrible shriek was heard; then the rush of feet, which raced across the upper floor and tore down the stairs at a rapid rate.

Next moment John burst into the room, white-faced and trembling violently.

"I saw it!" he cried. "It's no joke; I saw it with my own eyes. No sooner had I gone into the back room and turned off the light when I saw something rise from the floor like a puff of smoke and a black shape, like a giant football, rolled over and over towards me, as though someone was kicking it.

"The strange vapour, which looked like smoke, smelt abominably. It got into my mouth and nose and eyes and almost choked me. I wouldn't go into that room again for a thousand dollars!"

On Christmas Eve the spectre appeared to the children as they were playing round their tree.

A number of neighbours' children had gone to the Schill home to enjoy a party given by the youthful members of the household. Viola Lozynska, the young lady boarder, was helping the children to have a good time around the Christmas tree, which was hung with presents, sweets, and ornaments.

Little Isabelle Dodd, from a house a short distance away, suddenly paused in her play, and turned her head towards the stairs. Next moment she uttered a frightened scream, and ran breathless and gasping into another room.

"Take it away!" cried the child. "Oh! please take it away! Don't let it touch me."

When she had been quieted, the little girl said that when she turned her head she distinctly saw the white-gowned figure of a tiny baby standing in the semi-darkness on the stairs.

"It looked at me just a moment," said the girl, "and then it disappeared."

That night, after the Christmas Eve party had broken up, the ghost held forth in ghastly revelry. For an hour or more it laughed fiendishly in the upper part of the house, and once it seemed to be dropping heavy weights from a considerable height. It ran backwards and forwards along the floors, and ended its performance by emitting a terrifying shriek that could be heard throughout the neighbourhood.

Following the episode of Christmas Eve a more careful search than ever was made of the attic rooms of the "haunted house of Leading-road," as the place began to be called. The attic floor was gone over inch by inch, and when thus closely scrutinised it was noted that the floor was stained here and there with small dark spots, resembling blood. The search was even carried under the floor, and what was the surprise of Schill when, beneath the flooring, jammed in behind the clapboards, there was found a man's shirt, torn and bloodstained.

That same night, which was Friday, December 27, the ghost came forth as usual to haunt his old home. This time the Schills and the other people living in the house were kept awake for over an hour by the steady hair-raising "drip, drip, drip" of something on the attic floor. Presently this horrifying sound died away, and was followed by ten minutes of demoniac laughter. Someone seemed to be approaching the head of the stairs with heavy tread. At the landing the sound ceased and then, to the terror of all who heard, there came the sound of water splashing down the stairs in a veritable cataract. On investigation, however, the stairs were found to be perfectly dry.

Needless to say, the story of the "haunted house" spread through the neighbourhood like wildfire, and by the following Monday the whole city was conversant with the weird affair.

Several men, firmly convinced there were no such things as ghosts, bravely volunteered to go into the house and put the spectre to flight.

They went singly and in pairs and threes, but no one party ever paid more than one visit to the rendezvous of the awesome spook. One and all they fled precipitately, later telling tales of hearing awful whisperings, of hearing blood dripping on to the floor, and of seeing a large, black bear-like shape hurling itself at them from the corner of the attic room.

Among those who volunteered to spend the night in the haunted attic was a neighbour of the Schills, a man known to be most courageous in the face of ordinary danger. Armed with a revolver, he made his way into the attic, prepared to spend the night there. For two hours nothing happened, and the Schills retired, confident that the ghost, for that night at least, was going to remain in seclusion.

Shortly after midnight the whole household was awakened by a loud scraping sound that came from above; then a woman's shriek echoed through the house, followed by the scurrying of feet and the fall of a heavy body. The sound of hurrying feet crossed the floor to the upper landing and raced down the stairs, to the foot of which Schill dashed, his intention being to intercept the ghost.

Instead of the spectre, however, it was the neighbour who came clattering down the stairs, his eyes starting from their sockets in horror and his face pale as death.

Nothing would induce him to spend another night in the house, nor would he ever say what it was that he had seen.

"I cannot believe it myself," was all he could be induced to say. "It was too horrible—too ghastly."

*

Once, while a Mrs. Campfield lived in the house, she happened to mention to an Arabian woman who peddled goods in the neighbourhood that she had heard strange noises in the place. The Arabian woman nodded her head comprehendingly.

"Once," she said, "a man hurt his neck in the house. He bled—he die—he go away. But he come back sometimes, maybe."

The district soon became filled with strange rumours regarding the mystery of the haunted house. The most persistent rumour had it that a former tenant had been found in the attic with his throat cut, his head being almost severed from his body, and it was whispered that his ghost came back and tried to wash away the bloodstains on the attic floor.

Some who claim to have seen the spectre declare it is that of a headless man. Others are positive it is a giant animal shape, horribly grotesque, with fierce, malignant eyes set in a massive head, and with long powerful legs at whose extremities there are lance-like claws of great length.

Perhaps the most remarkable story of all is that related by Mrs. Campfield, who formerly occupied the haunted house, and who moved after the death of her little baby in August, 1912.

While she lived in the house Mrs. Campfield often heard strange, unaccountable noises at night, but at first she paid no particular attention to them. One night she was awakened from a sound sleep by what appeared to be the creaking of the boards in the attic floor. Then as the frightened woman sat bolt upright in bed listening, it seemed that someone was throwing a bucket of water down the hall.

"There was one night that I shall never forget," said Mrs. Campfield. "I was bathing the baby, and sent my little boy, Arthur, upstairs for something or other. I had told him nothing of the previous noises, nor had the word 'ghost' ever been mentioned to him. I heard him drop the article I had sent him for, and then he came downstairs screaming. I shall never forget the look of terror on his little face."

Mrs. Campfield turned to her boy, who is a bright little fellow of eight years.

"Tell what you saw, Arthur," she said.

"I went up to the attic, and had just found what mamma sent me for," said the little chap, "when I heard a funny noise. Then I saw something big and black coming towards me. It looked like a bear a little, only it was bigger. I ran as fast as I could. It looked as if it had nothing but a head."

"I know children often imagine they see things," continued the mother, as the little fellow finished, "so, wishing to show him there was nothing to be afraid of, I ran upstairs—and there, coming across the floor towards me, was the hideous black thing. As Arthur says, it looked something like a great bear."

The strange part of it is that this was no wraith of the darkness, born of an overwrought imagination. A gas-jet was burning in the room, and it was far from dark. Yet Mrs. Campfield saw the horrible, terrifying shape slowly advancing towards her, its eyes glinting menacingly, and its lips working into a smile of inscrutable, inhuman malice.

In the light of the gas-jet she saw its huge feet moving, sloth-like, along the floor, and she could hear the paws shuffling on the boards like sandpaper.

"It looked all head and shoulders," resumed the woman, "and as it came to the head of the stairs I ran. Picking up the baby from the tub, I wrapped it in my cloak, and fled with the children out the back way to the house next door. I am positive that the front door and screen were locked, but when my husband came we went back and found the front door wide open. I know that something went out. My husband laughed at me, but he has heard the noises too."

Mrs. Campfield paused, and her face paled a little.

"And—I don't like to tell this," she concluded in a whisper. "I saw the same black thing the night before my baby died."

The baby, it seems, had been ill only a short time, and the mother was watching over it when she heard a strange sound on the stairs. Looking up, she was horrified at seeing the same terrible, bear-like shape amble down the steps, pause at the bottom to turn its horrible face her way, and then shuffle past, out into the night.

Next moment, from the upper regions of the house, came a soul-chilling groan, followed by an unearthly shriek that made the windows rattle.

On Monday night, December 30, the Schill household was thrown into such a panic of fear that it was found necessary to send the children to the home of a neighbour.

All night long the fearsome noises continued. Doors and windows were opened by an unseen hand, and chairs were moved slowly, but perceptibly, across the floors.

From above came a low moaning, followed by the shuffling sound of feet. This was succeeded by a thumping noise as of someone dropping weights from a height of several feet.

Presently these noises died away, and when all had grown quiet it seemed to Schill and his wife and the other adult people that they could hear the whispering voices of children. Suddenly the whisperings grew more pronounced and ended in a soul-terrifying shrieking, which continued for several minutes, dying down at last into a dismal moan.

Another period of quiet followed, and then, with a suddenness that was startling, the shrieking commenced again, reaching such a pitch that the sounds seemed to cut into the listener's flesh.

Schill alone of the entire family kept his nerves together. He sat in the lower part of the house, listening to the awesome noises, while his wife, white-faced and trembling, tried to do her work.

Shortly before midnight a party of men, among whom were two doctors, called at the house by request, it having been decided that they should act as a jury to discover the cause of the strange manifestations.

At the time of their arrival the house was as silent as the grave, the ghost having apparently grown tired of groaning and shrieking.

The eleven men comprising the investigating committee made their way to the attic, where they were provided with a table and chairs and a few packs of cards with which to pass away the time.

A light was placed on the table, and the eleven men sat about the board, playing cards, talking, and awaiting the appearance of the ghost which had so long terrified those who lived in the house.

During the progress of the game the men were visibly nervous, but tried to cover it by jesting about the alleged spectre. Some laughingly suggested that it might be a hungry cat; another said it might be a big rat; while one man had a shrewd idea that it was nothing at all.

Suddenly, while the party were still discussing the phenomenon, a chill blast seemed to circle the room. The light of the lamp flickered for a moment and then burned bright again. From the hall came the sound of scraping feet and then a groan, like that of a man dying in terrible agony. The shuffling sound stopped outside the door, and the next moment, while all looked in breathless wonder, the door, which had been locked, slowly opened the mere fraction of an inch. Through the aperture there appeared a pungent, yellowish vapour, driving into the room for all the world like the breath of some large animal. The vapour carried with it an odour so abominable that the men were almost suffocated. Choking, they rose to their feet and made for the door.

Before anyone could reach it, however, the door slowly closed again, and when one of the men tried to open it he found, to the speechless astonishment of all, that it was locked!

Satisfied that someone was playing a joke on them, the jury returned to the table, but there was no talking or jesting now. Each of the eleven kept his eyes straight ahead and dared scarcely to breathe.

Ten minutes passed. No sound came to the ears of the anxious men. Another ten minutes went by, and still no sound was heard. Then, with a suddenness that caused all to turn deathly pale, came the horrible shrieking and groaning, and then the sound of a falling body. And, most remarkable of all, the sound seemed to be in their very midst—right in the same room!

When the shrieking and groaning had subsided there ensued a low scratching sound in a far corner of the room. All eyes were turned in that direction, and next moment a yellowish puff of smoke appeared rising from the floor. It rose higher and higher, spreading out as it did so, and from the very centre of the cloud they saw an animal face protruding. The vapour gradually thinned out, and as it did so the body of the monster appeared. The men rushed towards it, but before any of them could touch it the strange apparition had vanished.

The committee of investigators there upon adjourned *sine die*, nor did they pause to offer any opinions on what they thought of the horrifying manifestations.

A number of neighbours who had determined to keep watch with Schill and his wife together with other members of the family, lingered in the lower part of the house.

To their intense surprise the manifestations continued, the upper windows shaking and rattling and the floors squeaking in a truly remarkable manner.

The following day the entire family reached the conclusion that they would not spend another night in the haunted house. They accordingly departed to the homes of neighbours, leaving the furniture where it stood and it seems that the ghost, having regained the freedom of the place, held high revelry on the Tuesday night, wandering about the unoccupied rooms, rattling windows, opening and shutting doors, and banging the furniture about at a great rate.

Viola Lozynska, one of the last to lose her nerve by reason of the ghost's capers in the attic and other parts of the house, finally admitted that she believed there was something supernatural about it. At first she had attributed the noises to the sighing of the wind, to draughts, and to her imagination. She changed this opinion, however, when a glass of water vanished before her eyes!

The attic, which appears to be the favourite haunt of the spectre, is a room measuring about twelve by thirty feet. The walls and ceiling are unplastered, and the rafters are bare. All about the apartment are hooks, on which articles of clothing are hung, while the floors are piled high with boxes and barrels.

A careful scrutiny of the room failed to reveal any opening through which either a man or even a small animal could squeeze its way. No marks appear on the window sills to show that the sashes have been pried up or that anyone has climbed in. On the floor, however, there are a number of bloodstains, some apparently old, others fresh. One investigator going to the place in broad daylight, searched the upper part of the house carefully for hidden strings, cords, or any other trappings by means of which a practical joker could work. He found nothing. Even the boxes and barrels were searched, without result.

The investigator had been smoking while he scrutinised the attic and when ready to go below he thoughtlessly left his pipe on the window-sill. The window, it may be mentioned, was closed and fastened.

Having assured himself that there was no one in the upper part of the house the man went downstairs, closing and locking the door behind him. No sooner had he reached the lower floor than he heard the same peculiar sound that had startled members of the family for six weeks.

Hurrying upstairs, he unlocked the door leading into the attic and burst into the room. Everything was as he had left it, with the exception that his pipe, which he distinctly remembered having left on the window-sill, was now on a little shelf at the opposite side of the room!

The happenings at the "haunted house" developed into the sole topic of conversation of the inhabitants of that section of the city where it is located. Men known for their courage and disbelief in ghosts and other things uncanny have sought to solve the mystery by personal observation and investigation, but the mystery persists in remaining unsolved.

THE GHOST OF MOOR HALL
A CHRISTMAS GHOST STORY

M. E. Murray

Published in The Herald *(Tamworth), 26 December 1925*

There's frustratingly little to go on here regarding the identity of M. E. Murray. *Equal Rights Magazine* and *Country Life* make us aware of a Miss M. E. Murray during this time, who was English and possibly a librarian. Three M. E. Murray stories were written for *The Weekly Tale-Teller* in 1911 and 1912, then there follows a period of silence before a genre story was published in *The Westminster Gazette* called "Loveaday: A Peakland Ghost Story" (1922). "The Ghost of Moor Hall" followed in 1925, and then the trail goes cold. This isn't the only story about a Moor Hall ghost; there was one written in 1910 called "The Laying of the Moor Hall Ghost" by Ernest W. Dorner, but sadly, that story has a rather weak "it was all just a dream" ending.

While the identity of this author remains a mystery, it's very delightful to read a story that will be *exactly* one hundred years old on Boxing Day 2025, and it's one that has never been reprinted until now!

Christmas week at last, deep snow sparkling with frost, a clear sky overhead. Tom to meet me at the station with a young colt in the trap: and a holiday with the dearest girl in the world—what more could heart of man desire?

The clear, sharp air was glorious after the murk of town. Tom laughed when I told him what a lucky beggar he was; but there was a wry note in his pleasant voice.

"I couldn't live in a town," he said. "No, if I clear out I'll go to Canada." And then he looked at the many chimneys of his rambling tumble-down old house showing black over the hill against the red sunset. "I love every stone of the old place."

He and I were old pals: we knew more of each other in silence than most people do in years of talk. The old place was mortgaged nearly to the hilt, and the mortgagee coveted it. Tom had superhuman struggles to pay the interest. But Moor Hall without Moores—the thing was unendurable.

"Dash! There's the breeching gone again! Hold the reins, old man, the colt's not quite broken," he said, swinging down to mend the patched old harness.

We were in a cutting between two steep banks, where a side track led to the blacksmith's forge and a little cluster of cottages. The snow was piled high; the snow plough had been of no use here, and the drifts had been dug by hand. It was scarce a place to tempt anyone to walk on, but such an odd object came fluttering down the road that the colt would have bolted but for my hold and Tom's soothing words. He had repaired the breeching-strap by now, and turned to see what was wrong. And the odd creature, a frail little woman in a battered black bonnet, and a rusty crinoline, swooped towards him like a bat.

"Master Tom! Master Tom! Oh! Master Tom! Come and see bonny lady in the satin gown. Oh, the tags and tassels of gold! The tartan scarf and the blue ribbons. Bonny red gold! Just as my auntie told me," she piped.

"Why, it's Nanny," he said, gently. The poor old thing was eagerly clasping his arm. I could see her tiny, wrinkled white face with the grey elf locks framing it, and her China-blue eyes wide and beautiful as a kitten's.

"Oh! Master Tom, I've been waiting to take you, waiting and waiting! My auntie told me, she came while Nanny was in bed last night. Nay, to dream of the dead means sorrow to the living! And they wouldn't let me outside the door because of the storm," she whimpered. "Ninety-five my auntie was when she told me. But she never forgot the lady in blue, nor the lad that died in Carlisle Gaol, rest his soul! And the one that hanged hisself—I've seen him in the great barn, Master Tom. But they wouldn't let poor Nanny outside the door."

"Nay, I should think not, Nanny," Tom coaxed. "It is far too cold for you, let me see you home."

He led her carefully over the snow as she minced with fantastic steps like a young girl, clinging fast to his arm and prattling childishly. And the colt waited impatiently till he returned, although he was not long.

"Old Nanny lives in the end cottage with her great-granddaughter. Haven't you seen her before?" he asked. "She's a wonderful old body—very old—a hundred-and-two—got her second sight three years ago. Her great-granddaughter is forty. She was our nurse before she married."

"Second sight? Does she see visions and dream dreams?"

He laughed. "No, but the poor old thing was so blind she could scarcely grope her way, and her eyesight suddenly came back. She says it was all due to bathing her eyes in a holy well—it's a cattle trough now. But here we are, and here's Mall. He looks no worse for his influenza. What?" he called, as we neared Moor Hall and my girl came running down the terrace steps to meet us.

It was like home after years of exile to be there again. We sat in the inner hall, smoking and talking by the hearth, our feet on deer-skins and the fire-glow shining on guns and old armour hanging on the yellow-washed walls. Sometimes Mall charmed music from the yellowed, rattling keys of the square piano; sometimes Tom sang Jacobite ballads in his heart-reaching tenor.

The Moores had intermarried with Scotland intermittently for generations; they had been among the most loyal adherents of the Young Pretender; and the family fortunes had never quite recovered from the heavy sequestration following the '45. And then, in the midst of our harmony, the iron bell clanged; the door opened with a whirlwind of finely powdered snow, and no less a man than Gregory, the mortgagee, entered, begging a box of matches to light his lamps, which had blown out with the rising storm.

Careworn, middle-aged, lean-faced, with greedy eyes that went eagerly past Tom to Mall, standing slim and lovely by the hearth, in a gown as blue as her eyes.

He bowed, with a gleam of gold-filled teeth in his smiling mouth.

"I've had to fall back on the prehistoric horse, fair cousin," he said, over-lightly for real ease, and her eyebrows rose ever so slightly. The relationship was so distant it had never been recognised by the Moores. "My car could not get through the drifts tonight."

"Indeed?" she said, civilly. He lingered, though Tom had given him matches—and was waiting, door in hand, inhospitable for once.

"It's a dreadful night," said Gregory. "And your hearth is warm."

Neither brother nor sister spoke. He turned to go. Then he spoke very softly, over his shoulder. "My name is Gregory Moore by letters patent now. Soon—Moore of Moor Hall."

He passed into the night, and the door closed. Mall was shivering.

"I—I'm afraid of him," she said, sharply. "God forgive me, I hate him!"

"Let's forget the swine," said Tom. "Cheer up, Mall, old girl! There are hills beyond Pentland and firths beyond Forth," and he laughed. But our happiness fluttered on broken wings for the rest of the night, and I was glad to take my candle up the turnpike staircase and go to bed, for travelling and the past influenza had made me tired.

I had a whole staircase to myself; there were so many rooms and so few weather-tight. Mall had made the place cheerful with gay old Indian hangings on the four-poster bed and a great fire piled high with logs. But, though I slept as soon as my head touched the pillow, I was wandering in dreams all night. Wandering haggard with wild despair, searching for a Mall who was yet not my Mall. Up and down those old stairs, losing my way, finding myself in unfamiliar rooms and dim corridors, with old Nanny, candle in hand, peering through half-open doors to watch me. Tearing my hair because of my mad longing. Crazed with longing—and all in vain! When at last a dreadful calm, when, halter in hand, I made my way to the great barn.

It was daylight when I woke. They had let me sleep long after breakfast, thinking me still an invalid, but I laughed the idea to scorn, and went out through the fresh snow to help Tom and the two farm lads to shovel paths. And I made my way to the great barn. A gleam of sunlight shone golden through a crack in the roof; the great brown oaken beams looked like the ribs of some leviathan. Ropes of cobwebs, thick with dust, hung from the crossbeams; and I shivered. It was a trick of the sun, but I could have sworn I saw a man hanging. A man in brown with a writhing face, dying—horribly.

"You're cold, old man," said Tom. "Let's go indoors a 'noon-bit'. We never use this barn now—do all the threshing by steam of course. There's the old oak threshing floor, and you'll find an ash flail or two over there. By George, you could hit your head a mighty crack with a flail, learning to thresh by hand."

"Who's coming with me?" asked Mall after our early dinner. "I'm going to take Nanny her shawl if the road's cleared."

"Oh, I'm busy," said Tom, turning to his escritoire with an understanding grin. So we set out together. I wanted to ask many things; but she was silent about Gregory, and her silence told me far more than words. I could have kicked the fellow, but there! what good would it have done? Only satisfied my own little vanity and made him the more spiteful and vindictive. But I hated to see my girl afraid. I could only try to show her—no matter how haltingly and poorly, just a little of what was in my heart, and how I worshipped her.

"I'm thankful Miss Mall's in safe hands, sir, begging your pardon for making so free," said Mall's old nurse, a comely widow, while Mall talked with old Nanny, as happy as a child with her bright-coloured gift. "You've got a beauty in our Miss Mall, and as good as she's pretty, and indeed I wish you much happiness. But that Gregory—oh sir, he's a black heart. I don't trust him. Blood of the Moores he claims to be—but base born—my old gran could tell you a tale—eh, but it's far, far back. And he's always at the old lady to learn where the Miss Moore of that day hid her jewels. An heiress she was, and fell in love with a Highland gentleman that came with Prince Charlie. And she went to Carlisle—so they say—but the gentleman was hung there. Some says she never left her home at Moor Hall, though she was never seen again after that Christmas Eve. But there, how can you tell with things so far back as all that? It's far more likely she went off to France with what she had, and joined her gentleman's family there; for I've heard say they were exiled to foreign parts. But her cousin, Gregory (and this Moore Gregory—Gregory Moore he calls himself now, like his impudence)—claims kin with him through a village lass—well, Miss Moore's cousin Gregory, he went and hanged himself on Boxing Day in the great barn. They say he walks," she added mysteriously. "But this present Moore Gregory, as I was saying, is always at gran to get her to talk to him about old times. She'll rattle away reams long to anyone else, but mum as a fish with him. Never a word of her auntie and the lady in blue when he's in hearing, let him coax as he likes. A harmless creature, sir, and very lovable, my old gran, but a bit childish at times, and I've to keep her indoors for she'd wander out and get lost, poor soul."

She watched us out of sight; when we turned to wave our adieu, she was still standing at the open door, in a white apron, with Nanny's little old face smiling over her shoulder.

"It's going to snow again," said Mall, and she took my arm and came closer. The twilight was eerie; the great, snow-covered hills were very bleak and forlorn. We were all alone in a ghostly world; there was only love left in Pandora's box. And what might be the shadow of separation lay heavy on all of us.

"Here's to our last Christmas at Moor Hall," cried Tom, pouring a libation from the cut-glass thistle decanter. "Let's go through all the old rooms together. Mall let's leave our love and good wishes with every stone of the old place. For in March we go." His voice trailed into silence. We each linked an arm of Mall's, as, candle in hand, we traversed the dim passages and crooked stairs. The shadows fled before us like ghosts; there were so many old rooms with quaint furniture, so many more empty save for bats and rats and spiders. Birth and death and all that came between had passed in the old house; man's life, however long, was but a space to its age. Now the last of its children were going.

"There's still the Dower House, Tom," Mall whispered, holding closer to us both. "We can live there."

He shook his head. "I seek further hills if I leave Pentland," he said. "Now let's sing Auld Lang Syne, and take a stirrup cup in the hall."

But the stirrup must have been overstrong. My candle blew out on the staircase. I turned and turned, and twice tried to open doors in the wall, before I found my room, with its glowing fire. And there I sat by the hearth, drowsily nodding, but with my mind so clearly awake that I distinctly remember walking across the landing once more, and opening the door I had vainly tried to find, the door that was not there at all.

But it was there, and it opened into a room with a corner fireplace and a carved stone mantel. Mall stood beside it—Mall and yet not my Mall—Mall in a quilted gown with figures and tassels of gold, a ribbon of blue snooding her long curls and a scarf of tartan silk across her lovely shoulders. And facing her was the careworn man in brown, more hang-dog than ever—the Gregory Moore of those long past days.

She lifted a tall silver candle-stick and swept him a mocking curtsey. "You'd rob me, would you?" she asked. "Seek high, seek low, Cousin

Gregory! But you'll never find them. I, and mine, will live to enjoy them yet. I go to join my lad."

"Your lad'll rot in Carlisle Gaol," Gregory snarled. "Your bonnie Prince has turned his back on his friends—he's in retreat three weeks agone. Molly—listen to reason, girl! I love you."

"Love!" she echoed. "Oh, what a word from a spy, and a traitor," and her voice was terrible. But he did not seem to heed; he was grovelling at her feet, crazed with passion. For she was very beautiful.

"Molly, Molly! My heart's afire—it burns. Have mercy on me!" he said, thickly.

But she shook her skirts free of his clutching hands. Her eyes had grown afraid, and she turned; his face was demonic. And in turning her elbow struck the carved Tudor rose on the mantel jamb, and the stone swung back, and disclosed a narrow flight of descending stairs.

"Ah! Ah! You'd escape me, you jade! 'Tis here you've laid the jewels!" he screamed. And he rose in a whirlwind of passion and his clutching murderous hands crushed her slender throat. For just one second her eyes stared widely, bluely; it was but a second—the horror lasted but a second—yet it seemed an eternity. Then her head sank, and, as suddenly as he had seized her, his hands relaxed their hold, and she sank to the floor. And there he stood shaking over the dead body. Shaking and in dreadful pain and terror. And I saw him kneel beside her, and beg and pray, and all in vain. All in vain. She was dead, and he was an outcast. Outcast of Heaven and man.

And I saw him rise in the calm of despair and lift her dead body and carry it down that narrow stairway. And I saw him return, and beat his head against the wall. And stand motionless, listening as if she called. And beat his head on the wall again, and tear his clothes with crazy hands. And then gather the fire into the middle of the room and pile on the flames curtains and furniture…

And then I heard in the frost air the first faint cock crow of a dawn that had not yet come. And I awoke.

The fire had faded to a red glimmer, and I was stiff with cold. I groped to the mantel and found fresh candles, and lighted them. Then I crossed the landing once more; there was dead stone wall where once there had been a door. And I remembered it was an outer wall, storeys high; if the door had been there it would but have opened into space, since part of that wing had been burnt and rebuilt years ago. And I went back to the hearth and sat there till the carol singers came, and the house woke to the bustle of Christmas morning.

There were children crowding round the house place door for "fairings," but Tom beckoned me outside, and his face was anxious.

"Old Nanny slipped out in the night and wandered here," he said. "They've just found her. Come and help—but for Heaven's sake don't let Mall hear a word," and he led the way to a ruined old brewhouse that stood some distance from the rear of the house.

The roof had fallen under the weight of the snow; the walls were cracked, and part of the floor had capsized. Nanny was lying there, stiff and cold, with a shred of faded blue satin and a tarnished tassel of gold in her hand. And, in the broken archway beneath her feet lay what had once been a woman, still in her bravery of quilted satin petticoat and tartan scarf, and oh, pitiful, pitiful, still with her wealth of lustrous silken curls, though most else of beauty had perished.

"Don't let Mall see," said Tom. "Poor old Nanny! Here is her lady in blue. Poor girl, she never went to Carlisle. But look—look here," and he held up a fragment of tattered satin. "She had quilted her jewels into her petticoat. Oh! Molly Moore, there'll be Moores of Moor Hall still. May you rest in peace."

And rest she did, for the lady in blue was never seen again. But there are still Moores at Moor Hall, and a sturdy Tom and a blue-eyed fairly Mall at the Dower House with Mall and me. Though there are hills beyond Pentland and firths beyond Forth, our own hills are dearest to us, and we are thankful to remain with them.

"THE MALIGNANT THING"
A CHRISTMAS EVE GHOST STORY
Vincent Cornier

Published in The Mackay Daily Mercury, *Christmas supplement (Queensland), 22 December 1928*

Born William Vincent Corner (1898–1976) in Yorkshire, Vincent became an author of weird and detective fiction, who was labelled an "unclassifiable maverick" by his fellow mystery writer Francis M. Nevins. This is not his only Christmas-themed story; "Among Those Present Was Santa Claus" (1952) can be found in *Who Killed Father Christmas? and Other Seasonal Mysteries* (ed. Martin Edwards, British Library, 2023). A collection of his occult-flavoured mystery tales featuring his detective Barnabas Hildreth, *The Duel of Shadows*, was published in 2011 (ed. Mike Ashley, Crippen and Landru). An author who is finally due his time out of the shadows, I hope that the reprinting of this story, for the first time in ninety-seven years, showcases his singular talent and acerbic style.

COLONEL Petersham took a long pull at his cigar, pressed his feet nearer the blazing fire of the billiard room, and laughed.

"I think, Summerson," he said, "you should be labelled and put away—y'know the kind of thing. 'Excellent specimen of genus homme… highly non-intellectual; probably tenth century; very rare.'"

Summerson, his host, laughed. Nothing that a Petersham could say could halt that fount of lazy geniality which only Petersham could excite to full laughter. Summerson usually chuckled in a drily impudent way, when his sense of humour was made alert. The third of the party, Professor Tankerley, did not like to hear that laugh.

"I say—I say," he broke in, "don't you think this subject has been rather dragged about? We'll only end up in bad odour, one with the other, and then—"

"My dear Tankerley," Summerson's voice, lazier than his laughter, smoothly took the words off the Professor's lips, "don't worry… I'm used by now to the Petershams of this world! Our gallant old soul believes, and rightly too, that nothing of the invisible should dare to affront the corporeal. As a matter of fact, I also think the thing's in deuced bad taste. But, there you are—I've told you all about our pet spook—it's a true 'un right enough, as sailors say."

"I—I don't give a tin damn what sailors say, Summerson, what I, as a soldier say, is simple: show me one proof, one proof is all I ask, that your place is haunted and I'd not only retract all I've said, but I'll apologise to the tune of a pony to any charity you're interested in, old man."

"A fair enough offer," Summerson began.

"A—a simply idiotic proposal," rapped out Professor Tankerley, "and one, for the sake of two souls, Summerson, you must not dream of accepting!"

The Colonel's blue eyes opened wide beneath his bristled brows. He took a gasping gulp at his whisky and soda.

"Good Lord," he shot out, "do you also range yourself on the side of such nonsensical—"

"Nonsensical be hanged!" The Professor was so earnest now that his cheeks paled. "Essentially a soldier, Petersham, you deal only with stark elementals. Try for a moment to let some other type of intelligence dominate you… try, if you can, to assess the whole affair by the eerily cold light of a hundred thousand years of human tradition.

"Here you have Summerson telling you, in all seriousness, that for four centuries at least a malignant thing—call it a thing of Hell, a demon, a spectre, a shadow, what you will—has terrorised to death, at a modest estimate, a score of folk, even as you and I…

"Because of its horrible presence, a whole wing of this house has been closed up for nearly forty years… the last time it appeared as Summerson has said, was when the house was so full with a Christmas house-party that a valet was pushed away into that alleged haunted chamber. Apparently, poor soul, he did not know the common chit-chat of his master's friends sufficiently well to realise that a fortune would not have attempted any guest to occupy the place.

"Right—we have this valet in the room; probably he slept for an hour or so; he awakes—yells out that something is with him, screams and hammers the door.

"The whole house is aroused… the unfortunate servant is found in a corner of the room, talking to himself, drawing diagrams with his wet fingers on the wall… white-haired, druling in idiotic laughter… a shattered madman.

"That's but the last manifestation of the thing. For two hundred years so far back of course, as reliable testimony can extend, upwards of ten people have either been driven mad in that room, or killed by fright. I ask you in all earnestness, Colonel Petersham, not only to let the subject drop, but to—forget it entirely. Believe me, my researches into the phenomena of existence only have gone to prove demoniac survivals about us… there are such things as—as ghosts, and I—"

Colonel Petersham drank the last of his whisky with a flourish that was actually an impertinence. The white grave face of the scientist flushed before the action. Professor Tankerley drew back in the chair—and got to his feet.

"I think I'd better bid you both 'good night,'" he suavely murmured. "I—I am a little tired."

"So'm I," grunted the Colonel into his glass, "of a lot of damn fool tommy-rot and bunkum!… Don't want to upset you in any way, Tankerley, old man, but somehow such yarns get me by the throat and I almost choke. It's a failing of mine, I know. Sorry I can't get over it, and all that—but I've knocked about this earth for nearly sixty years now and I'm dashed if ever I've seen anything worse than myself."

"I sincerely hope," Professor Tankerley smoothly rejoined, "you never do. Pardon me—I'll be off now. A Merry Christmas to you in the morning."

Nothing could shake the old scientist's determination to retire. In less than ten minutes he was upstairs… He felt that he had gone too far, and had made a fool of himself. Not a pleasant state of mind for the famous Professor Tankerley to be in—he tumbled into bed, and brooded.

Probably two hours had passed. Tankerley had not slept. Now he sat up in bed and listened to vague chucklings, rough voices and clattering.

"My God," he muttered, his skin suddenly damp, "I believe that fool of a man has actually induced Summerson to have the bricks that wall off the empty west wing broken down! Surely the madman does not intend to sleep in that room after all—after its forty years of emptiness?"

Really concerned, Tankerley got out of bed, slipped on a dressing gown and scuttled as quickly as his slippers would allow him along the polished floor of the corridor and toward the hitherto blank wall that had for so long cut off the sinister wing. A couple of keepers had been brought in. Between them they had demolished the greater part of the wall. Summerson and the Colonel, both under the influence of too much whisky, stood laughing and jesting before the aperture. Along in the foul silences of the west wing glowed a great orange light. Clouds of dust flew from out of the room that was haunted. Servants were busy inside it—they had lighted a fire in it and were cleaning it out.

Professor Tankerley drew up to the twain. He queried—pleaded—argued… nothing was of avail. The Colonel had a bunch of candles and a bottle of whisky; in a pocket of his huge dressing gown he carried a fully loaded service revolver. He had wagered Summerson £50… he was going to spend the night in that room—yes if the Devil himself came into it with him.

And so Professor Tankerley quietly gave up his task of conviction. He held out his hand to the Colonel… For a moment that man was sobered by the solemnity of the gesture; but then the whisky took hold of his brain once more.

As the Professor moved away to bed for the second time, Petersham was uproariously laughing with Summerson at the antics of a servant attempting to pull bedding through the hole in the wall.

Half an hour later the servants, all, had gone. Only Summerson remained with the Colonel in the haunted room. They had opened the second bottle of whisky and were having one final tot before the host left the guest to whatever horrors he dared. The fire blazed violently, as though the roaring chimney, silent for so long, hungered for flame. A dozen candles flickered about the place… all was cheerful; all was sombrely calm.

Summerson went his ways. The Colonel placed his revolver close to his hand and tumbled into the makeshift bed. He drank a little more and smoked a little more. Nothing happened; he had no fear.

Then, suddenly he grinned and jumped out of bed.

Of course—of course—that cunning devil Summerson was going to play a practical joke on him! That was the idea—eh. That was why Summerson had advised that the door of the room should be left open an inch or two—not, the Colonel chuckled, because the room was oppressively musty—no, the man was going to steal in during the night and scare him. Um, if that was the game, the Colonel decided he'd soon stop it!

Over to the massive door he went. He closed it tightly and locked it. The key he slipped into his pyjama pocket.

His scalp twitched… someone sighed, as if in relief.

No, damn it all—no! It was the wind. Right—hang the stuffiness, he would close the windows. He closed them—again the sibilant sigh, as of satisfaction.

"I'd bet another fiver that clever joker's just outside!" The Colonel chuckled again and had more whisky. "He sees the game's up."

And now, for no reason but restless desire it seemed, the Colonel explored and locked up an old powder closet that stood in a corner of the older room… and then a tiny door that was let into the panelling to close on an alcove in which there lurked a mirror. He looked in the mirror before he closed it from his sight… Jove, how queer its old glass had gone! How strangely green, like the light of dead fish, it made the fire! Ugh, he shuddered in a sudden draught, the place was dank with cold… He latched that little door and faced the room.

"Ah," he gloated, "not a single entry; no practical joking now—not a single crevice left that a rat could get through… Locked, bolted, and barred, b'gad—absolutely alone."

Something seemed to roar up at him—a sullen cloud, a grisly horrible and deathly cold mass of putrescent vapour… the fire was gone… God, the candles had gone… the room was a laughing tumult; a place of Hell—haunted!

"Yes," snarled a voice into his failing ears… "Alone!"

THE SPECTRE BRIDEGROOM
A CHRISTMAS STORY

Mrs. Gordon Smythies

Published in The Tasmanian News, *supplement, 23 December 1884*

Harriet Maria Smythies (1813–1883) was "the Queen of the domestic novel"* with more than twenty novels to her name. The (amazing) titles include: *A Warning to Wives: or, The Platonic Lover* (1847), *The Male Flirt: or, "Ladies, Beware of Him"* (1860) and *The Sleep-walker; or, Lady Theresa's Trials*, which was serialised between 1865 and 1866. Her son, William Gordon Smythies, a noted barrister and poet who died in 1909, was survived by his father.

"The Spectre Bridegroom" is a fun romp which shares its title with several nineteenth-century tales on this theme, including Washington Irving's 1819 story, inspired by German legends, and another folklore-inspired tale in Robert Hunt's *Popular Romances of the West of England, or, The Drolls, Traditions, and Superstitions of Old Cornwall* (1865). But, I have to say, while some of us might believe in ghosts, the notion that *anyone* but Tom Cruise could fall 80 feet and *survive* (for a short while), is preposterous! I present the first reprinting of this story since 1884.

---

* "Publications", *Morning Herald* (London), 26 August 1861.

CHAPTER I

THE wedding bells were ringing in the cold clear air, and every leaf, twig, and blade of grass, crusted with hoar-frost, sparkled in the pale wintry sun.

It was Christmas Eve.

Strange to say, this day had been fixed upon for the marriage of Mary de Lisle and Sir Gabriel Ellesmere. It was an old custom in the De Lisle family to marry on Christmas Eve.

Mary was the last of the De Lisles—a once wealthy, powerful family, now much impoverished. Mary lived with her widowed mother in the old manor house where she was born, and which she was to quit for the grandeur of Ellesmere Hall, one of the noblest of "the stately homes of England."

Mary was in her own chamber. She stood before the old-fashioned oval toilet-glass, with its carved oaken frame.

That glass had reflected the beauty and blushes of many generations of brides of a family celebrated for the loveliness of its daughters.

Mary de Lisle was eighteen. She was passionately in love with her bridegroom, trembling with a joy too deep for utterance, and yet clinging to the fond, proud mother, who, now that the object of her hopes was all but attained, was very pale and hysterical with emotion as she folded her darling in her arms, and rested that delicate and blushing face on her maternal and full bosom.

"Is he come, mamma?" faltered Mary.

"No, dearest; but Dr. Trebeck, who arrived last night too late to come here says Sir Gabriel's directions to him were to escort us to church, if he were not here himself by ten o'clock, as the church is so much nearer to the hall than to his house, and Gabriel had some very important business to transact this morning. He thought that arrangement would save time."

"What business could he have to take him away at such a time, mamma? He never told me of any."

Mrs. de Lisle was silent. She knew that Sir Gabriel Ellesmere, young, handsome, and at one time very gay, had been entangled before he was of age, in a very unfortunate attachment to a poor girl, who had sacrificed everything for his sake—home, name, fame, and peace of mind, and that the unhappy creature was a mother.

In strict confidence Trebeck, who was related to Sir Gabriel, and in fact was his next of kin, had revealed this sad story to Mrs. de Lisle, who therefore understood that the bridegroom might have business to transact which he could not confide to his intended.

A message from the vicar and the young doctor, sent by Mary's little maid, compelled Mary to leave her room.

Leaning on her mother's arm she glided like a sunbeam down the broad old black oak staircase, and entered the dining-hall, where the little wedding party awaited her.

The *déjeuner* was tastefully set out, and a superb wedding-cake, presented by Dr. Trebeck, and brought down by himself from Gunter's, glittered like a mimic Mont Blanc in the Christmas sun.

It was a mile and a half to the church. All the way uphill, and the roads rutty and bad.

"We must set out at once," said the vicar.

The carriages were at the gate.

Trebeck escorted the bride; Dr. Vernon gave his arm to her mother; and the two bridesmaids—not very well pleased—followed arm in arm.

"Who ever heard of having two bridesmaids and one bridesman at a wedding?" said the elder Miss Vernon, who, rather on the wane, was growing angular in form and sharp in temper. "What a miserable affair!"

Dr. Trebeck folded an ermine mantle round the bride. She looked pale and shivered; yet the sun shone brightly.

The air, though frosty, was not very keen, and the merry peals of the church bells, ringing loudly and gaily out, in honour of the wedding day of the squire, Sir Gabriel, and Mary de Lisle, the belle of the village, enlivened the quiet drive through the hills.

CHAPTER II

At the entrance to the church, the school children, and all the villagers, in their Sunday best, were assembled. The path from the churchyard gate to the porch, was strewn with flowers. Every cottage window had been put under contribution.

The beautiful bridal carriage and four, with the postilions in blue satin jackets, and with huge white favours, was at the gate.

"Gabriel is here, then, before us, Dr. Trebeck," said, Mary, joyfully.

"No," replied Trebeck. "At his request I ordered the bridal carriage from B—— to be here to meet him. He was to drive over from the hall in his own brougham."

When they had waited some time, the vicar drew Dr. Trebeck aside.

"Had we not better send a man on horseback to the hall?" he said; "and another to the station. Heaven grant there may have been no accident!"

"Oh, we should have heard of it by this time!" said Dr. Trebeck. "Such news travels swiftly."

"The ten o'clock train has been in more than half an hour," said the vicar. "The next train does not reach Ellesmere till 11.45. What if he should arrive after canonical hours!"

Dr. Trebeck sent the bridal carriage off full gallop to the hall, and despatched Topper, Sir Gabriel's new valet, who was in the rumble, to the station. Topper was to telegraph to Sir Gabriel's lodgings in St. James's street, and to bring back the reply.

Meanwhile, Dr. Trebeck, by Mrs. de Lisle's desire, kept close to the bride, who grew paler and paler every minute.

She bore up, however, till the bridal carriage returned from the hall and Sir Gabriel's valet from the station.

Sir Gabriel had not arrived at the hall.

The answer to the telegram was—

Sir Gabriel left us, we understood, for the continent, yesterday, at 3 p.m.

When Mary heard these words, a cry of agony burst from her white lips.

"Oh, mother!" she exclaimed.

And as Mrs. de Lisle rushed forward to support her, Dr. Trebeck extended his arms, and caught the sinking form of the bride, who had fainted.

It was a long time before all the skill of Dr. Trebeck—and he was very skillful—could restore Mary to life and misery.

By the time consciousness had returned, the hour of twelve had struck. The unhappy girl was driven home to the old manor house in company with her mother and Dr. Trebeck.

In spite of all Dr. Trebeck could do, Mary's agony of mind brought on the brain fever. At one time even he despaired of her life; and had she been his own intended, he could not have been more devoted, more intensely anxious.

In her delirium, she constantly apostrophised Sir Gabriel, and persisted in asserting that he was by her bedside.

"What is that crimson stain on your waistcoat, Gabriel?" she would say. "Why do you not speak to me, Gabriel? Why do you glare on me thus? Why is your cheek so pale? Speak to me! He beckons! I must follow him!"

Then she would try to rise; but with the effort she would sink back exhausted and insensible.

But Mary's time was not yet come. Dr. Trebeck watched her through the terrible crisis. Mrs. de Lisle averred that his skill and care alone had saved her darling's life.

The long midsummer days found Mary the ghost of her former self, slowly gliding like a shadow about the old manor house, where so lately she had flitted like a sunbeam, pacing the quaint, formal gardens, or watching the water-lilies floating on the dark, deep waters of the moat, beneath the old trees and older walls.

But wherever she went, or whatever she was doing, it seemed to Mary that ere long a shadowy form would steal to her side. The form of Sir Gabriel!

She told her mother of this strange sense of invisible companionship, and added that a cold, sepulchral draught of air always seemed to usher in the invisible presence.

Mrs. de Lisle confided this strange hallucination to Dr. Trebeck, who treated it as hypochondriasis, quoted many learned authorities and parallel cases, and prescribed travelling, and an entire change of air, scene, and the habits of life.

"Alas, dear doctor!" said Mrs. de Lisle, "you know how small my income is at best, and now the breaking of M——'s bank has deprived me of my little capital, while last year's bad harvest makes it impossible for old Grimes to pay his rent. How, then, can I give my poor girl the advantages you advocate?"

"By giving her to me, dear friend," said Dr. Trebeck, "I love her still—not with the wild passion I felt for her when she was in all the radiant bloom of her beauty, but more tenderly, more deeply, for all she has suffered."

"But will she consent? Does she not love that false, bad man?" said Mrs. de Lisle.

"Show her that letter he wrote her the day after that fixed for the wedding," said Trebeck.

"Is there no fear of a relapse? Mary is proud," said the mother.

"And to her pride I look for her cure," said Dr. Trebeck. "She is now full of illusions about Sir Gabriel. That letter will destroy them all."

Thus urged, Mrs. de Lisle sought Mary in her own room, and, after tenderly embracing the wasted form of her darling, she put the letter into her hand, saying—

"Oh, Mary, had you a male relative of any kind, this villain must have been punished."

Mary read as follows—

I have deceived you, Mary, but not intentionally. I thought I loved you. Alas! At the eleventh hour I find I deceived myself. Another has taught me what love really is. You cannot forgive me, I know, for I cannot forgive myself. Still, let me make what poor atonement I can. One who has so loved Gabriel Ellesmere must never want. Your cheque, then shall be honoured to the amount of £200 p.a. at Lloyds and Leverett's, Lombard street. This will keep you, and one dearer to you than yourself, in comfort. May heaven bless you both! Farewell for ever!

G. E.

Dr. Trebeck was right. The agony was intense, the wrench was terrible; but from amid the ruins of Mary's half-broken heart the idol was cast out.

This letter proved Sir Gabriel to be mean and cruel, and Mary felt ashamed of loving, of dying for such a man.

Before the winter came again, Mary was affianced to Dr. Trebeck.

The wedding-day was fixed, as before, for Christmas Eve, and Dr. Trebeck, who had a large house at Bridgewater was gone away for a few days to get all ready for his bride.

Mary was resigned; but she was not happy. Nothing crushes the heart like the fall of an idol. Her mother's prayers, Trebeck's devotion, the grim poverty that threatened her beloved parent, and the desire to show to Gabriel and the world that she was cured of her love for him—all united to make her accept Trebeck.

It was the day before that fixed for the wedding. Mary, dejected, and yet excited, and with that strange sense of invisible companionship which had never ceased to haunt her since her illness, strolled out into the country, and rambled on till she came to a wild heath, on which was a clump of trees, and a flat stone, which had been a favourite resting-place with Sir Gabriel and herself.

It had been noon, and the August sun was shining with a brassy glare on the golden gorse, and on the little pink bells of the heather. The bees were gathering their sweetest nectar from those bells, and warm air was fragrant of the honey they distilled.

Not a creature was to be seen, not a sound to be heard save the hum of those bees and as Mary stooped down to gather a harebell, she felt the short, dry sod warm to her cold hand.

Mary was now always cold and pale. Her heart was dead in her breast.

In the distance she saw the spire of Ellesmere church, and the tower and battlements of Ellesmere Hall. The past came vividly before her; and as she approached the clump of trees and the flat stone, her knees trembled, and she sank down upon the stone.

Sir Gabriel had carved on that stone his own and Mary's initials. Was it her diseased fancy, or was it really so? To Mary it seemed that the letters "G. E." were now blood-red!

CHAPTER III

Dr. Trebeck, young as he was, had gained the esteem and confidence of Bridgewater and its neighbourhood. He had an excellent practice, and of his skill there was no doubt. He had studied very hard, and few rising physicians had given the time and attention to anatomy which he had given. Then, too, his character stood so high; his conduct was so steady; he was so good to the poor.

All Bridgewater had resented Mary de Lisle's preference of Sir Gabriel, and now all rejoiced in the approaching wedding. Everyone knew how their young doctor had idolised Mary de Lisle.

The large old house, which had belonged to Trebeck's ancestor (a celebrated physician in the time of James I), was now newly decorated and richly furnished. It had a formal garden in front, with two single yew-trees cut into the shape of storks. The crest of the Trebecks was a stork *passant*.

Dr. Trebeck had an underground study, laboratory, surgery, and dissecting-room, the latter lighted by skylight, and communicating with the sluggish waters of the river Parrot, which flowed past the back entrance to the house. Dr. Trebeck's study was partly fitted up as a dressing-room, partly as a library. It contained two large, dark closets, and in them were skulls, bones, bottles containing nondescript horrors, parts of the human body preserved in spirits, on which he had made experiments, and two ghastly skeletons, reduced to that state by his own hands after dissection, and adroitly put together again by wires, till they looked, as they hung in that dark closet, like the King of Terrors himself.

It was evening, Dr. Trebeck was alone in his study. On a couch at hand his wedding clothes were spread out. He had tried them on; they fitted beautifully. A cheval glass stood close by, with telescope sconces and two wax candles, not yet lighted.

Everything had gone well so far. Mary was to be his on the morrow. Fortune smiled. His wedding clothes fitted to a "t," and yet a deep dejection bowed the glossy and curly head of the young doctor.

"A regular attack of the blues," he said. "I'm hipped, that's all—worn out, overwrought, over-excited, and cold as death."

He had a kettle on the hob. He took a bottle and a tumbler from the cupboard, and mixed a stiff glass of brandy-and-water.

He felt his pulse—low, thin, and fluttering—and, drawing his easy chair to the fire, he drank off the brandy-and-water he had mixed, and not feeling much warmed and cheered, he filled and emptied the glass again, and yet again.

He stirred the fire, and leaned back in his chair. There was now no light in the room but that of the flickering flame.

Did he dream? or did he really see the door of the dark closet opposite to him at the farther end of the room slowly open, and one of the skeletons hanging there step out of the black recess?

The doctor's well-curled hair stiffened and stood erect, his eyeballs glared; his limbs grew rigid; a cold perspiration burst out all over him. He could not speak—his tongue clove to the roof of his mouth. He could not move—he was paralysed.

A cold wind filled the room, as the skeleton—or so it seemed to him—advanced, and stood before the cheval glass. The wax tapers seemed to light up of themselves; and gradually Dr. Trebeck beheld in the glass that skeleton form clothe itself, by some mysterious invisible process, with all that constitutes that complicated machine called "man."

Over all stole by degrees the soft and tinted skin. The polished skull resumed its coating of flesh and its rich waves of auburn hair. The ghastly, bony hollows were once more bright with beautiful blue eyes. And at length the fine face and noble form of Sir Gabriel Ellesmere was reflected in that cheval glass; and those eyes gazed mournfully and reproachfully at Trebeck's.

The skeleton, having thus resumed its hues and proportions, arrayed itself deliberately in the fine embroidered shirt, and in fact, in all the articles prepared for Dr. Trebeck's wedding toilet.

With, if possible, increased horror he saw the double-breasted white waistcoat assume a small red spot over the region of the heart, and that spot spread in size, and deepen in hue, till it became a dark crimson stain, as large as the palm of his hand.

Sir Gabriel then walked to the hearth, Dr. Trebeck's glossy new hat on his head, his white gloves and scented handkerchief in his hand, and holding the latter to his heart. Suddenly, he stood on the rug, with his back to the fire, in an attitude familiar to him in life. In a hollow, sepulchral voice, he thus addressed Trebeck—

"Murderer! You shall never wed Mary de Lisle. I go to warn her, to claim her as my bride, and to denounce you. You availed yourself of my trust to stab me in my sleep as I lay on that couch. You reduced this form to a skeleton, and hid it in yon dark closet, side by side with that of a hospital patient, killed by your cruel experiments. You had the charge of my wedding clothes, which you burnt to ashes. Exchange is no robbery; and, therefore, I have appropriated yours. You gave to the high-born Mary de Lisle a letter I confided to you for poor Mary May, the unhappy victim of my youthful passion and her own fond frailty. So crafty have you been in your fierce passion for my bride elect, your hatred of me, your jealousy, your remorseless cruelty, that the law cannot touch you. You have eluded even suspicion, and yet, villain, it is all in vain. To defeat and to punish monsters like you, Nature suspends her laws, and the invisible world resumes it ancient power. Mary de Lisle shall yet be mine, and mine only; and your bride shall be death! There is no escape for you, Trebeck! All earthly secrets are known in that bourne whence I have just returned; and of your vile deed there was a witness unseen by you. His evidence shall convict you yet!"

With these words Sir Gabriel disappeared, the same cold, sepulchral air which attended his entrance stirring as he did so.

At midnight Dr. Trebeck's man-servant, alarmed at not seeing his master, sought him, and found him lying insensible, and cold as death, on the rug before the now extinguished fire.

He raised his master, poured some brandy down his throat, succeeded in restoring him to life, and helped him to his room, and to bed.

"Only a swoon from over-exertion, James," said Dr. Trebeck; but James told the maid he was sure it was a fit.

CHAPTER IV

While Dr. Trebeck was lying insensible on the hearth in his underground study, Mary de Lisle—the bride elect—was sitting alone in the old dining hall of the manor house. She had wished her fond mother good night, and both had retired to their own apartments; but Mary could not rest. A presentiment of evil weighed down her spirit. Her bridal dress, wreath, and veil—presents from Trebeck—had remained unlooked at in a packing case; but now Mary felt a strange desire to try them on.

As she stood before the glass, it seemed to her that she gazed on the ghost of that blooming bride who had been mirrored in that glass a year ago. Suddenly a thought crossed her mind.

In an antique escritoire in the dining-hall were the letters Sir Gabriel Ellesmere had written to her, and several bunches of dead violets—once fresh as her beauty and her affection, now withered like her hopes and her heart.

Mary was very conscientious. She felt she ought to destroy those relics before she became another's bride. The clock struck twelve as she stole down stairs, and into the old hall.

Mary's escritoire was in a recess near the large Gothic window. There it was her custom to sit formerly to write to Gabriel, to indulge in happy dreams and wild hopes; but of late only to weep and pray.

Mary took out the little packet of letters and the treasured knots of faded violets.

"I will burn them in the fireplace," she said to herself, "all but the last; that I will keep to remind me of what he really was."

She read that terrible letter over again, to strengthen her in her resolution; and, as she did so, a deadly faintness came over her, and with the packet of letters in her hand, as she arose to approach the hearth, her strength failed her, and she sank on her knees before her chair. As she did so a cold wind, smelling of vaults and graves, lifted her long, dishevelled tresses and made her shiver.

Slowly she turned her head. Her eyes were distended, her limbs rigid. She could not move, she could not scream; but she could think, she could see, she could shudder.

"Is this a trance?" she said to herself; "or do I really see my ancestors in their armour, descending from their niches, and their eyes glaring fiercely on me through the bars of their vizors? Do I see Sir Adam and Sir Launcelot, with their solemn dames, move, and their eyes flash, and their breasts heave? And do they really step down from their frames?"

Mary tried to scream, but she had no power to utter a sound.

"Gabriel!" she would have shrieked, had not her voice failed her, for it seemed to her that the hall door opened slowly, and that her beloved, dressed for his bridal, looking larger and taller than when she saw him last, but very pale, and with cold, glassy eyes glaring upon her, advanced into the hall, holding his handkerchief to a wound in his breast, the blood from which had stained his shirt and waistcoat.

The knights and dames, and the old warriors in their coats of mail, advanced to meet Sir Gabriel. The knights bowed low, the dames curtseyed to the ground.

Sir Gabriel solemnly returned their salutations, and led the way to the recess, where Mary knelt.

"Bravo knights and noble dames!" he said, in a hollow voice, "I come to clear my honour of the foul charge of falsehood and inconstancy to my bride elect, the last of the De Lisles. I come to beg you to join me in forbidding the marriage of a daughter of your house with a murderer!"

The knights and dames drew nearer.

"I denounce Dr. Trebeck as my murderer! He sent to my bride, my beloved, a letter I confided to him for a poor girl, Mary May, whom in my early youth I had wooed and won. Mary de Lisle, will you wed this murderer? Knights and dames of this ancient house, do you not forbid this union?"

Mary's white lips vainly essayed to form the word "Never!"

A hollow sounding, "We do!" from the ghostly knights and dames seemed to reach her ear.

"Is she not mine?—mine only—mine for ever?" asked Sir Gabriel of the knights and dames or, to Mary's entranced, bewildered senses, he seemed to say those words; and she thought they answered, "Aye, verily," and bowed low in assent.

Then did she fancy that Sir Gabriel, extending his arms, cried, "Mary, my love, my bride, I claim you! Come," and that she rose from her knees and fell upon his breast.

Now the thought of her mother rushed through her mind, and she said—

"Let me write one line of farewell and of explanation to that dearest, best of mothers! Let me tell her that you have come back to claim me, and that I go with you!"

Sir Gabriel bowed assent, and Mary had just written a few lines to her mother, when her lamp went out.

That window was found wide open by the housemaid in the morning, and Mary's note to her mother lay on the escritoire.

CHAPTER V

"What a strange nightmare was that I had last evening in my study!" said Dr. Trebeck to himself, as he sprang out of bed on his wedding morning. "The effect of three glasses of brandy-and-water on a brain not seasoned!"

He rang for James.

"Bring me my wedding clothes," he said, gaily. "I shall dress here."

Somehow he did not like the idea of his study. He glanced rather nervously at the shirt and waistcoat. They were spotless.

It was a green Yule; but the soft west wind brought the merry peal of the church bells to his ear.

As the bridal carriage and four drove up to the manor house gates, the scarlet satin jackets and white favours of the postilions contrasted prettily with the dark evergreens of the avenue.

Dr. Trebeck looked eagerly from the carriage window. He expected to see the bride at her open casement, looking out for him. What he did see was a crowd gathered round the moat.

He cried to the postilions to stop.

"What is that crowd?" he said. "What are they about?"

"They zeem, zur, to be dragging the moat," said the Somersetshire lad he had addressed. "For all the world az if zomum wor drowned."

"Drive on," cried Dr. Trebeck; "drive to the spot."

It was soon reached.

Dr. Trebeck sprang from the carriage. His eye had lighted on Mrs. de Lisle, deadly pale, tearing her hair, beating her breast, and rushing wildly along the bank.

Dr. Trebeck hurried towards her.

At this moment one of the men engaged in dragging the moat cried out—

"Hold hard! Lend a hand, Zam!"

The fair young face and slender form of Mary de Lisle rose to the surface. She was dead!

They laid her on the bank, her bridal wreath and wedding-dress hung with green slime and duckweed, and in her dead grasp a packet of letters, which Dr. Trebeck at a glance recognised as Sir Gabriel's.

Mrs. de Lisle fell insensible on her daughter's breast.

By this time the crowd had increased tenfold, and Dr. Trebeck, having ascertained that Mary was indeed dead, was giving orders to the men who had dragged the moat to carry Mrs. de Lisle to her chamber, and to convey Mary's remains to the dining-hall, when a heavy hand was laid on his shoulder, and the voice of a Bow street officer said—

"Dr. Trebeck, I arrest you in the Queen's name, on the charge of murdering Sir Gabriel Ellesmere."

"It is false!" said Dr. Trebeck. "Touch me at your peril."

And he clenched his fists, and put himself in a posture of defence.

"Here's my warrant, doctor," said the officer. "I don't want to make things unpleasant; but I must do my duty. So come along, like a good gentleman. I've a carriage at the gate."

"Never!" said Dr. Trebeck. "You shall kill me first."

"That ain't my work. That's for Jack Ketch to do."

And then, as Dr. Trebeck still refused and resisted, other officers came up, and slipped a pair of handcuffs on his wrists, and dragged him away.

On inquiry, Dr. Trebeck learned that Sir Gabriel's bankers and solicitors, surprised and alarmed at hearing nothing of him, and at his drawing no money for a whole year, began to suspect some accident or some foul play.

Unable to obtain any information, they consulted a celebrated London detective.

His private inquiries at Sir Gabriel's lodgings in St. James's street, and of Mary May, who had been driven by utter destitution into the union with her child, confirmed their worst suspicions.

The detective came privately down to Bridgewater. He found out a wretch who had been in the habit of supplying Dr. Trebeck with dead bodies for dissection, and of assisting him in his experiments.

This wretch had once forged Trebeck's name to a cheque for twenty pounds. This crime threw him into the doctor's power. He did not prosecute him, but he made him his slave.

The wretch, whose name was Jukes, having robbed a grave, and the police being on his track, hid himself in one of Dr. Trebeck's closets, and thus was a witness of the murder of Sir Gabriel. Not feeling safe where he was, he escaped to New York, and had returned to Bridgewater only the day before that fixed for the wedding.

A reward of three hundred pounds offered by Government tempted Jukes to betray Dr. Trebeck. The doctor was taken before a magistrate, and on the evidence produced was committed to prison. The police had much difficulty in preventing the mob from tearing the handsome doctor to pieces. In prison he protested his innocence, and appeared sanguine of acquittal. But the night before his trial he adroitly effected his escape from his cell, and got on to the roof of the prison. In trying to drop from the roof into the road, his foot slipped, and he fell into the stone courtyard, a height of 80 feet.

There he was found in the morning, one thigh and one arm fractured, and insensible from concussion of the brain.

He lingered for some days and when consciousness returned he was in horrible agony; but no word of penitence or prayer passed his lips.

When he did speak, it was to apostrophise two "bodiless creatures," whom he called Gabriel and Mary, and whom he declared he saw from the open window (open on account of the heat of the weather) by moonlight, gliding hand in hand through the clear evening sky. The doctors said he died raving mad.

    Mrs. de Lisle only survived her daughter one year; and since her death the old manor house has been uninhabited, the garden is a waste, and all the country people say the place is Haunted.

A CHRISTMAS GHOST STORY
Bessie May Tobin-Montague

First published in Modern Culture, *December 1901*

In the "Jottings" section of an undated copy of *The Bohemian*, a look back at the first issue of the magazine from 1899 noted that Bessie May Tobin-Montague (1868–1938) was "the sweet poet and noted story-builder of the old Palmetto State".* In another issue of the same magazine it stated that: "she was born during the dark period which succeeded the Civil War; but being blessed with a joyous, sunny nature, she grew and revelled and thrived in the sunshine of her own making." She wrote several other stories for *Modern Culture* magazine, and her poetry was featured in newspapers from all over America. She died in San Diego at the home of her daughter in January 1938 after an "extended illness".

This is a story offering a twist on the tradition of the haunted house at Christmas, reprinted here for the first time since 1901.

---

* "Palmetto State" is a nickname for South Carolina. During the Civil War, SC played a significant role in the conflict, which included the attack on Fort Sumter and naval operations in Charleston Harbor.

I

I F John's great uncle, Richard Havergall, an octogenarian, who had lived for a number of years in close retirement, while he probed and dug and quite submerged himself in all that was occult and mystic and impossible—an alchemist, he would have been called in the thirteenth century; a wizard he was called by his townspeople—if this great uncle had not died and bequeathed to John the great, dark, uncanny old place called Mock Orange, this story had probably never been written.

It was a grand old place, John said; if a little gloomy, he had the grace to supplement. Many a day had he spent within those walls when his aunt and his cousin Dick were alive. He and Dick were fast friends when they were little chaps. He had never been there since Dick's death. The loss of this friend had been a great blow to John.

After losing both wife and son, the old man, always erratic and shaky as to his mental underpinnings, went quite to pieces, and wandered away into psychological fanaticism. All that he loved were in the spirit world. I suppose he naturally went groping after them.

And so the old man died too at last; and the old place and belongings—the old books and pictures, and curios; the antiquated furniture, as hideous as it was rare; the heavy old-fashioned plate, with the Havergall crest—all came down to John. Perhaps they came for love of this one nephew; perhaps because there was nobody else so closely allied by blood; for blood is a strong factor when it comes to the bestowal of a legacy. I have seen it push love and preference quite out of the way.

It was John, of course, that conceived the idea of our spending Christmas there. Christmas was never Christmas to John away from the South. And it had been ten years since he had enjoyed a Southern Christmas. I did not think it would be a bit nice.

I had heard of these old worm-eaten Southern Seats, and had my opinion on the subject deeply rooted. I was not to be carried away by John's voluminous panegyrics upon the charm, and solemn picturesqueness of this one in particular. I believed it to be depressing, dingy, full of spiders and perhaps—ghosts.

And not two months had elapsed since the soul of a mysterious old being had passed away within those walls and he, you might say, hand-in-glove with the black art and the—Devil! I shuddered at the bare thought.

But John insisted that it would be great. He had to show up there some time, sooner or later, to investigate matters concerning the property, so why not, he argued, go now.

"Take a crowd of young friends along and make a house party, and spend a regular "fore de war' Christmas."

The friends apprised of the scheme acclaimed, with a voice, their delight, and would not hear of any backing down.

When John spoke of a wonderful Black Swamp, in the vicinity, and belonging, in part, to the Mock Orange estate, which he described as practically howling with game of all kinds, ranging all the way from wild hog to the majestic stag, with field and brake and fen galore with partridge, duck, and turkey, I could not stem the tide. I yielded.

However, one stipulation I adhered to—that the sportsmen be restricted to the limitations of the actual premises after sundown, ghoulish individuals not being supposed to roam abroad prior to that hour.

So the guests were seriously invited, and a list made of all the things we were to take along. Charles (our man-servant) must go. Charles was a man of parts, who could cook as well as serve meals very satisfactorily; and Fanny (my maid) of course would go too. Fanny was also a good servant and an indefatigable worker. They would be dispatched ahead with most of the luggage and the dogs, perhaps John's two, at any rate, and we would follow when all was in readiness for our reception. The care-taker of the old place would give them all the necessary information and perhaps be pressed into service for something. Besides, the village was conveniently at hand for needful purchases.

Maud, my sister, would go, and Jack Fletcher. I had a mind to make a match there, and thought—Oh, well, since then the match has been happily consummated, so I will confess to the innocent intrigue.

Halcourt Meredith and Minnie must go. They were such a jolly couple. Besides Halcourt had a prize dog which accentuated his desirability from John's point of view.

Frank Baker also had a good dog, besides being possessed of many admirable qualities in himself; and Julia Steene—of course I would have a woman for each man, being wise in my generation—Rob Patton and Kitty Floyd; John and me. That was the sum of us. Two married couples ought to be chaperonage enough, I thought. A good healthy crowd we were all round. Young but not unsupportably so.

And such a crowd as we were, we found ourselves, in due course of time, rumbling into Brighton, a considerable little village in Southwestern South Carolina—a pretty village, with white houses and many trees of the vividest green imaginable. Mock orange, John said they were—very like the sweet orange in foliage.

Another thing that attracted our attention was the profusion of flowers in the gardens. John, our staff interpreter, explained that they were japonicas—and winter flowers. There were huge trees of them of every shade, from snow-white to crimson. It was a ravishing sight for the dead middle of winter to one accustomed only to snow drifts and sleet at this time of the year.

It was just the beginning of dusk when we actually arrived at the entrance gate of our newly-acquired ancestral home; which was quite at the edge of, almost outside, the village.

All day quite lowering, and dark, it began to drizzle a fine mist, like ether spray, stinging the face as our party, ten strong, emerged from the capacious maw of the village bus and stood, ere we gathered ourselves together, contemplating the dark and frowning pile of stone and masonry that was to shelter us for the next few weeks—with portentous thumpings at heart, to speak for myself.

A momentary glance took in the towering structure, outlined against a murky twilight sky. Great fluted columns arose from the balustraded portico, supporting a heavy gabled roof above, which was heavily ornamented, and dark with weatherstain. I could make out a queer, grewsome, centre piece—once white, but now greatly discoloured—of a monstrous figure, in relief, half human and half bird, with wings rampant—an appalling sight; while, in sympathetic character, the corners of the roof were set with hideous gargoyles—human heads with yawning mouths, from which the rain water trickled like spittle, falling with a gurgle to the ground below. On every side were the vivid green mock orange trees.

The windows were of curious shape and device, an architecture belonging to some long gone time, below prison-like turrets, and abutments. Evidently the structure was built in grotesque and laboured imitation, of some baronial hall, of the middle ages, constructed by its erratic proprietor with a view to inspire awe or suggest mystery.

Above the tall chimney-posts, however, smoke was to be seen, attesting faithfully to the warm oak fires within. And above the sweep of broad stone steps Charles the punctilious and Fanny the timid stood, with doors thrown wide, to bid us welcome. We lost no further time, but trooped up the steps, and into the great wide hall.

The men were concerned for their own welfare and in haste to gain comfortable quarters, while we, the women, and the inevitably curious, were disposed to linger a moment to gaze about us. We saw an immense hall, darkly wainscoted with mahogany, an imposing stairway of the same rich wood, heavily carved and panelled, very broad and sweeping up, with a beautiful curve, past a lofty ceiling, monstrously ornamented with designs in relief. Great dark doors mahogany panelled, were to right and left of us. One of these Charles now rolled back, and we were ushered past a dimly lighted reception room into the parlour proper, an immense room, stuffy and hideously furnished in red mahogany and black mohair, with heavy dark hangings, cabinets, and escritoires impossibly high, bow-legged, and claw-footed tables and chairs. Three huge old-fashioned settees and a big square piano. But above all we enjoyed the tremendously wide fireplace; in it was a gorgeous fire roaring up the chimney. There we took up positions, refusing to budge, and toasted ourselves. Chatting, and discussing volubly and in concert all that had befallen us and what might befall us ere we saw the end of our adventurous enterprise. We got into an uproar finally, impelled by mixed emotions, in which I believe was a predominance of nervousness. We were gratified to see Charles and Fanny appear bearing samovar and tea things, chafing dish, and tray of refreshments.

We subsided at once, and made tea and concocted something good and hot in the chafing dish. Inspecting the appetising-looking tray Fanny had placed upon the centre table, we discovered all kinds of enchanting edibles, which we fell upon and devoured, like so many voracious wolves. After supper, Minnie Meredith opened the old piano, that probably had not heard its own voice for ages and favoured us with a loud, though scarcely tuneful, selection from Chopin; while we prowled about, inspecting things, laughing about everything and nothing, feeling all the while, to speak for myself, as though we were laughing in the face of death.

As hostess, I felt it incumbent upon me to make a show of inspecting the sleeping apartments, which I had found to be all above stairs except one, which had been set apart for me, upon the parlour floor. I did not fancy so much isolation, but it was a small matter.

Fanny went ahead, bearing a candle, assuring me all the while that everything was in readiness, from under her own hand. The rooms were pretty much the same—all large and gloomy with no trickeries to make them cosy. Unsightly old rooms, I thought, with a shiver. But the carpets were soft under foot, and the fires truly cheerful.

Everything bore evidence of careful keeping, and preservation. Fanny explained that there had been an old housekeeper, grown very old in the service of this benighted old master. She had remained after her master's death, and cared for things in a feeble way until the news of our projected invasion of her territory had frightened her away.

We were glad enough when at last we all said good night, and sought our couches.

I went to sleep and dreamed all night of a weird apparition, in sweeping cerements of grey, like smoke that bent over me, as I slept, whispering unutterable things, that froze my blood in my veins.

II

Everything was astir betimes next morning to get the sportsmen a-field. The dogs were barking and rushing about distracted at sight of the guns. After a hurried meal they all set out. Our men looked very smart in their hunting rigs—high rubber boots and brown corduroy suits, duly belted and cartridged—some laughably new, some positively bought for the occasion.

We were glad to see them off at last, for we were our own maids and needed to take a peep into the disgruntled condition of our wardrobes. Nothing in that way had been unpacked, and we intended to be in regulation garments at dinner, which was to be served in the great, old dining room, with due formality. So we closeted ourselves for hours, reappearing at luncheon, which was set for one o'clock; after which Maud suggested that we, in a body, investigate the old house from attic to cellar. We all agreed heartily and set about it at once. We spent several hours wandering around in the dark old rooms and long, cold corridors, peeping at the inscrutable old faces upon the walls and the queer stuffed birds and animals that ornamented the dusky corners; keeping up a great chatter all the while, but quite ready to jump out of our several skins at the first sound or the sight of a mouse across our path.

The billiard room was really the most habitable and cosy room in the house, being on the sunny side and blessed with many windows.

There was a narrow passage that led to the old master's own private quarters—a suite of three rooms—study, bedroom, and laboratory (I call it that, for want of a better name). It was a queer little room furnished with curious apparatus for chemical experiments, all in great disorder, and emitting a tragic smell. We shut the door leading thereto quickly, with exclamations of disgust, and hurried into the study. Poor old man! Here was where he took up his last stand ere death seized him; for here, they said, he had died. Books and papers were scattered about just as he had left them, the very last book that his dim eyes had scanned lying open upon his desk. The walls were lined with fine old pictures, mostly by Landseer. The book-cabinets, filled with handsome volumes, reached almost to the ceiling.

I was filled at once with pity and horror at the thought of this lonely old man that had lived and died in these rooms working alway and ever in life-long pursuance of what? An *ignis fatuus*, perhaps, who could tell? Perhaps valuable manuscripts from his pen were hidden away in a dusty corner, which would come to light some day and give this old doubting world an insight into things of which, now, it little dreamed. It was sad to think of his long and busy life utterly unavailing.

A third stairway led darkly into the attic. We did not explore that, however, content to leave it to the spiders and dust. We descended to the basement and inspected the kitchen and servants' quarters and chatted with the care-taker, old black Maurice, busy with wood and saw in the kitchen yard. He told us many interesting things about the old place and the departed landlord. About an hour after sundown our men returned with a rich spoil of partridges and ducks and one 'coon, which last we were to look at, and then it was to be given to the dogs. The men were not so crisp and jaunty as when they had set out in the morning. They were decidedly fagged, and rejoiced at the hint that dinner would be ready for them as soon as they were in proper condition to receive it. They lost no time in making their toilets, and positively bolted for the dining-room at the first sign from Charles, with a fine disregard of the conventionalities.

After dinner we spent a really delightful evening in the billiard room, which, by my instructions, had been charmingly heated and illuminated.

We all played, and did some very good scoring, retiring at an early hour, however, for the men were glad to get to their beds. I was awakened in the night by the sense of an unrecognised presence. Every one has felt it numbers of times. We cannot explain it, but it is there. I was lying upon my back and had been dreaming deeply. I opened my eyes in the darkness. A wasted moon was probably setting, and through a broken shutter in the window sent a red shaft of light directly across what appeared to be a human head suspended from the ceiling. Face and features were clearly outlined against the dark background, showing sunken, glowing eyes and an ashen, withered countenance. Then, slowly emerging from the darkness, a dim weird ghostly form, to which it belonged, could be traced.

It stood motionless in the centre of the room, gazing, not at me, but absently at the little red ray which was gleaming through the broken blind. My blood froze within me! I was powerless to move or to articulate. Soon the figure moved slowly out of the line of light and floated away into the darkness of the room. The shaft of light withdrew, as the moon dropt below the horizon, and the room was enveloped in unrelieved darkness.

How long I lay there petrified, I know not. At last I gathered my faculties sufficiently to reach out a hand and clutch John's arm. He awoke instantly, being a very light sleeper, and when he spoke I burst into violent weeping. In a moment he had lighted a lamp, knowing that would soonest reassure me. I had a habit of getting terrified at night. He had been over the ground before, and knew the signs.

When I told him my story, however, he laughed and pooh-poohed the idea altogether. Then he looked grave, and said he would have the doctor look into my nervousness. I held my ground stoutly; reiterated that it was not a chimera, but he would hear none of it. However, he went so far as to examine the door, and finding it securely locked, he laughed again. He said I would not soon hear the last of this exploit. I begged him not to tell the others, and finally wrung from him a promise that he would not, for I hate being laughed at. I tried to think it was an hallucination, superinduced by indigestion; but I slept no more that night, and thankful, oh, so thankful, was I to see the dawn of day.

John was faithful to his promise; nothing was said of my ghostly encounter. But for days the horror of it was upon me. The time went merrily enough, the men spending most of it in wood and field, while the women amused themselves by various methods. We felt a little lonely and deserted sometimes, and wished we had cultivated a taste and skill for hunting. However, the evenings were very festive and enjoyable, and we had sumptuous dinners, with always music and sometimes dancing, in a small way, afterwards.

At length the day came around which was settled upon for the great deer hunt. A man who knew the swamp thoroughly had been engaged to conduct the hunt. There was a great clatter and clamour attendant upon the preparation for this glorious occasion, unusual preliminaries having to be got through with. At length the lusty sportsmen marched grandly away to chase the fleet-footed buck; not one of the innocents having been within gunshot of the noble game outside a city park. Just before dusk it began to rain. All day it had threatened; the sky had been grey as lead. Soon it began to pour. As twilight advanced we became anxious about the belated hunters. Tragedies so often befall men in the field. Five expectant faces were pressed against as many cold panes, as we gazed out into the increasing gloom in the direction whence must soon come our husbands and lovers.

At length we descried them looming up through the gloom of pelting raindrops. I fancied I made out my dear one's familiar figure in advance of the others. Seizing an umbrella I rushed out recklessly to meet him, by way of the side-entrance gate. At sight of him I fell back aghast. He was dishevelled and bloody! I almost swooned, but when I saw that he was laughing, I was in a measure reassured.

"I am the hero of the occasion," he said, appropriating me and the umbrella and hurrying me along. "I have slain a noble buck, and as it was my first, they have blooded me; nothing more serious."

I knew nothing of the ethics of the chase, but I pronounced this an unwarrantable proceeding.

"I was given the most indescribable stand, and I beat them all. Baker had a shot, and lost. A big buck ran nearly over Jack. I think he took refuge behind a tree, more frightened than the deer. But it was great! The music of the dogs when they 'open up' beats all your operas."

They looked like a gang of old-seasoned tramps, as they grouped around the big hall stove. We women inspected them to see if they really were intact and possessed of all their members; while they talked volubly of their experiences, John looking, meantime, very consequential.

After awhile we all repaired to the back veranda to inspect the trophy of the day—the toothsome venison, which two men had placed there. That night I had a fearful dream. I dreamed that John had met his death upon the hunting field. There was a great ghastly wound in his chest. His heart was exposed and I watched the pulsations that told his life out. A great load of shot was in his breast. I felt the pain, the weight of it in my own. I felt as though a cannon ball had penetrated my breast, and that it was bearing me down, down—I awoke. The weight was still there; there upon my heart. I could scarcely breathe. Something was leaning heavily upon me. It was death, I knew; it could only be death. At last, in the almost complete darkness I could discern a horrid form that leant heavily upon me, its gaunt hands upon my breast crushing out my power of speech and thought; while the intense eye scrutinised my own, and the ashen lips murmured words I could not comprehend. I shivered and sank into unconsciousness.

When my faculties returned it was quite day. Then a horror seized me. With a gasping cry, once more I sank into a deep swoon, this time for hours. I opened my eyes in a darkened room. I heard whispers and soft footsteps. John and Maud were beside the bed, and the village doctor—a kindly old gentleman with a peculiarly soft voice. I went to sleep naturally then, and was very comfortable. The next day I was better and sat up in bed and had chicken broth and toast. I had forgotten. When I remembered, I began to cry bitterly. Instantly Maud was beside me with a horrid draught. And John made me lie down quietly and go to sleep without a word.

When I narrated my terrible adventure, the doctor looked very grave. Clearly he thought I was ill or going out of my senses.

After awhile I almost came around to the opinion that perhaps I was demented, or at least a victim of dreadful nightmare. Nobody believed my story, though I found Maud and Kitty had taken the precaution to occupy the same bed.

In the corner of my room stood crosswise a great wardrobe or press. When I got up I peeped behind it. I found, as I had suspected while lying in bed, that a door was there, leading into an ante-room. I locked it securely. Before long I was quite well again, and felt rather ashamed of myself for having broken so unpleasantly into the general enjoyment of the occasion.

III

It was the day before Christmas. Old Maurice, who was thoroughly versed in the habits of wild turkeys, had led the sportsmen at daybreak to a roost at the edge of a dark lagoon, and they had secured an immense gobbler, which was to grace the Christmas dinner.

All the preparations for the festal day were in progress. Great branches of holly, festoons of bamboo and wild smilax, beautiful clusters of waxy mistletoe were procured for decoration. Every man and woman of us kept busy as bees the entire day, turning the old house into a bewildering dream of loveliness; while below stairs Christmas cakes and all good things a-making sent up savoury wafts through the dumb waiter.

John had hidden away a very mysterious box, which he had received by express, the which contained charming souvenirs for every plate at breakfast Christmas morning. We were as merry as children over it all.

But alack! Christmas day dawned dark and drear and bitterly cold. The rain poured in torrents, and the wind howled around the dark old gables and corners horridly.

All day long it poured. The habitual gloom of the place was intensified tenfold by the darkness of the sky, which, added to the impossibility of getting the huge rooms comfortably warmed, tended to dispirit and disappoint us. Early in the afternoon it became so dark that the light of the lamps was a necessity, and under the blaze of light a gorgeously set picture emerged out of the gloom, as by the touch of Aladdin. The spirit of our enthusiasm returned at sight of it. We rushed away to make ourselves regal for the sumptuous dinner which was to be served at eight. We met to await the announcement of dinner in the parlour.

For once the old room was a charming picture, metamorphosed by its habiliment of green. Over everything the wild smilax trailed, intertwined with the branches of Christmas berries and glistening mistletoe; while a huge bunch of the latter hung from the large, prismed chandelier in the centre of the room, reflected on all sides by the tall pier-glasses which reached to the ceiling.

We chatted away like magpies in ecstasies of admiration of our handiwork. At length, at a sign, we marched grandly and ceremoniously away towards the dining room.

There we met with a surprise. John had out-Neroed Nero in the splendour there revealed. The table was an Eden of the loveliest of hothouse flowers, which John, sly fellow, had surreptitiously ordered from the city and himself arranged, with a view to overwhelming us with the luxury of roses, carnations, hyacinths, outlined with delicate ferns, in fragrant and rich profusion. In spite of our intention to observe a suitable decorum, very soon formality had been flung to the winds and we were in high glee, it becoming an actual carousal as the dinner advanced. I think Charles was distinctly scandalised. Everyone was toasted. Finally Hal Meredith arose, and with great solemnity proposed a toast to the health and fortune and long life of Mrs. John Havergall's ghost. Of course, there was an uproar. However, the toast was never drunk, for at that moment the door was flung unceremoniously open and Fanny, wild-eyed and terror-stricken, rushed into our midst. We were tremendously startled and disconcerted.

"It's in Miss Floyd's room!" Fanny exclaimed in breathless incoherency "It's a spirit! I saw it! I was seeing to the rooms. I opened the door. In the middle of the room it was, all in grey. It pointed a long, bony finger at me and said: 'You must die!' Oh!" Here she burst into tears and retired behind a lace curtain, with which she proceeded to stifle her sobs.

Charles stood straight and rigid against the wall. He would have suffered a wolf to gnaw his vitals ere he would have so relaxed his dignity. Before John or I had time to collect ourselves sufficiently to frame a reply to Fanny's theatrical outburst, at an exclamation from some one, our attention was again turned towards the open doorway. We were electrified with horror, for there, between the dark curtains, stood the figure of a tall, gaunt old woman; wizen and wrinkled. She was clothed in a loose gown of grey, torn and soiled. Her hair, thin and white, was dishevelled and unkempt, and filled with wisps of straw. Her maniacal eyes gleamed redly beneath her white shaggy brows. She stood quite still in the embrasure, and smiled demonically upon the petrified assembly before her.

"I have come unbidden to the feast. It is my master's table. *I* have surprised you, eh? *I* have come to warn you. *I* have come to drive you away. *I* have control here." At every personal pronoun she touched her heart with one gaunt finger. "You must go. I will kill you!" With a lean finger and a nod and glance she included each one of us, severally, under the direful ban.

"You are intruders. This is my master's house, and the house of my mistress. Twenty years I have lived within these walls. I will not have it. I have come to warn you."

There is no describing the horror that her peculiar mien and rasping but child-like voice, inspired.

"You," and she pointed a ghastly finger at me, "you sleep in my bed, while I sleep in a bed of straw in the attic. You sit at my master's table, while I creep about at night to snatch a crumb of food."

All at once she became livid with frenzy.

"I will kill you! *Kill* you! *Kill* you!" With clenched hands and distorted face, she made a lunge forward. Instantly John and the other men sprang to overpower her.

With a fearful shriek, which resounded to the uttermost part of that old house, she turned and sped up the dark stairway, as if a legion of demons was pursuing her. A fearful climax this to our dinner party! Poor old soul! When they found her, at last, in her retreat in the attic, she was lying across a pile of straw and rubbish in one corner quite dead. It was pitiable to think of the many desolate nights she had lain there in the cold, hungry and miserable, broken in heart and mind: while those who had known her, thought she was happy in the country with her loved ones. Like a cat she had clung to the old place and life. She was too old to make a new home. The strain had been too great. Death was merciful.

Her friends came by and by, and took her away. It was all very sad and miserable.

One good thing, I concluded, came out of the incident, nay two things. The fact that I can sometimes speak the truth has been established. And it is a comfort to know that I am not threatened with mental discrepancy.

Very soon, we set our faces homeward: and it will be some time before John will suggest another house party at Mock Orange.

THE GHOST OF APPLEDORE POOL
OR THE IRON CHEST AT THE BARNSTAPLE BAR

J. Y. T.

First published in The North Devon Herald, *28 December 1893*

This is a story I've become rather fond of. As I live in Devon, I've travelled up to Appledore where this is set. Sadly, the Braunton Lighthouse is no longer there, but if you stand by the water, the sky will suddenly become darker; there'll be a clap of thunder and you might see yourself a ghost…

As to the mysterious author, "J. Y. T., of Braunton", "Appledore Pool" wasn't the only ghostly tale they wrote for *The North Devon Herald*.* There's an additional festive treat called "The Midnight Ghost and the Christmas Rose Tree" published in 1892 and another, "The Ghost of Saunton Sands" from 1891. "The Ghost of Appledore Pool" has never been reprinted.

---

* Below the story's title in the paper runs the line: *"Written expressly for the North Devon Herald."*

"OH! Grandmother dear, do tell us a story—a real good one, a thorough Christmas story, as it is Christmas time." These words were spoken by a little girl about nine years of age, and were addressed to an old lady, who had weathered the storms of life for over eighty-six years. It was in a cosy little room, not far from the town of Braunton, where this little party was assembled on Christmas Eve.

"I know Grandmother can spin a good one," said a bright-eyed little boy about twelve, brother to the little maiden already mentioned, "she told us a good one last Christmas, and I have not forgotten it yet."

"Well, well," said the old lady, "I suppose I must gratify you. Now, my dears, what kind of story would you like?"

"A real true one," said the youngster, while his sister pleaded for "a ghost story."

"Well, you shall both have your wishes," replied the old dame.

"When I was a very little girl," she commenced, "just about your age, Dottie, I went to stay with my grandmother for a little time at Appledore. The whole town then was talking about a singular occurrence that had recently taken place, according to the statement of a poor ferryman, who used to take passengers to and fro the Broad Sands, on the Braunton side of the river, and Appledore.

"Now, my pets," said our grandmother, "my grandmother who told me this story, possessed a remarkable memory. She told me how, many years ago, she remembered well a strange incident happening in Appledore Pool. It was a very dark and stormy night. You could scarcely see a yard in front of you, and the wind was blowing with hurricane force, as it had before ten o'clock at night. The waves were lashing and dashing, breaking with a roar on the Barnstable Bar, and now and again vivid flashes of lightning divided the dark masses of cloud overhead, which concealed from view the moon. Ever and anon there would be a lull in the storm, as if the elements were collecting their forces for a fiercer effort, and, during one of these lulls, a person was heard shouting across the river from the Braunton side, and these were the words which the crowd collected on Appledore Quay distinctly heard: 'Boat ahoy! Boat ahoy!!' Again and again the same cry was repeated, and between the gusts of wind, and above the roar of the breakers, the cry 'Boat ahoy! Boat ahoy!!' rang out. It was evidently someone wishing to cross the estuary, but the sailors and mariners on the Quay, looked at each other and then at the troubled waters below them, and it was evident that, notwithstanding their eagerness to secure the fare, they did not wish to risk their lives and boats on the raging waters on such a night. The gale increased, the wind whistled shriller, and the waves ran higher, and as eagerly as ever swept forward to the shore, but still as loud as beforetime rang out that voice, 'Boat ahoy! Boat ahoy!!' Among those gathered on the Quay was a weather-beaten old salt, who had listened with as deep interest as the others to the shout, and at last he muttered, 'I don't like the job, but still I think I'll have to try. I dare say 'e'll pay me well, if I succeed in bringing him safe across.'

"'You must be mad,' said his mates gathered round, 'to risk your life in such a foolhardy manner, for it's sure and certain death to you. No boat could live in such a sea.' 'Boat ahoy! Boat ahoy!!' again resounded the voice, and there was a flash as from a brilliant light on the Broad Sands. 'I'll go,' said Oatway, for that was his name, 'be the consequences what they may. I have a wife and six dear little ones at home, and trade has not been of the best this season, and I have no doubt the gent will pay me well.' With that he ran down the beach, and, with the assistance of one of his mates, launched the little craft into the raging waters. With all speed he pulled away, towards the cry or shout from the individual on the other side. The wind still blew harder, and swept along in still more furious gusts, and it was with great difficulty that those on shore could retain their footing while they strained their eyes in trying to pierce the darkness, and, with the help of the blinding lightning, to follow the progress of their comrade on his perilous way.

Time wore on, and the little crowd momentarily grew larger, and among the knots of women on the Quay was the wife of Oatway, who had learnt of the perilous errand on which her husband had ventured. In the pouring rain, which was dashed along in blinding showers by the storm, the wife knelt down on the Quay, in the presence of the anxious crowd, and offered up a fervent prayer to the One who has control over the deep, and holds the waters of the earth in the hollow of His hand, that He would watch over her husband and bring him back safely once more. The bystanders stood near in silent sympathy, and gazed with pity on the sorrow-stricken wife, while many a bronzed mariner was not ashamed to wipe a tear away in the darkness as he thought of his own loved ones.

Presently there came a welcome shout across the river from Oatway, high above the storm, announcing that he had arrived safely at the other side, and that, with his passenger, he had re-embarked on the return journey. The wife heard the tidings, but she still continued to offer up her supplications, and now the crowd was eagerly discussing the pros and cons of the possibility of Oatway's return journey. The weary moments wore on, and they were anxious ones for Oatway, as he endeavoured to guide his boat to the Quay. Presently a shout went up below the crowd from Oatway, and his mates ran down over the slip to the rocks to help him to secure his boat.

"'Where is your passenger?' they asked in surprise, as they assisted him to land. 'I have a strange story to tell you presently, but first let me secure the boat,' rejoined he. When Oatway arrived at the spot on which the Custom House now stands, he addressed his eager audience as follows, 'I would not go through again what I have tonight, not for a fortune; nor, if I was to be made the richest gentleman in England. When I arrived at Broad Sands there stood a gentleman who carried a dark or black bag, and had an overcoat on. I asked him if he wished to go to Appledore or Instow? "Land me," he said, "at Appledore, near the 'Bad Step,' as I have an important business there." As soon as I got into the boat, I looked at him as well as I could in the darkness of the night, and I noticed he was of very sorrowful countenance. I don't think, in the whole experience of my life, I ever saw a sadder face. He noticed that I was taking stock of him, and said, "Row faster, as my time is precious, and you kept me lingering long enough here." "But consider the weather, sir," I said, "I had the greatest difficulty in getting across." "Nothing to be compared with what we shall have to contend against in going back," replied the gentleman, nor was it. The wind increased, and blew with such fury, that many times I thought my little boat would be swamped, and if ever I prayed to a living God, to bring me safe back to Appledore, then it was tonight. Just as we were in the middle of the river, there was a tremendous flash of lightning, and I thought for a moment I was gone. The boat appeared to sink beneath the foaming waves, and when she righted herself, my passenger—would you believe it?—had vanished—vanished with the terrific flash of lightning.'"

"Where had he gone?" asked the little boy.

"Now, my dears, you must not interrupt me," said the old lady, "until I have finished my story."

"All serene," retorted the youngster, "but I didn't know men could ride on lightning."

"Well," proceeded his grandmother, "Oatway said to his people he would never cross again for anyone, after nightfall, even if it were 'the King of England, in such a storm,' and everyone seemed inclined to fall in with Oatway's opinion. When the storm abated, and the morning dawned, a large vessel was seen to have drifted on to the North Tail, at the Barnstable Bar, and during the night every soul perished, as no one living was found on board her when the mariners from Appledore rowed out in the morning. She proved to be the *Parisian*, a large French vessel, and from the document afterwards found, it appeared she had been driven out of her course by the terrific storm. She had come from Australia, and had brought away a valuable cargo, consisting mainly of bars of gold, gold dust, specie, and precious stones. The bodies of several persons were washed up on the beach by the old Braunton lighthouse, inside the Barnstaple Bar, amongst them being those of two females, evidently by their clothing, a lady and her servant. There was also the body of a black servant, clasped in whose arms, as though he had made a desperate attempt to reach the shore, was a fine little boy about four years old. The remains of the unfortunates were conveyed to Braunton, and buried in the churchyard, but it was said that, before so doing, some of the sailors at Appledore rifled the corpses. Amongst them was a man called Bowden, and it was rumoured that he secured among the papers some valuable documents, and a bunch of keys. The vessel the following tide broke up, and her cargo was scattered on both sides of the Bar."

"I wish I had been there," put in the little boy, "and then I should have filled my school-bag with gold. It would be such a treat, I should never have to work so hard as pa does now."

"You would not be a thief," said his grandmother, "it is wicked and sinful to plunder, you know, but many, I am sorry to say, were like what you would have been. They made a good haul, as Appledore people term it; they earned a rich harvest. But Appledore people were not the only folks who profited thereby. It is said that a certain farmer, living at Northam, had such a large quantity, that he buried it, and left a rich fortune to his family, who became the wealthiest people in North Devon. And a certain woman at Braunton, who was a widow, secured enough gold to buy a large ship for each of her sons."

Here the little girl intervened with, "But, grandmother, where was pa all this time? Could not he get to this gold?" The old lady smiled as she answered, "You forget, my dears, that *I* was not born then, when this vessel went ashore, much more than your father."

"Oh, I see, it was years and years ago," return the little girl.

"Yes, people are more honourable in these days, and a greater quantity of the salvage would have been recovered and handed over to the authorities. But, it is said, that even to this day, tons of gold lie buried near the entrance to the Barnstaple Bar.

"But I must go back to my story," continued Grandma. "Whenever there were indications of a coming storm, the cries in Appledore Pool would be heard at nightfall from across the river: 'Boat ahoy! Boat ahoy!!' Many times the poor boatmen, or fishermen, put out with a view of taking their supposed passenger across, but the passenger always disappeared in a flame of fire in the centre of the Pool, or else he leaped overboard unseen by the boatman. Many people living at the present day—old people I mean, like myself—have heard the cry in their earlier days, and can remember more even about the strange story than I can. But one night, Oatway broke his vow and went across the second time to secure his passenger. 'I'll be upsides of him this time' said Oatway as he put off. 'Where for?' he shouted to the individual whom he recognised to be the same person who played such an important part in his former journey. But the man with one spring leaped into the boat. 'Pull me,' he said, 'and land me at Bad Steps.' 'But, sir,' said Oatway, 'one word with you please. Many of my mates have come over here to convey a passenger across and some have even landed him, so they say, but never a brass farthing have we received for our labours, and, you'll pardon me being plain, sir—we Appledore people are, but we mean no offence—I prefer to have the tin before I take you across. Once bit, twice shy is our rule here you know.' 'Row me, I tell you, to Bad Step,' loftily returned his fare, 'don't waste my time with your vain talk. I have an important engagement and my time is precious.' 'And *my* time is precious too,' said Oatway, 'and I'll not budge an inch till I see the colour of your money.' The night became suddenly darker, and there was a loud clap of thunder. 'I'm in for it now,' thought Oatway, 'but I won't go. I don't half like the looks of him, but I won't change my mind.' At this moment Oatway heard a boat passing up the river towards Barnstaple, and on hailing it, he found, to his delight, it contained one of his mates called Williams, who demanded to know 'What's up?' 'Pull in here' said Oatway. 'I have got a queer customer to deal with.' Williams tried to comply with his friend's request, but found to his amazement, that he could not, owing to some mountainous seas which pressed him back, and, try as he would, he could not land at the Crow. Then there came another grand display of Heaven's artillery, and after the flash and the deafening roar had died away, Oatway discovered not only that he had lost his passenger, but that 'his boat,' which he had pulled up on the beach, had also vanished. 'I say' he shouted to Williams, 'for God's sake pull in, my boat and passenger have both disappeared.' To his surprise, Williams was now enabled to pull to shore with comparative ease, and Oatway was rowed home; but, from that time to this, nothing has been seen or heard of Oatway's boat."

"Did they see the ghost again?" queried the boy.

"Yes" returned the old lady, "I am coming to that. He appeared several times and at different places to vessels making their way to Pool's Mouth entering the river at Braunton Pill. Many declared they had heard of this strange visitor, and at times some affirmed that they heard a splashing of the water close to their ship, and as if a boat were passing below them, rowed by four men; but though many asserted that the boat was passing close to them, it could never be seen. People became very timid, and some would not visit Broad Sands after dark, even though their business called them that way.

"Soon after this another frightful storm swept over the coast. It was Christmas Eve, and, after the storm had abated, a heavy fall of snow set in, which covered everything with a mantle of the purest white. It was real Christmas weather in those days we used to get, you see nothing like it now. Toward evening, the voice was heard calling, 'Boat ahoy! Boat ahoy!!' Now it happened that a strange man had taken up his residence at Appledore, and had started a ferry in opposition to Oatway, and, in so doing, had incurred the displeasure of many of the residents. Hence they did not tell him of the trick that had been played on so many of the ferrymen. So Jenkins (that was the man's name), rowed with all speed to the Broad Sands. Having shipped his passenger, he rowed him to Bad Steps. 'What time will you return, sir, and I'm at your service at any time,' said Jenkins, in the well-known phraseology of Appledore ferrymen. 'You are a very obliging man,' returned the passenger, 'I shall not be long.' Jenkins afterwards related this to his mates, but did not tell the sequel. As soon as the stranger landed, he was joined by a man of rather stout build. Jenkins, being of an inquisitive turn of mind, contrived, in the darkness, to approach them sufficiently near to overhear the conversation which ensued between these worthies.

"'You have kept me waiting long enough' said the stout one to the ghost who had been the passenger of the listener. 'It's not been my fault' replied he with the black bag, 'I have tried and tried *and* tried, again and again *and* again, to cross the river, but fate has been against me. Something has cropped up and prevented me each time I tried to land here in safety, since the fatal wreck on Barnstaple Bar, when our ship the *Parisian*, went to pieces, and all of us were lost.' 'Have you brought the keys of the chest that you had?' asked the bulky one. 'That is the point. You knew our chest rests buried in the sands, not far from Hairy Point, close by the old walls. There lies all that we have worked for, for many and many a year, although you know as well as I do that there lies hidden the hardly earned wealth of many a poor fellow who, after toiling so earnestly for the gold and precious stones, succumbed to us. Several times the Appledore and Braunton men have discovered the chest at dead low water; but their unaided efforts have been useless, and by the time assistance and appliances have been procured, the sea has covered it again. Night after night I have wandered about, guarding our treasure, for you swore as you know, in the goldfields, that we should share it together if ever we reached the shores of England. That promise holds as good today as ever, and it's through making that solemn compact that you and I can't rest. The gold *has* reached the shores of England, but not in the way *we* expected.'

"'What good can the keys do?' he asked. 'Well the money will be no use to me or you, but we have sworn to divide the money and share it.' 'I will,' replied the stout individual, 'and then we may try to rest in peace, or in such peace as can be obtained.' 'I will never, no never, deliver the keys up to you,' shouted he who had crossed the river, with a demoniacal laugh. 'Then that is the reason you have delayed your visit to me; you won't give me the keys.' Jenkins grew horror-stricken as he saw with dismay, that the anger of these two supernatural beings was rising, and at last reached such a pitch, that one drew a sword from its sheath. Up to this time the watcher had not noticed they were armed.

"A desperate duel now raged with fearful malignity on both sides, and at length Jenkins covered his face trying to shut out the terrible sight. Once more he watched this fearful midnight encounter, when suddenly they both fell, and at the same instant a frightful flash and its accompanying deafening roar, half-stunned him, but he perceived for a moment, and only for a moment, the forms of two men, with cutlasses embedded in their hearts, stretched on the Strand. Recovering from his fright, he moved forward, when a hand was placed on his shoulder, and turning round he saw a female form clothed in white.

"'Touch them not,' said the apparition, 'it is sure and certain death. These two deep-dyed villains have much to answer for, with their ill-gotten wealth. They came home in the same ship as I did, and the child clasped in the arms of the black servant was my child. I know what is passing through your thoughts, Jenkins. We in the unseen world have the advantage over you; we understand your thoughts. You may think it a strange sight you have just witnessed—the duel between two ghosts, and the reason that one was on one side of the river, and the other on the other. I will explain it to you. The body of the man on the Braunton side was washed ashore on this side, and so he was only allowed to trouble that side of the river, while the man washed ashore on the Northam side, was also confined to his particular locality.' 'Will they ever appear again?' asked Jenkins. 'I don't think they will,' replied the apparition. 'They were two desperate characters in their lives, and have made an enormous fortune on foreign shores, which they had secured in a large iron chest, fastened by three immense locks. There are the keys lying close by that bunch of seaweed, near which those bodies fell. Their treasure lies buried near the old walls, on the Braunton side of the Barnstaple Bar. You may take those keys, I don't see it's any good letting them remain where they are. If you should ever find the chest, you will observe, on one of the locks, the letter *A*, turn it "nine" times; on the next you will find the letter *B*, turn it "nineteen" times while on the last of the three, you will find the letter C, and turn that "ninety-nine" times. Make no mistake about this, and when you have secured the contents, it will make you one of the richest millionaires under the sun. Mind I shall never appear again to you, or anyone else; but there is danger in your path, and to no one must you relate this, or it will be at your peril; keep it a close secret.' Jenkins rubbed his eyes to assure himself he was a living man, and that all he had gone through was not a dream, but to his surprise he found the draped figure, which had so amazed him with its stupendous revelations, had vanished, with the supernatural visitor and his accomplice in crime.

"Nevertheless the black bag and keys brought across by the passenger, lay there, and these Jenkins conveyed home. In the bag he found some paper, but the hieroglyphics traced on them he could not understand, and, being afraid to take them to anyone who might be able to read them, in consequence of the fear of detection, he burned them. All this had produced a strong impression on Jenkins' mind, and he became a strangely reserved and solemn man. He was ever wandering on the beach at the Braunton side of the river, near where the old lighthouse stood, watching the sea, at dead low water, looking for the iron chest which was to make him a millionaire."

"Did he ever find it?" asked the little boy.

"Yes," answered the old lady, "one night he came across it, at dead low water, and what a monstrous chest it was. Jenkins went all round it and tried to move it. Yes, there, sure enough, were the locks, containing the letters, just as the apparition had told him, on the most important day of his life. 'I am a thorough millionaire,' he exclaimed, 'I shall not care now two pins for the ill-feelings of the ferrymen at Appledore. They have sneered at me enough in times gone by, but now I shall be able to keep my own servants, and drive my carriage and six greys.' He hastily put his hands into his pockets to feel for the keys, when he found, to his great dismay, that he had left them at home. He instantly rushed towards Appledore as fast as he could to secure the keys, and the inhabitants there seized this as an occasion to remark that his recent strange behaviour and seclusion constituted a sure proof that he had lost his reason. Securing the keys, and returning with all speed, Jenkins found to his disappointment that the tide had risen and had hid his El Dorado from his reach. This untoward circumstance still further increased Jenkins' melancholia, and the neighbours would shake their heads in a very wise manner, as they talked across the narrow streets of how the poor fellow could not be anything but insane. The weight of his secret was gradually crushing him, and so Jenkins made up his mind to unburden himself, and one day, several months after meeting Oatway on the Braunton side, he ignored the warning given by the apparition, and he said: 'Look here, old fellow, I can't keep my secret any longer. We have been bad friends long enough. There lies buried near the foot of the Barnstaple Bar, gold enough to make all Appledore rich, if we could only lift a chest that lies out there.' 'Have you seen it?' said Oatway. 'I have, and, what is more, I know the secret of it and here are the keys to open it.' He then related his strange story, and the two men shook hands for the first time, swearing to be friends until their dying day, and provided that the wealth in the chest could be obtained, they swore to equally divide it.

"Oatway and Jenkins were ever afterwards inseparable. What had caused this change in the feelings of this couple, naturally furnished the good people of Appledore with an ever-fresh subject for comment, and many were the opinions ventured as to the cause of the midnight excursions of these two, always at dead low water, in the direction of the old walls. The lighthouse-keeper at the Braunton side had often observed them strolling away together as he was at his post, and so one night he followed them, and this happened at the time of dead low water. The seekers this time had at last discovered the chest, and as the watcher crept nearer he noticed they were unlocking it. But Oatway had nourished the hope of obtaining the whole of the treasure, and hence, as Jenkins was unlocking the last lock, which he had to turn ninety-nine times, he nervously fingered a large club which he carried, and just as his companion was approaching the end of his task he stepped forward and struck him a fearful blow on the head.

"'You villain,' shouted Pow, the lighthouse-keeper, 'do you wish to murder him?' for Jenkins had sunk senseless to the ground without a moan on receiving the treacherous blow. Pow dashed forward and caught up the unconscious man, and after he had carried him up on the sand-hills, he returned and seized the keys which had fallen from the hands of the stricken man. Oatway made a rush for him, and Pow threw the precious keys far out into the ocean.

"'You are both here,' said Pow, 'for the purpose of unlawfully securing plunder.' When Oatway realised that the chest was still locked, and that Pow had destroyed the only means of reaching the treasure, he raged up and down like a demon, cursing and swearing in a fearful manner, until he at last turned, and, with the greatest ferocity, attacked the lighthouse-keeper. But, though possessed ordinarily of strong physical powers, which were increased tenfold by his present disappointment and anger, he found his match in Pow, and the motionless form of poor Jenkins in the rear, formed a strange contrast to the desperate struggle which was taking place on the beach. In spite of his superior strength, Pow was at length forced to retreat before his opponent, and he shouted wildly for assistance. Several of his companions, who were at the lighthouse, came to his assistance just in time. Oatway seized the opportunity that offered itself by dismay at the discovery of Jenkins, to effect his escape. The poor unfortunate Jenkins was conveyed to the lighthouse, but, in spite of medical skill called in, died without recovering consciousness.

"Oatway, who had contrived to escape in the darkness, was never heard of more in Appledore.

"The chest still remains buried at Barnstaple Bar, and though the old cry of 'Boat ahoy! Boat ahoy!!' had ceased, and the strange passenger had also vanished, a form was often seen wandering about on lonely spots on the approach of a storm, and sometimes it was accompanied by a female apparition. The spot where the iron chest lay buried was the place most frequented by the forms, and at last, as one after another met the supernatural forms, the discovery was made that one bore a strange resemblance to Jenkins. So frequent did these appearances become that it was deemed advisable to have 'the ghost of Jenkins laid.' Nine clergymen were engaged from different parishes, and they came from Northam, Bideford, Instow, Barnstaple, Pilton, Fremington, Ashford, Braunton and Georgeham, and they congregated at the spot most frequented by the unwelcome marauder. The rev. gentlemen were approached by the apparition, but before they could begin the ceremony, the subject of their quest related its remarkable story, how he became possessed of the keys of the iron chest, and the adventures, terminating in his death, which resulted therefrom. 'You are going to try to lay my spirit,' he sneeringly ended, 'but I tell you there is not a man among you high-learned enough.' Then, with a blood-curdling laugh, the apparition disappeared. The clergymen were nonplussed, and eventually, after the conference, it was decided to write the Bishop for instructions. The following night, when the lighthouse-keeper went to trim his lamps, he found that the task had already been performed. Then every fortnight, when the water was at its lowest ebb, the ghost of Jenkins was always to be seen, and anyone whose path lay over the burrows or sand-hills was sure of meeting him. Then, too, often enough, the keepers at the lighthouse would find their work had already been performed, and endless were the tricks played on them, until at last, several men in succession resigned their posts rather than be subject to the whims of this supernatural being. This state of things was intolerable, so it was resolved to make another attempt to 'lay' the spirit of Jenkins, but this time the services were engaged of a clergyman living at Ilfracombe, who was reputed among his brethren for the extent of his knowledge of the black art. On the spirit of Jenkins appearing, this holy man of Ilfracombe asked him if he would grant him the favour of doing one thing if he (the clergyman) would not attempt to lay his ghost. The apparition assented. 'Now I have caught you,' gleefully shouted the parson, 'ghosts can't tell lies, and you shall bind me nine bundles of sand from the surrounding Braunton sand-hills, and you shall use beams made of the same material to secure them.' The apparition gave a woeful howl of disappointment as he vanished, and for several years he could be seen to attempt, at rarer and rarer intervals, to complete his impossible task. And now for many a long year the passenger hailing Appledore with 'Boat ahoy! Boat ahoy!!'

has ceased to trouble Appledore Pool, while no longer does the erstwhile troubled spirit of Jenkins terrify the Braunton lighthouse-keepers."

"But Grandmother," said the little boy, as she ceased her narrative, "is the chest still lying at the Barnstaple Bar?"

"There is not the shadow of a doubt about it" returned she. "I have been told, but I cannot vouch for the truth of the statement, that the iron chest has been seen not many years since at the Barnstaple Bar, but no good luck seems to attend anyone who endeavours to raise it."

Thus ends our strange story, which was told by an old lady, who had it from her grandmother, to her grandchildren in a cottage near Braunton, a few years since. There are many living at the present day who believe in the existence of the Iron Chest at the Barnstaple Bar, and that it still lies buried in the sea there.

THE LADY OF THE MISTLETOE
A CHRISTMAS GHOST STORY

Mary Hall

First published in The Pittsburgh Gazette, *7 December 1902*

Mary Hall Leonard (1847–1921) was the inaugural Principal and First Instructor at Winthrop Training School for Teachers in Columbia, South Carolina, taking the then student population from 19 to 100 from 1886–1894. Once she left she became a noted historian and author. Her books include *The Story of Portus and Songs of the Southland, Grammar and Its Reasons, Moral Training in Public Schools* and *The Days of the Swamp-Angel*. She was also the author of several heavily syndicated short stories. She died at her home in Rochester, Massachusetts, after a short illness.

Now, to this tale, originally "written for The Sunday Gazette" as the byline reads. It's not *exactly* a "lost" story, but it absolutely was when I rescued it from the shadows for my anthology *Remember the Dead at Halloween and Christmas* (Black Shuck Books, 2019). It was one of my favourites of that (limited edition, now out of print) book, it hasn't been reprinted since that time, and I *really* wanted to bring it back for this volume as it truly is a spooky one!

WHEN I was about thirty years old, I found myself in the possession of two very desirable things—a comfortable fortune and a successful love affair.

As Ellice and I were agreed that we wished to live in the country, merely going into the city once in a while for shopping and theatres and so on, I began in the summer to look about for a home—a comfortable roomy mansion, as old as possible, and which would yet lend itself to modern addition of luxury and comfort.

For Ellice had the craze for old-fashioned things very badly. At last, late in the season, I discovered just what I wished. And strange to say, it had belonged to an old man of my own name, Derston. It lay on the outskirts of a little town called Derston, and was already known as Derston Hall.

What more could we have asked? "Derston of Derston" sounded so delightfully English that Ellice nearly wept with joy, and I began hunting up our family records and discovered that old John Derston was really the first cousin of my grandfather.

That fact made the people living round about still more friendly than they had already shown themselves, and by the time I had the old place fixed up with modern plumbing and a furnace to help out the big old fireplaces, and decided to give a Christmas house party to introduce it to everybody, I was on excellent terms with my neighbours.

Ellice, with her mother and married sister, Mrs. Mayne, came down on the Saturday before Christmas, which fell on Tuesday that year, and they helped us decorate the old house for this, its first festivity in many years.

On Sunday evening, Mrs. Bird, a quaint, bright little lady, who had known John Derston and his cousin, my grandfather, well, drove over and inspected the decorations.

She peered about every corner, nodding as she looked.

Then she turned to me with a funny little expression in her bright old eyes.

"You've got more respect for tradition than I should have given you credit for, Tom Derston," she exclaimed. "You've left out the mistletoe right enough."

I stared at her and Ellice laughed. "That's the thorn in our rose, Mrs. Bird," she said brightly, "I was to bring it and I forgot. You see I've passed beyond the need of it and didn't think of the others."

But while the rest of us were laughing Mrs. Bird looked sober. "It may have been a very lucky thing for you that you did," she said shortly, and was unusually silent until she went away.

And in the morning our want was supplied. Ned Waters, who had to go south and refuse our invitation, sent us a mass of mistletoe that would have made most dealers envious.

Ellice and I were in raptures, and she took especial delight in fastening a great branch to the quaint old lantern of iron that hung above the library fireplace. It was a queer old lantern and like many other things in the house, had been bought with the house.

We fixed the biggest branch of all to the lantern and stood beneath it, watching our serious-faced butler, as from the top of a stepladder he tied the last bit of crimson ribbon that held it in place. As he climbed down and departed, I heard Ellice give a little sigh—such a strange heartbroken sigh.

I turned and took the tribute of mistletoe.

"Why did you sigh so, dear?" I asked, and was puzzled when she said, "I didn't. I have had no chance to sigh since last June."

Now that was a very pretty speech indeed, as it was June when we became engaged, and I expressed my thanks in the most appropriate manner, but still I was rather astonished. For I had heard that sigh quite plainly. But we went away, and the time flew until afternoon, when our guests were coming.

I stood waiting for them in the great dim old library. A fire of logs burned in the fireplace, and I stood before it, under the mistletoe, when suddenly there was a silken swish beside me, and before I could turn, a soft arm stole round my neck and two sweet lips had kissed me.

"You little witch," I cried, and swung round to catch her. But—there was nobody there.

I ran to the hall, calling, and reached the foot of the stairs just in time to see the tail of a familiar grey gown vanishing around the upper landing. I would have followed, but the door of the dining room opened, letting in a flood of light and the butler appeared with the information that he could hear the sleighs coming, and there was no time to go chasing saucy sweethearts—I had to stay and receive my guests. There were eleven of them—Ellice's father, Morgan Dunlap, the great banker; Charles Mayne, his son-in-law; my cousins the Elliott girls, Maud and Mary; pretty Kitty Kenton, Bob Truscot, her devoted slave; Morris Slayton and Tremain Lloyd, and the Binghams, the gayest, merriest young couple that ever helped make other folks happy, and my Uncle, James Derston, who had been my guardian since I was ten. But though Mr. Dunlap and Mrs. Mayne were there, welcoming everybody, and helping the girls off with their furs, nowhere could I catch sight of Ellice, and I was surprised, and a little hurt. I knew she was dressed. Why did she not come down to welcome her friends in the home that would soon be hers as well as mine?

But I did not see her until dinner, and then she looked as though she had been crying. It astonished me as much as the question she asked me, "Where is your other guest?"

"Why, they're all here," I answered, and wondered as her eyes darkened, and she turned to Tremain Lloyd. She did not speak to me again throughout the evening.

Long after the others had gone to bed I went to the library and sat before the fire, pondering over her strange freak. At last I rose, and yawning, threw my arms above my head. I was right beneath the mistletoe. Again, I heard that strange, heartbroken little sigh—again came the slight, silky rustling, and the thought leaped through mine, "Ellice is sorry, she has come to make up." And I was very glad. But surely the long, lithe body I felt against me was not Ellice's pretty, petite little self. And the arms around my neck were bare, and the flesh so smooth and soft and cold it made me tremble. And then came a face, pressed close to mine, and the pressure of the lips—so passionate and yet so chill that I stood dazed with the horror, for my upraised arms had fallen upon a form I could not see.

There was someone there, I knew. I could feel her breath upon my neck, the soft sweep of her hair against my face, her lips, her body—and yet—I could see nothing.

With an exclamation of horror I tried to tear myself away, and so stepped without the shadow of the mistletoe. Instantly the presence slipped from me. It was like a dream, and I turned, almost certain I had been asleep, and saw Ellice standing in the doorway. But there was no love in her eyes. They were full of scorn and anger, and before I could speak she was gone.

Turning out the lights, I went too, and tossed from side to side of my bed all night, trying to understand what it was that had happened to me, after all.

Suddenly like a vision of help and comfort came the little voice of Mrs. Bird: "You've got more respect for tradition than I should have given you credit for. You've left out the mistletoe," and I remembered too, the odd little look on my uncle's face when I told him of my purchase, his half-uttered sentence, "There's fate in it all—the Derston fate—" and the reluctance with which he had consented to come to my Christmas party. There was a family story somewhere, and I must have it.

A family ghost? Maybe that too, though I laughed at the thought as I lay there in my comfortable nineteenth-century bed with the dim glow of a modern gas jet in the room and the knob of an electric bell staring at me from the wall.

Still, the thought comforted me, and I got a bit of sleep before breakfast.

I had time to see that Bob Truscot was unhappy, and that Kitty had been crying, but Ellice's face was as cold as the morning light, and I was too much absorbed with my own troubles to fuss with Bob's and Kitty's.

It was a busy day for me. There was to be a dance in the house that night, and I simply couldn't get my uncle aside to talk with him. From the few words I did manage to have I imagined he knew very little anyhow, and grew gloomier and gloomier.

Mrs. Bird was the first to arrive that evening, and I led her to the library to find a comfortable chair.

But as soon as her eyes fell on the huge spray of mistletoe, and glancing through the rooms she saw other bits of gleaming waxen berries, she sprang to her feet.

"Tom Derston," she cried, "what are you doing with mistletoe in this house—and above all things, hanging on that lantern? I thought that having a party here on Christmas night was enough—but this! Oh, well, I suppose I'm an old fool. And I was a child when it happened. It hasn't been tried for years. Maybe the curse has been worn out," and she laughed a strange, excited little laugh.

"Mrs. Bird," I exclaimed, "I haven't an idea what you are talking about. What hasn't been tried? What is the curse? What happened? Why shouldn't I have mistletoe in my house at Christmas, and a party, too, if I wish? What—" but before I could add another to my list of questions, the people from upstairs trooped down in a body, and a sleigh-load of guests drove up to the door. I was swept away, and only saw Mrs. Bird carefully walk around the old iron lantern and hurry from the room.

Things all went wrong. The natural gas flickered and twinkled in a way that drove me wild, and once it nearly went out. The musicians seemed excited and played badly, the guests talked and whispered in groups together, and, worst of all to me, Kitty and Ellice clung close to each other, so I could not get a word with Ellice, try as I might, and could only grip Bob's hand sympathetically when I saw him eyeing the same pair with a face as despairing as my own.

Somehow the night dragged on. The guests grew more and more uneasy. I could feel a whisper was running round among them. But I had not ordered supper until midnight, and they could not leave.

And they all voided the mistletoe. I was watching, alert for every movement, and noticed that not once did the young men from the neighbourhood lead their partners beneath the branches of white berries. What was the mystery that hung over my home?

And then suddenly, as the great cathedral clock in the hallway chimed twelve, there was a gust of chilling air that swept through the rooms, from where we could not tell, and with a ghastly flicker the lights flared redly and then fell into blackness. The music stopped with a crash and far above the frightened voices of my Christmas guests came a cry, so pitiful, that I tremble now when I remember it.

Silent, awestricken, we stood together in the darkness.

It seemed that the power of speech and movement, too, was taken from us, while around we felt a strange invisible presence, and rustlings in the Christmas greenery that sounded like the whisperings of many spirits. And then a voice, not loud, but very terrible in its intensity, that cried, "A curse on any Derston that brings Christmas cheer or Christmas music to this stricken house. And a curse on him that stands beneath the mistletoe!"

Suddenly, as swiftly as they had gone out, the lights leaped up again, we saw each other—a pale-faced, stricken crowd, with here and there a fainting woman, and the marks of terror on us all.

Mrs. Bird and my uncle ran to the library.

There lay Bob Truscot, stretched beneath the mistletoe. And at first we thought him dead.

But as he slowly struggled back to consciousness, with Kitty close beside him, I turned to see my guests. And they were gone. Not one of them remained save Mrs. Bird, who sat beside the fireplace in the library, looking old and worn and troubled. And I noticed that the great branch of mistletoe had vanished. It had been wrenched from the lantern, for the gay red ribbons hung there still, with tattered ends.

"It is my fault," she murmured, as she saw me. "All my fault, my boy. I never thought you didn't know. And I admired your courage, and I thought that now such things could not occur. It is so many years. Yes, I'll tell you now—when it's almost too late to serve:

"John Derston's grandfather built this house when he was young, and brought his bride to live here. And his brother came to visit him, and he too had a beautiful young wife, a strange, tall woman, with a slender, graceful body, long and lithe, and people said she looked like a snake, and that there was a snakelike glitter in her great dark eyes. At any rate she loved John Derston, not the brother she had married, Ned, and she tried to win him too, and when he repulsed her fiercely, she but loved him all the more, and hated her husband, and the other bride, Alice Derston.

"So things went on till Christmas, when there was to be a Christmas ball, and the house was filled with Christmas greens. A branch of mistletoe was hung to that very lantern there—it has been there many, many years.

"Judith Derston, coming down the stairs, saw John standing just beneath it, and crept over to him. All is fair beneath the mistletoe, and she caught him there, and held him, and kissed him, and he turning to put her off, threw his arms about her as his wife came down the stairway and saw them. She was not strong. She gave a cry, and fell. They never knew what happened, but as the guests were coming they carried her up the stairs, and there she died, and all she said was, 'the mistletoe—the mistletoe,' over and over again, till she was dead. She died at midnight, and the guests went home, frightened, as they were tonight. But the tragedy was not ended. Alice alone had not seen them there. Ned Derston had seen it, too, but he had seen it all, and he knew his brother was not to blame—that it was his own wife.

"He found her there, beneath that very mistletoe, and when he told her, she taunted him with her love for his brother, and now that the other wife was dead that she would win John's love, and kiss him there, beneath the mistletoe, on every Christmas Even, in honour of that first kiss that she had stolen from him.

"Already blind with passion, Ned caught her. No one was there and he never told all that happened. But he killed her—there beneath the mistletoe, where she had taunted him, and given the kiss that killed his brother's wife. Then things were not as they were now, and Ned was never brought to trial.

"From that time on the two brothers lived alone in the house. John's baby son was not brought up here. He rarely saw his father.

"The two men lived solitary and alone, and never once did any woman come within the place while they lived, and Christmas was quite banished from their lives. Never would either touch a sprig of mistletoe. At last John died, but no one knew it till a servant who brought them what they needed now and then could not get in, and breaking down the doors they found John lying in his bed and Ned—hanging from that lantern there. He had died where he had killed his wife.

"And in the will which young John Derston found there was a clause that never should the house belong to any man who did not bear the Derston name, and that never should Christmas revels be held beneath its roof or sprays of mistletoe be brought within its doors.

"All laughed at that, and young John Derston, father of the one who lived here last, tried it—once. I heard of it. My mother was at the ball. And the same thing happened that happened here tonight. And then again his son tried, the third John Derston, and once more Judith Derston and the brothers came back to wreak their vengeance on the man who dared to throw aside their wishes. There, that is all. I should have told you sooner. They say that Judith can be seen—but by women only. That when a man stands beneath the mistletoe, by the library fireplace, she comes to him and kisses him, as she kissed John Derston years ago, and that only if the man's sweetheart can see her.

"I never believed it all—before. I thought the people had been frightened somehow, and the stories had grown larger. But tonight—I have seen. Give me your arm, Tom Derston. I am going home." In the morning we went, too. And though the mansion still stands in my name, never since have its dark doors opened for me or mine.

The ghosts of all the Derstons that are gone may use it, if they like. It is not a place for living folk.

THE GHOST OF CHELDON COURT
A CHRISTMAS GHOST STORY

May Wynne

Published in The Chronicle (Adelaide), *13 December 1924*

Mabel Winifred Knowles (1875–1949) was a British missionary, author and early pioneer of female science fiction writing. Born in Streatham, London, Mabel was home educated and the family moved to a large mansion on the edge of Hayes Common when she was twenty. Early detective, genre and love short stories were sold to *Cassell's Family Magazine*, *The Novel Magazine*, *The Red Magazine*, *Love Story Magazine* and countless newspapers. Her first books were written under the pseudonym May Wynne (*A King's Tragedy* (1905) and *Maid of Brittany* (1906)) and other pseudonyms include Lester Lurgan, Mark Winchester and Michael Kaye. Under the name Lester Lurgan she co-wrote the "tie-in" to the very first British sci-fi film, *A Message from Mars* (1913), based on the stage play by Richard Ganthony. The proceeds from over 300 books and countless short stories went back into her church work. She died while preparing a mission for women. I'm honoured to present this lost ghost story by an early science fiction pioneer for the first time in its one-hundred-year history.

"You won't be late, Jack," pleaded the little wife. "You won't forget that in two days' time it will be Christmas. And Robbie and Pam are looking forward to such a happy time."

John Rigdean laughed. He was such a big, jolly fellow, such a splendid good sort, always ready to lend a helping hand to do a kind turn. His small son and daughter adored him, his pretty wife loved him as dearly as in the days of courtship, and the whole of life might have been a rose-tinted idyll if it had not been for that fated streak which he seemed to have inherited as surely as the old Grange itself, with its quaint gables, straight clipped yews, and ancestral glamour.

It was the fated streak which had brought that wistful anxiety to the little wife's brown eyes, and given her pretty face the stamp of lurking fear which one sees in the expression of those who have had reason for their trick of anticipating evil.

"Never fear, Mollie," laughed Jack as he kissed the upturned face. "I'm going to be the model of discretion. A regular Puritan. I owe it to you, dear. I owe it to the best little wife in the world. I've been a rotter. You needn't deny it. And you've never rubbed it in! It would have served me right if you'd become a regular shrew. Not a bit of it! I never saw such a girl. I shall be home early, ladybird, but don't wait up for me. I should fuss my soul out if I thought you were. Ta-ta. Tell the young rustlers we'll have a regular Wild West show for Christmas Eve—and snapdragon galore!"

So he rode away, and Mollie—despite winter cold—stood in the porch crying. For half a dozen words had warned how much faith to place in Jack's promise. "But don't wait up for me" told its own tale.

He went—with brand-new resolves all ready to be swept away by those boon companions she hated and dreaded.

Bart Wilfex, as host, provided an excellent dinner. Thus far they remembered it was Christmas time. The season for feasting! The Stilton was worthy of the port wine. The wine worthy of a perfect cheese. The bottle was empty as the party adjourned to a snuggery nearby. Wilfex drew attention to the fact that lone bachelorhood has its privileges. The Trenleens cheered uproariously. They, too, were bachelors, and intended to remain so till heiresses smiled on them. But your up-to-date heiress is remarkably sharp in requiring a *quid pro quo*—and neither Roger nor Keith had anything to show but a lively aptitude to play the leech. It was amazing that the finely-polished Wilfex tolerated them. But he did more! They were his friends.

Jack Rigdean sat down to play in a frame of mind which was at once virtuous and genial.

Up to a certain point he meant to be good comrade. Wasn't it Christmas time, eh? And a man is a man—not a mere appendage to his wife's apron strings, or a nursery maid to his children. Mollie was prejudiced. All the same, he meant to consider her. Hang it all! He fixed eleven o'clock as a reasonable hour for departure.

In the meantime he intended to enjoy himself.

The stakes were not too high. Wilfex preferred deep gambling in other people's houses. He intended to get an invite out of old Rigdean in spite of the little prig of a wife. Odd, how our courteous Bart disliked poor Mollie! There was a reason, of course. But Mollie had kept a tale of unwelcome flirtation and curt snubbing to herself.

Eleven o'clock struck! Rigdean pushed back his chair. His mood was gay—very gay. Owing, no doubt, to the excellence of the whisky. He hated going, but—well, fact was, he had to remember he was a married man.

Wilfex laughed.

"Rot!" he retorted, "we're out for a spree. Another drink, old chap. Let's chuck the cards. We're fairly quits, eh? I'm in the humour for a razzle. What particular spot can we paint red?"

He had a slight drawl in his speech, a way of self-mockery which made listeners wonder if he were in earnest.

"We might climb the church steeple, eh?" giggled young Chartling, "and leave Rogers' hat on top. Ha, ha! Or rail the Manor and start dancing in the gallery. Get the fire engine out, put the men to bed, and gallop the old engine through the village. Ha, ha!"

"Capital," applauded the sneering Wilfex. "I'll wager ten to one against your carrying out the Manor joke. Any other suggestions?"

"What about the Court?" asked one of the Trenleens, yawning. "It's haunted, you know. Special Christmas number, too. What's the tale, Wigmartin? It's your uncle's place."

Horace Wigmartin looked doubtful.

"Fact is," he admitted, "I'm not quite game there. Reserve a sort of respect for the ghost. My uncle Wilfred, who owns the place, will never live there during the winter. Old Charlton and his wife take care of it, and get village girls in to clean round during the day. I'm not superstitious, but I'd not sleep the night in the haunted room at Cheldon Court for a fortune."

Wilfex laughed that charmingly mocking laugh of his.

"Here's the game," said he; "I'll lay a thousand to eight against any man spending the night tonight in that haunted room."

Instinctively his dark eyes appraised the Trenleens. Here was a gold mine for hangers on. But the Trenleens hung back. Your leech is generally a coward. The Trenleens had sound reasons against—er—sleeping in unaired sheets. The rest of the company remained silent.

"What?" he queried; "is it a pukka funk? Two thousand to eight. If no one accepts I'll try the trick myself."

He looked at Rigdean.

"Of course," he added silkily, "married men are exempt. You were talking of your wife, Jack, eh?"

Jack Rigdean had been drinking. Of all the company, too, he was the only one whose debts were considerable after the play. His mood was queer. His temper jangled. Somehow he knew Wilfex hated Mollie—and was deliberately attempting to make her suffer. Yet, in quite contradiction of his own wish to quit, rang the challenge of this man.

Wine makes fools. Whisky inspires the mad spirit of the desperado.

Jack Rigdean laughed uncertainly. His hand clutched the back of a chair. He knew he hated that smiling devil, but he had to do what he wished.

"I accept your challenge," said he.

Cheldon Court lay remote, at the further end of the village. A fine old place, but aloof, mysterious, shadowed by its own awesome reputation.

Yet the strangest part of the whole story of haunting was that ghost and tale remained unknown.

Young Wigmartin reluctantly told them that much as he parted from his comrades at the gates.

This mad buffoonery had jarred his sense of respect to what had always been a dark, grim shadow in family history.

"The room had always been called Humphrey's room," he told them, "but the story has never been recorded. The room has not been slept in for generations, or… or rather those who have slept have never told the tale of what they saw. One died, two were found… maniacs babbling on their knees… one kept silence and became a missionary. If Rigdean takes my advice he will chuck a mad wager, or he'll lose more than he bargains for."

Wilfex laughed softly.

"You hear, Jack?" he asked. "Is the bet off?"

He knew the Rigdean breed. And he did not mistake. Rigdean's reply was curt.

He was out to win that bet.

After Wigmartin had gone the escort became boisterous. The avenue with its snow-wrapped trees rang with catch tunes bawled lustily.

They entered the old hall, with its gloom—its bare boards, bagged curtains, forlorn air of desertion.

Carols were impossible.

Even the Trenleens came short of such profanity.

But bottles were produced, and the jest carried far.

Old Charlton and his wife were respectable folk, but they knew Mr. Wilfex for a gentleman, and his wine was as nice as his manners. So they drank the toasts suggested, and grew sleepy over-soon.

The Trenleens took charge of them with Scotch Tammar, who wheedled them back to their own snug apartment, and left them sleeping soundly in the chairs from which the coming of the mob had dragged them.

It was Wilfex who led the way upstairs. He was a curious fellow, this Bart, and knew all he wanted to know. He had reason for having discovered beforehand which was the room with reputation.

Jack Rigdean stood on the threshold undismayed. He had also to forget Mollie till morning. From thenceforward he would be the model of perfection.

Hang it all! He had told her not to wait up for him.

The room with the reputation was not particularly sinister. The bed was old-fashioned and canopied; the floor, with time-darkened boards, was bare. There were wardrobe, chairs, and a long mirror facing the door. That was all. No tapestries, chests, or other paraphernalia of ancestral chambers.

The door had been locked, but the key was in the lock. The window of the room boasted neither blinds nor curtains. Roger Trenleen had thrown back the shutters.

"Moonlight," said he. "Luck for you, Jack. After all, it will be a cheap two thou."

He spoke regretfully. What a fool he had been not to take the odds offered by Bart Wilfex. The latter was smiling as he looked at Rigdean. He seemed curiously fascinated by this dare-devil escapade.

He had heard Wigmartin talk of the people who had slept in Humphrey's room. And his interest in the occult was as strong as his dislike for Rigdean's wife. Two birds at a stone.

"Look here, Jack," he drawled; "all the cards on the table. Do you object to our locking the door—outside?"

Trenleen giggled, and officiously opened the wardrobe, while his brother looked under the bed.

Jack Rigdean looked at the man who hated him.

"Not in the least," he replied, "so long as you'll guarantee I shall be free by seven in the morning—or my wife may be sending for the police."

"I will guarantee it," said Wilfex.

The noisy rabble trooped out. Odd, how quietly they went. An old bed, a wardrobe, and few chairs could surely not have worked the marvel. The Trenleens went first—rather too hastily. One jostled the other and cursed. Bart Wilfex was the only one to look back.

"Pleasant thoughts," he purred; "I won't suggest dreams—nor do I recommend the bed. I doubt if it is aired. Don't risk your health, John."

"I will not," retorted Rigdean; "I want to be fit to enjoy that two thou'. By-bye."

He heard the key turn in the door.

Peace and goodwill! Turkey and plum pudding! What a time he meant to have with the kids. He seated himself in the deep embrasure of the window. After all, this was an easy way of coining a pot of money. He would explain to Mollie. He deliberately planned to think of Mollie as he fixed his eyes on the white sheen of a wonder world.

There was no need to look back into the room at all!

Mollie and those kids. Some of the best! He had not been too fair to poor old Mollie, but this two thou' would grease a number of wheels. What about the Riviera, eh? Snakes! How cold it was. Even in his great-coat he was chilly! What a splendid lot of trees the Court gardens boasted. In spite of the snow he could see that. Magnificent! Those deodars. He wondered old Wigmartin ever left the place. All bosh about being hustled out by an annual and ancestral ghost.

No sober-sided, normal man believed in ghosts!

He was a sceptic himself.

How cold it was!

And the glare of whiteness made his eyes ache. He had to turn back to look into the room to soothe the strain of the eyeballs. The room itself was light—in patches. The bed remained in shadow, but the glass of the mirror showed like silver, reflecting the door. As Rigdean looked, his gaze drawn by that silver sheen, he noticed the door was ajar.

Impossible!

He had heard Wilfex lock it.

He did not look towards the door. His gaze remained on the mirror which reflected the opposite side of the room.

The door was opening.

He did not move.

The idea took him that Wilfex was playing a trick, or else that young Wigmartin had come to urge him to clear out.

Should he do so?

Had Rigdean been frozen in his place he could not have felt colder. His limbs seemed stiff. A trance held him. He could not have moved had he dared.

But he would have given the wagered two thousand twice over to have been able to reach the door. Still, could that be a ghost? It was too real, too substantial in appearance.

He could see the silken stockings and buckled shoes, the delicate lace and fine buttons. He could presently see the face of the man who had entered and closed the door.

Beads of perspiration gathered on Rigdean's face and rolled down to his neck.

The face of the visitor was colourless. His eyes terrible.

Fear sickened in the watcher's heart. But he had to look.

The man in dainty court suit did not seem to see him, though he came and stood by the window. The moonlight showed the wan, agonised features, the dreadful purpose in the tired eyes.

Rigdean knew what was coming, and would have given all he possessed to stop it.

Death was on that young face.

What did it mean? Why did that figure stand there if… it did not belong to life and the things of life?

Could it not sleep… after all… these years?

Cards fluttered to the ground… had the delicate hand scattered them there? They lay… mute witnesses, to form the clue to that coming tragedy. They lay in the dust under the watcher's gaze and told the tale of a gambler's last hour of life.

A last hour of despair. A last hour…

John Rigdean could have shrieked in his horror. His brain reeled.

He recalled the fate of others… who had watched. He understood why they had found their own tragedy in this room.

The atmosphere of some vital force of suffering filled the apartment. The tense, supreme suffering of a young, virile man who deliberately sets himself in the spirit of reckless cowardice on the threshold of an unknown world.

The horror left the air cold.

With all his might Rigdean tried to close his eyes… to pray… He could think of nothing, do nothing but watch the man in that old-world dress raise the fatal weapon to his breast.

Then… Then…

Was it the echo of a lost sigh drifting back from the realms of eternity?

The door was opening.

Rigdean, his gaze again on the mirror, saw it was so. His soul swelled in the impotent longing to scream a command aloud.

"Go back! Go back!"

He could not speak. A woman had entered the room. A woman, young, sweet, very lovely, with soft, fair curls gathered under a mob cap; there were ribbons on the cap, ribbons on the bosom of her kerchief. The flowered silk of her sacque gown showed a dainty pattern. It was the prettiest figure from the past, in all but expression. As she came forward Rigdean knew what she would be seeking. He saw the wistful suffering in the blue eyes, the tense pain about the lips. He realised as he never could have done before what it meant to be a gambler's wife. And the woman was young. The soft curve of her cheek should have been dimpled by smiles. Instead, it would soon be followed by the sickness of long strain.

Rigdean's mouth grew dry. He longed to cry "go back!" He dreaded the moment when the dainty seeker found… found… that…

She had found him.

A cloud sailed over the midnight moon. A curtain seemed to have been drawn across the window of that haunted room. Rigdean felt his mental balance tottering.

Mollie! Mollie!

The name was an anchor.

Mollie!

The light had returned. He saw the girlish figure which bent in agony of suffering over the other.

The woman's arms were about a dead gambler. The dark head lay pillowed against the filmy lace of her kerchief.

Across the dead body of the man she had loved in the long ago the ghost-woman looked at John Rigdean.

And the latter saw the reflected anguish of a heart broken centuries before. Broken by the selfish madness of a reckless gamester who had dared tell her he loved her.

John Rigdean put out his hands.

"Forgive," he sobbed. "Mollie forgive."

Then darkness closed around him.

It was the day of Christmas Eve. The children of the Grange were already calling each other from their cots, telling of all they were going to do this day. Mollie Rigdean rose from her knees and drew back the curtain. Dawn had come after an all-night vigil.

She had waited in vain.

As she looked from the window a man came up the drive—on foot. She herself went down to greet him.

It was Jack.

He did not speak, but allowed her to lead him to the dining-room and pour him out wine. She tried, poor little soul, to hide her fears.

"You are ill, dear," she said, and laid her lips to his grey cheek.

Her tenderness broke the spell.

Laying his head down in his arms, John Rigdean broke into tears. His shoulders shook. But the passion of emotion saved—his reason.

When old Charlton had found him an hour since crouched by the window of Humphrey's room he had believed another victim's name had been added to the grim roll laid to a ghost's account.

But—this man's reason was spared. He owed it to the love of his young wife.

She heard the tale of confession—later. She heard the story of a long passed tragedy. The secret of an untold tale was learned at last.

Afterwards it was Mollie who spoke.

Her hands were clasped, and her brown eyes held a deep and reverent pity.

"I should like," she whispered… "to tell that other woman… I thank her."

John Rigdean knew there was no need for him to make promises.

Bart Wilfex, smiling to hide his inward rage at baulking, rode to the Grange to pay a debt. Rigdean stood on the steps with his arm about his wife's waist.

"I will not take your money, Mr. Wilfex," said he, "and the account of our friendship is closed. You were right last night. Married men have their responsibilities. I wish you goodbye."

Leaving the man to curse as he rode away, Mollie's husband brought Mollie back to the fireside. The children were shouting with laughter as they came to play. Their father would not refuse them.

But this moment was his own.

He drew Mollie into his arms.

"God bless the women," he whispered, "and teach their men to see… this side of the grave… what the cost is… to them."

"Amen," said Mollie, softly.

Over the fields Christmas bells were ringing.

THAT TERRIBLE DENTIST
A STORY OF THE STRAND

Anonymous

First published in London Society, *December 1880*

This story was published alongside "Sandy the Tinker" by Mrs. J. H. Riddell and "The American's Tale" by Arthur Conan Doyle in the *London Society* Christmas Annual. Dentists and Christmas. It makes for a heady, horrific mix. One of those stories that I'd give my right arm to know who had written it, and where I'm surprised it's never been reprinted before now, because it truly is an open goal for any editor who would choose it. I'm proud to present it to you for the first time in one hundred and forty-five years.

I suppose no one would imagine that anything particularly horrible or ghastly could arise out of a mere ordinary visit to the dentist. That is altogether so commonplace and everyday an occurrence that, though you naturally regard it with painful apprehensiveness and repugnance, you do not see how anything extraordinarily horrid could possibly spring from it. Nevertheless the most terrible adventure that it has ever been my lot to pass through resulted simply from my going to have a tooth extracted.

The tale I am about to relate may seem to be somewhat prosaic in its materials, but it is at least a true narration of an incident that befell me, and one that was impressed so forcibly upon my mind as to leave a vivid remembrance behind it; vivid, indeed, even yet, though years have elapsed since it happened. My story rests upon a rather rare case in medicine, occurring at an odd moment, and when the combination of circumstances rendered it—to me at least—appalling and terrible. But you shall judge for yourselves.

It was the afternoon before Christmas Day, in the year 186–, and I had left the office and was strolling along the Strand towards Hungerford Bridge, intending to take the train from Waterloo to Richmond, where my sister and brother-in-law lived, with whom I had arranged to spend my Christmas holiday. The afternoon was still young—it being only about two o'clock, I think—and I was not really due until shortly before seven, my sister's dinner-hour. Accordingly, I was in no particular hurry; and being reminded by the sight of a bill-of-fare temptingly displayed in the window of a restaurant that I had not as yet lunched, I turned into the place to get a snack of something.

Whether it was that the meat at this establishment was unusually tough, or whether it was simply my destiny, I do not know; but one thing is certain, that while eating I was unhappy enough to break a tooth. It was one of my back teeth, molars, an old offender that for long before had caused me trouble at times, and that had now chosen the most unpropitious possible moment to break off by the gum, and, worse than all, to plunge me straightway into all the torments of an aggravated attack of toothache.

What was to be done? Here was I, just starting forth to meet a merry assemblage of Christmas guests, old and young, bound to be jolly from the moment of my arrival and for several days to come, bound to eat, drink, and be merry among the merry, as English people consider necessary at this season. And who was to be jovial, or even cheerful, I should like to know, with a raging, racking, rasping toothache causing one endless misery all the time? There was no help for it now; the long-postponed visit to the dentist could be deferred no longer: I must go and get my aching stump extracted, and go down to Richmond without it, and also without, as I fervently trusted, the pain that was now consuming me.

So, having made up my mind, I called the waiter and paid for my half-unfinished lunch, telling that commiserating official of my misfortune, and inquiring whether he knew of a good dentist in the near neighbourhood to whom he could direct me.

"Dentist, sir? Yessir!" he replied, after the manner of waiters, and as though taking an order for some comestible: "'eaps of dentists round about 'ere, sir. There's a gentleman hoppersite, but 'e's away by now; and, you see, sir, bein' as it's 'oliday time, and has most of 'em honly 'as consultin'-rooms in the Strand, and lives somewheres helse, I don't know as you'll heasily find one close by 'ere. But I'll ask the chief waiter, sir; I dessay 'e'll know of one."

The chief waiter being appealed to did know of one, a Mr. Masseter, let us call him, who was in the habit of dining at the restaurant very frequently, and who lived close by. His address was No. – Lewis street, one of those small streets leading off the Strand down towards the river, and he was most likely to be found at home.

"And," added the waiter, pocketing my douceur, "don't you take no notice of 'is looks, sir; 'e's a queer un to look at, is little Mr. Masseter, but a good un at 'is business, so I've 'eard, and cheap, sir; and I 'opes you'll get relief of your pain, sir; and a merry Christmas, thankee, sir."

I turned away and sought the street I had been directed to, finding it with some trifling difficulty; but once in Lewis street I had no trouble in discovering the house I sought, since a brass plate bearing the inscription, "MASSETER, SURGEON-DENTIST," sufficiently indicated it. It was an ordinary dull brick dwelling-house, uniform with its neighbours; and in the murky December atmosphere, the whole narrow street looked about as uninteresting and uninviting for a place of residence as any that intersect that quarter.

I rang the bell, and presently the door was opened by a person, whom, from the waiter's brief description of him, I had no difficulty in recognising as the dentist himself.

"Ah," he remarked, when I had explained the reason of my call, "you are lucky to be just in time. I was intending to go out of town till Monday, and, not expecting any patients, I was just about to start. My housekeeper and servant are gone as it is, so, if you had been half an hour later, you would have found only an empty house. But step in and come upstairs."

So saying, he ushered me up to what he jocularly termed his "torture-chamber;" remarking, as he did so, that Christmas was an unseasonable time at which to be suffering from toothache, since such an extra amount of mastication was supposed to be required then.

"But never mind," he added, "we'll soon be all right now, and ready for any amount of turkey and goose."

Mr. Masseter indeed was, as the waiter at the dining-rooms had intimated to me, a most extraordinary-looking man. He was short and small, not much over five feet in height, I should think, and he was also somewhat deformed. He had a humpback, or at least much the appearance of one given him by a pair of high sloping shoulders, a projecting neck, and what is generally called a pigeon-breast. His legs were bowed, and his feet unshapely, while his arms were of unusual length, and terminated in large, bony, knuckly hands. Unfortunately for him, poor man, the list of deformities did not end here, but was augmented by the appearance of the head and face. The little gentleman's head was large and long; he was bald over the forehead, and his hair, clipped short and bristly, showed a surprising field of bumps and excrescences; interesting, no doubt, to a phrenologist, but unsightly enough to an ordinary beholder. Then his eyes were small and beady, a trifle crossed I fancied, but bright and twinkling like a ferret's. His beard was thick and full, but was trimmed to a point that appeared unusually elevated in advance of the rest of his person, and so made more remarkable the long lank face. Hair and beard, and also a pair of beetling eyebrows, were of a peculiar rusty-red colour, that showed up in sickly contrast against a shiny sallow skin, and somehow seemed to remind me of rotten apples.

The room into which the dentist led me was what Londoners call the "first-floor-front." There was nothing unusual in it beyond what one commonly sees in a dentist's consulting-room. It was furnished sombrely and heavily, with leather-covered chairs, ponderous bookcases, and dark coloured hangings and carpet. There were two windows, and a sort of table secretaire stood below one of them, loaded with dental instruments and appliances. Another table occupied a corner, bearing several mahogany cases of suspicious appearance; while a movable gas-lamp of unusual shape stood on a stand near it. The mantelpiece, above a fireplace in which a small fire was apparently dying out, and various brackets and bookshelves were piled with plaster-casts and other general dental litter.

With exception of these particulars the apartment presented the general aspect of a study or sitting-room. Stay, no! I have omitted one detail of importance. In the centre of the room, and facing one of the windows, stood THE CHAIR; that horrid combination of bolts and bars, sliding-rests and screws, that a carious generation knows only too well.

I looked at this engine with much the same feelings that a heretic in the judgment-hall of the Inquisition might be supposed to regard the sheeted rack in the dark corner. There it stood, seeming to carry an air of infernal triumph about it, and wearing a wolfish look in every joint and screw. I think some dim presentiment of what was to happen to myself mingled with those nervous apprehensions that any one may experience when they set eyes on the dentist's chair.

Flanking the chair on either side were two pillar-like stands, the one containing the usual water conveniences, and the other being, as I afterwards discovered, a receptacle for the apparatus used in generating and administering protoxide of nitrogen or "laughing-gas," as it is popularly called.

In these days, when a visit to a dentist is no uncommon occurrence in the lives of any of us—worse luck!—I daresay you are surprised at my retaining for so many years such a full remembrance of the little details with which I have just furnished you. But if you will have patience to bear with me to the end of my story, I think you will see no reason to wonder that my memory has been so precise.

By the way, have you ever observed the curious transformation that comes over you directly the door closes behind you, and you are once fairly within the dentist's sanctum? That you have left your toothache behind you in the street, or in what schoolboys aptly term "the funking-room," is an experience that surely no one will gainsay; but there is a further manifestation of the same feeling that I would draw your attention to. At the moment when the door has closed, and you feel that you are now entirely in the power of the gentleman who is about to operate on your offending "ivories," you become conscious of a feeling of moral abasement taking possession of you.

However mild-mannered be the individual dentist you confront—and these gentlemen are pre-eminent for their suavity—you have a singular desire to treat him with most exaggerated courtesy. You would like to bow constantly, and address him as "Sir!" You laugh feverishly and inordinately at the tamest and stupidest joke he may emit. You abase yourself before him, feeling that he is to be your executioner in some sort, and that you are helplessly and utterly in his power. I had all that feeling on the occasion I am telling of, and I think it was somewhat more absorbing than common; for I remember having some very unusual thrills of nervous agitation, though there was nothing in especial to have caused them. I suppose it was presentiment of my coming fate.

Well, after a few preliminary questions, which he scarcely permitted me to answer, Mr. Masseter, with the dexterity of his craft, adroitly piloted me into the chair. Once safely within its embrace, I became like plastic dough under his manipulation. He hovered over me, examining my mouth, in a ghoul-like manner that was in itself sufficiently discomposing; and while he kept up a perpetual undercurrent of—"Now, I'm not going to hurt you in the least! It's perfectly painless! Won't pain you at all! Now don't be afraid; I won't hurt you, won't hurt you!" he yet prodded and tapped with relentless and coldblooded ferocity, putting me to excruciating and indescribable agony.

I recalled to mind the waiter's eulogies on this operator, and as he kept up the monologue just mentioned and its accompanying practical disproof, I thought to myself that there could be no mistake: Mr. Masseter evidently did "know his business."

"Now," said the little man, after he had finished his explorations, "I'll tell you what, sir: that's a very awkward stump of yours! It may give me a little trouble to extract; and come out it must, if you are to be freed from pain. Now what do you say to taking the gas, eh? It's perfectly harmless; effects don't last ten minutes; and it will save all pain. Luckily the apparatus is all ready, as I was using it this morning; and I won't charge you anything extra for it. Come now, what do you say?"

This he accented with divers grins and gestures that he probably meant to be cordial and persuasive, but that only served, unfortunately, to render his singular appearance more uncouth if possible. However, I felt his proposition to be so reasonable and kind that I at once assented to it.

Immediately that I had signified my willingness to be put under the influence of the gas, Mr. Masseter opened the stand or case that I mentioned, and having arranged the apparatus within it, he drew from it a coil of tube, one end of which was in connection with the gas-receiver, and the other was furnished with a sort of mouth and nosepiece. This mouthpiece he adjusted to my face as I sat back in the chair, telling me to respire gently.

I daresay many of you have taken the gas at one time or another, and pretty well know what the experience is like; but I may as well describe to you the effects it had upon me.

I was first of all conscious of a kind of half-choking sensation in the throat and some uneasiness in the chest, but that quickly passed off. Then I began to get gradually more and more exhilarated in mind—somewhat like dram-drinking would affect one, but of course quicker, and also more easily and buoyantly. I wanted to talk, but the infernal mouthpiece prevented me. I seemed conscious that I had lots of things to say that were really very witty; but no, I could not get utterance for them. All sorts of humorous ideas struggled vaguely in my mind; and though I felt I was growing very silly, yet I wished to let the feeling increase. Then it appeared to me to be necessary that I should get up in order to give free vent to my mirthful tendencies; but no, the dentist held me down in the chair, and kept the mouthpiece still over my face. I struggled to get free, and fought with my hands to release myself; for I felt that there was a whole tempest of laughter within me that ought to be let out. Every moment, too, the dentist himself and the whole situation seemed to become more and more ludicrous to my mind, and I strove and strove with the little man, who was fairly lying on top of me now, until I suppose I lost consciousness more or less.

I came to all of a sudden, with a singular feeling of shame and contrition, as it were, for the foolishness I had been guilty of. But one consideration bore all others down before it. The pain in my jaw was intensified instead of being relieved.

Mr. Masseter was standing in front of me, looking rather rueful.

"Have you got it out?" I gasped.

"No," he said smilingly. "The fact is you are a little rough under the gas. It excited you a good deal; and so, as you kept moving and struggling with me, I did not get a chance to operate till just as you were coming round again."

"Well, what's to be done? What do you propose?" I said querulously.

"Oh," he replied, "it will be all right if you'll only just permit me to do what is needful in cases of a similar idiosyncrasy to your own."

"What is that?" I questioned.

"Nothing that need discompose you, sir," he answered; "merely to let me fasten your limbs for the moment, so that I may get at your mouth when you are under the gas. I've several times had to do just the same thing to lady-patients."

"Fasten me up!" I said, in amazement. "I never heard of such a thing before! It's very unusual, is it not?"

"Unusual, yes, in a general way; but every dentist who employs the gas must sometimes have recourse to it, or else operate without the gas at all; which, in your own case, would be very painful, as I have told you."

"How do you mean to do it, then?" I asked him.

"In this way," he answered: "I have here two collars or bracelets united by a short chain. Now if you will pass your hands behind the back of the chair, and permit me to fasten your wrists with this contrivance, I shall be able to get to your mouth without your fighting with me when you are under the influence of the gas. There is a bar here, too, that I can shut down over your knees to control them, and a strap to pass across your shins and keep you from kicking."

My jaw was now aching so furiously that I was ready to close with any plan that offered speedy relief.

"Fire away," I said. "Do what you like, only rid me of this pain."

So, in a minute or two, I was made securely captive in the chair, in the manner as aforesaid. I am not a suspicious man, and as everything seemed natural enough, I had not the least reason for objecting to the plan. Certainly I felt a little foolish, and the thought crossed my mind that, if the unprepossessing little man who was busying himself about me meant foul play of any sort, he had me most completely in his power. But there was no excuse for harbouring such a notion; and if events had taken the course they were intended to, I should have had no occasion to grumble at my temporary bonds. That they did not do so the sequel of my tale will quickly show, but of course I could have no prevision at that moment of what actually was to follow.

So it was with perfect composure and acquiescence that I again felt the mouthpiece put over my face, and that I recommenced inhaling the gas. I underwent much the same succession of feelings on this second occasion as before, with this difference, that my bonds prevented my struggling and interfering with the dentist in the performance of his work. When I recovered from the gas, therefore, I found, to my delight, that the job was over, my offending member gone, and my pain with it. Mr. Masseter was holding a glass of water to my mouth, and I felt altogether in a state of tranquil blessedness.

So far, then, things had gone according to settled plan and intention; now they were quickly to assume a course extraordinary.

What fiend prompted him to do it, I do not know; but, just at this juncture, Mr. Masseter asked me to let him take a cast of my upper jaw. It was from the lower, you understand, that the broken stump had just been extracted. The reason of his request was that I have a peculiar arrangement, or disarrangement if you like, of the teeth, and the dentist, so he told me, was desirous to have a cast of the jaw.

As you may suppose, the request, my compliance with it, and its execution occupied such a short moment, that I never thought to ask for release from my bonds first; and, to do the poor little man justice, I am perfectly sure it never occurred to him either.

Everything being in readiness, Mr. Masseter stepped over to me, and, telling me to open my mouth to its widest extent, he placed in it a sort of little spoon or trowel filled with some composition resembling putty in consistence. This spoon was flat at the bottom, and shaped so as to fit the mouth, which it nearly filled. By raising and manipulating it a little the composition came in contact with the palate and upper teeth, and being soft, moulded itself to their shape.

Just at the precise moment when my teeth were fixed in the composition in this way, the dentist moved to the table to reach a spatula or probe or some such instrument. He said something, but I failed to catch what it was, as he moved away from me. Then, to my utter amazement, he suddenly fell to the ground, turning partially towards me as he sank, so that his head and back came up against the panelling below the window in front of me, and were supported by it.

Naturally I thought he had but tripped over the carpet or something, and I instinctively made an effort to rise and help him. Of course I could not do that, fixed as I was, and I was rather amused at the *contretemps*. I looked to see him spring up again at once, as a man would under the circumstances. For several moments I watched him, all the while seeing nothing but the ridiculous in the incident. Then my mirth gradually gave way to concern, and that became in its turn actual alarm. What could be the matter? The man did not move a muscle or even speak!

There he lay, or rather crouched, without visible motion of any kind, just as he had fallen; one leg was drawn up under him, the other extended; his back and shoulders were resting against the wall, his arms hanging loosely down, and his face fully turned in my direction. His eyes and mouth were open, the former fixed and staring, with a certain glassiness coming into them, while his complexion was beginning to assume a more ghastly and livid look. What on earth could be the matter with the man? I asked myself. Was he in a fit of some sort? Hardly, for there was none of that convulsive motion one usually associates with the idea of a fit. Then what *was* it? Could it be possible—that—the man—was—dead?

I had enough knowledge of medical science to know that these deformed subjects, born into the world with a body that had seemingly been the sport of creative nature, were often gifted with emotional capacities of a very extraordinary kind. In other words, it sometimes happened that a body, physically a structural abortion, might contain nervous centres and organisations capable of singularly delicate sensation and faculty. Again, I knew that persons, in whom was this hypersensitive nervous power, were peculiarly liable or predisposed to a class of diseases not ordinarily met with among others, and which, too, might be manifested in them in a strange and inexplicable manner. All this, and more that I need not weary you with, existed in my mind in a confused and hazy sort of way.

You will wonder what I was doing all this time. Briefly, then, I was making the strongest and most frantic efforts to free myself from my unfortunate position.

This is how I was situated. I was sitting in the chair, which was like an ordinary solidly built large armchair. The back had been let down to a considerable angle, so that I was really in a half-reclining posture. My arms were held round the back of the chair, behind and partially below me, and were fastened at the wrists in the manner already described. So tightly were the bracelets buckled round my wrists, that it was impossible to slip them off; while the coupling-chain between them had apparently been passed through a ring attached to the chair itself.

Across my knees was a bar that passed through the arms of the chair, and that was immovably fixed; while over my shins was a strap, completing the bonds that held me most securely fast.

To add to the miseries of my position, the spoon and its contents yet remained in my mouth, nor was any effort of mine able to dislodge it. Biting made no impression on the metal spoon, while every movement of tongue and teeth only forced the composition into my cheeks and gave it a firmer hold. I was simply bound and gagged in the securest possible manner. Had I been a slighter-built man, I might have contrived to wriggle my legs upwards, and so possibly I might have twisted myself free; but, being large and heavy as I am, this was wholly impossible. Indeed, the chair seemed to hold me as though it had been fitted to my body, and I filled my bonds without an inch of room to spare.

Of course my first impulse, after the whole horror of the situation had forced itself upon me, was to struggle to release myself. I prolonged my efforts with frantic persistence until the perspiration streamed from every pore—cold as the weather was—and until I was thoroughly exhausted, but without relieving my position in the smallest degree. After every conceivable endeavour, after exercising my strength and ingenuity to the utmost, I still remained as at first, helplessly bound, hopelessly gagged.

I had been primarily excited to try and release myself by the desire of assisting that poor little man, who had been struck down before my eyes so suddenly, so strangely, and so awfully; but I soon began almost to forget him in alarm for my own case. Clearly I must remain where I was until somebody came to the rescue, nor could I shout to summon aid, or make any noise sufficient to attract attention.

I remembered that Mr. Masseter had told me he was alone in the house. His servants had gone away to make holiday with their friends, and he himself had just been going off somewhere when I arrived. Yet, surely, I thought somebody would come to the house before long; some servant would return, some tradesman or messenger at least would call presently, and I should be relieved. Surely, I argued with myself, here, in the very heart of London, I could not remain undiscovered.

Much as I pitied the unfortunate object before me, the outlines of whose figure I could just perceive through the gathering gloom—for by this time the light had waned very much—deeply though I deplored his sudden and fearful fate, my mind was now fully occupied with my own personal concerns.

I thought of the party that was expecting me, whose members would shortly be commencing their Christmas Eve festivities, probably with much wonder at my non-appearance, and, likely enough, with plenty of jests at the expense of the laggard. When—O, *when!*—might I expect to join them? There was a disagreeable apprehension stealing into my head that was momentarily increasing into a terrifying certainty. The morrow was Christmas Day, and the day following was Sunday. Doubtless the dentist's servants had received leave of absence until Monday, or perhaps till Tuesday. These were days on which there would be no likelihood of tradesmen, patients, or other callers coming to the house, and consequently but small chance of any one discovering my situation. My prospect of liberty, therefore, depended on myself, or on my succeeding in attracting the attention of some passer-by in the street. It was a horrible conclusion to arrive at, just as I was panting with the futile efforts I had already made to release myself.

Again, and yet again, I strove and fought for liberty; struggling until my wrists were swelled and raw, until my arms were strained as if they had been drawn out upon the rack, until every muscle of my body and limbs seemed wrenched and torn. The muscles of my cheeks and throat were cramped and painful; my lips and tongue became swollen, tense, and bled with the strenuous efforts I made to eject that infernal spoonful of plaster from my mouth. And when exhaustion and torture precluded all further attempts, I found all had been to no purpose—I had not gained an inch. Weakened and racked with pain, I lay in my bondage; and I am not ashamed to say that tears of despair and mortification welled from my eyes as, half choked and panting, I lay there in the darkness.

Now commenced a time in which my suffering was so acute that the living reality of it seems present with me still. That period of horrible anguish has left an ineffaceable brand upon my memory that will remain with me always. I may as well tell you at this point of my tale that I remained a prisoner until late on the Monday following—only some seventy short hours in all, but, O God, hours that to me seemed unending years!

I cannot describe to you separately each hour as it passed, each night or each day; that first night was, perhaps, the easiest of all. Gagged and bound to that fearful chair, I reclined a tortured prisoner. Prostrated by unusual exertion, my body and limbs were alternately numbed with cold or seized with cramps that would have caused me to scream if I had had the power to do so. By and by I was assailed with intensest thirst, and anon with hunger also; and these, added to the pain I suffered from the immovable constraint of my position, the aching sores and bruises my struggles had left me, and the horrid cramps that griped my limbs, effectually banished all chance of sleep.

But the wretchedness of my physical condition was intensified by the mental misery I endured. Realise my position to yourselves if you can, and you may form some idea of my state of mind. As the slow hours passed on and on, bringing no relief with them, and my torments grew worse and worse, I began to lose hope, and to harbour apprehensions that I might not be found until too late. Imagine the thinking and thinking I continued to endure all that horrible time, the growing despondency, the utter depression, the sense of isolation there, close to the Strand and Charing Cross, the very centre of London.

And, worst of all, I am a nervous man; and my situation was such as might have wrought upon the courage of the strongest nerved. For do not forget the silent watcher who all the time crouched opposite to me. I could not see him by night, yet I knew he was there; and with the first streaks of daylight came the gradual growing shape, joining itself among the shadows until the dead glassy eyes sprang suddenly out of the gloom and fixed themselves on mine. Though dull and cold, their immovable stare had a weirdly awful expression that fearfully excited my imagination. If I closed my eyes I still seemed to see the ghastly form through the lids; and the unquenchable fixity of that horrible gaze impelled me to turn my eyes to it.

Sounds of life were around me in plenty; and perhaps that may have kept me from going actually mad. It was a quiet street, with little or no traffic through it; but the nervous tension of my faculties made me alive to noises that one would scarcely notice in general. Moreover, after a bit, I began to link the sounds I heard to strange effects of imagination; they became living things to me, and part of the dismal nightmare through which I was passing.

By night I heard the constant chiming of Big Ben and other clocks, the occasional distant rattle of a cab, the solemn tramp of the policeman on his beat, the voice or song of some returning reveller. Then the jangle of the milkman's cans would usher in the dawn, and gradually life would awake into abundant noise. Then, too, I would be aroused to consciousness of the ghastly sentinel who watched over me; and under the dead fascination of his motionless eyes I would hear the noises of the day. The voices and laughter, the noise of people moving in the street or in the neighbouring houses, seemed unnatural and weird; the jarring and incessant clang of a hundred different church bells filled me with gloomy thoughts, and powerfully increased the nervous terrors of my fevered mind. There was no cheerful sunshine to exhilarate my senses, but that dim murky fog that London knows so well in winter. And when through it there arose the discordant iteration of street-sellers' cries, it seemed to my imagination, circumstanced as I was, that these were the howls of tormenting fiends.

You see that my mind was becoming distraught as the anguish of my body and the still constraint of my position affected it. All sorts of horrible ideas kept thronging into my brain; and as the hours crept slowly on, and still my odious captor held his basilisk gaze upon me, and fed on my mental life, was it any wonder that my reason became enthralled like that of one in *delirium tremens?*

So, what seemed interminable ages wore on, and weaker, with faculties fast becoming more and more estranged under the torture of body and misery of mind, my stay in purgatory drew to a close. It was the Monday afternoon, though I knew it not.

A wild terrifying notion seized me that the body before me had been entered by a demon, whose special mission it was to subject me to greater and yet inconceivable torture. Through an endless time I watched the shapeless form, the detestable face, the horror-striking eyes—watched and waited in all the anguish of prolonged suspense for the awful climax of my doom.

At length came the supreme moment. I saw the dreadful eyes rapidly flicker and move; I saw a red flush spring to the dead man's cheeks, a movement to the lips, a stealthy twitching to the limbs and body. It seemed to me that the moment was come I had been expecting through a lifetime. Without astonishment, but with immense, unutterable, overwhelming horror, I saw the dead man spring lightly to his feet, and, with outstretched arms, move towards me. He spoke: the tones were Masseter's, the voice was the demon's. What the words were I know not; they brought to my mind the last tremendous shock of awful fear, under whose appalling terror I happily sank into unconsciousness.

*

Yes, it was a case of catalepsy, so they told me at the hospital weeks afterwards, when they judged me able to hear of it; for I was long ill with brain fever as a sequel to my adventure. Mr. Masseter had been subject to fits of this kind formerly, but had supposed his liability to them to have ceased. He told the hospital physicians that he had felt no premonitory symptoms whatever, and that on awakening to consciousness he merely thought he had fallen, neither knowing he had had a fit, nor being sensible of the lapse of time. Finding me ill and in a swoon, he at once released me, and, not succeeding in his efforts to bring me round, feared he knew not what, and bore me off to the nearest hospital. There he discovered the real date of the day, and so became alive to what had actually occurred. The physicians were much interested in his case, so prolonged a trance being rare, though the usual symptoms of catalepsy were well known to them. The affair made some noise at the time, owing to the singular coincidence of my captivity; and, in consequence of that, and of his own morbid sensibility, poor little Masseter shortly afterwards left Lewis street. I have not seen him since, nor do I wish to do so; not that I bear him any ill-will—God forbid, poor little man!—but simply because a sight of his face would too vividly renew my remembrance of an event that, besides having such a terrible effect upon me at the time, has left its fatal impress upon me for the rest of my life, and has burdened my memory with an ineffaceable nightmare load of horror that I suppose I must carry to my grave.

So ends my tale. If its details appear commonplace to you, at least reflect how terrible and all-absorbing the endurance and memory of them must be to me.

CLAUS AND DEFECT
William J. Koen

First published in The Boston College Stylus, *December 1927*

As to the author, I've not been able to find out much about the life of William J. Koen, as the name is quite a popular one in America. Researchers looking for prominent William J. Koens will find one from Salem who was the President Elect of the Lens and Tripod Club and another who was a jeweller on the board of directors of the Austin National Bank. Our William J. Koen edited the *Sub Turri* yearbook for Boston College in 1913, as well as the *Boston College Heights* (c.1929) and wrote several tales and poems for *The Boston College Stylus*. His tales include "Nebulous Nothings" and "Dream Fancies". "Claus and Defect" is another favourite story of mine. A non-scary one, but when you have a tale with a ghostly Santa Claus who claims to have given Charles Dickens his inspiration for *A Christmas Carol*, you know you're in for a treat! This story is one for the writers out there trying to chase their Christmas deadlines and is being reprinted for the first time since 1927.

THE Author was drowned in deep despair. For weeks had he wandered around the streets, seeing nothing, speaking to no one… thinking… wondering. He would lie awake at night, searching the inmost reaches of his hitherto imaginative mind. To no avail, this searching? So it seemed. But wait, what was that little thought that would creep in from behind some huge void in the Author's brain, and insinuate itself into his feverish fancy? And the Author would always send it back to its corner, saying, "There is no room for you; anything else—anything." And he groaned.

What price groaning! To what avail tears and sighs? The Author was daily more and more despondent. Never before had his imagination failed him; never before had his mind refused to yield up plots, characters, and new ideas, which he might piece together and write into a story.

"Why, it was only last year," he thought, "when I wrote three Christmas stories during the last of November, and at that time I had already sold a dozen which I had written the previous summer. But those were the old type, written when I was an amateur, so to speak. Then I kept writing the same old stuff they all write. An indiscriminate public will read whatever is in the magazines. If they cannot get something good, they are forced to be content with what is mediocre. I'm through with the *hoi polloi*. I simply refuse to write the same old stories. Last year I had, if I remember correctly, five Santa Claus stories—that was when I foolishly believed in Santa Claus; two about the little rich boy who never had the Spirit of Christmas until the fifth paragraph from the last; and a couple of others, in the same category—Christmas trees, holly, bright shop windows, snow, and all the old hokum. Thank goodness, I have learned a new type of story, and now only the ultra modern will do. However, if I don't find a satisfactory plot, I feel that I shall have to go back to the old style for a Christmas space filler."

The next day, a note came from the editor of the *Register*, telling the Author to send his Christmas contribution as soon as possible, since the Christmas number of the magazine *must* go to press sometime before February!

The immediate answer was (we do *not* excuse it) a lie, to the effect that the Author was hard at work on a contribution which would, when finished, take up sixteen typewritten pages. One of the Author's mottoes was borrowed from such sources as Police Headquarters and Public Hospitals: "When nothing has been done, report progress."

In truth, the Author rejected one plot after another—too childish, common, not modern enough, or too Christmassy (it really mentioned holly twice!)—until he was at his wit's end.

The editor gave him a week in which to submit his story, or else be dropped from the staff. The night the editor's epistle was received, the Author had almost given up hope, and decided that on the morrow he would surely start a story, even if it had to be about Santa Claus and Christmas tree.

The Author, being ultra-modern, as we have previously stated, would have refused to employ plots at all, except that the *Register* demanded them. So, of course, he refused to write about Santa Claus. Not because he was compelled to use plots, but because he was ultra-modern. It was his firm belief, as we have also stated, that the old fellow did not exist.

In fact, he was so disrespectful towards the jolly saint that he frequently referred to him (satirically) as "The adverbial—pardon me, I meant Santa—clause." Or, "I wonder whom Santa Claws"; or again, he referred in an article which he had had published to "St. Nick—the Old Nick canonised." And so, *ad nauseam*.

Now when the Author slept, he usually did so in a large four-poster bed with a tester, and drawn side-curtains. After he had decided to write a Santa

Claus story, he removed the typewriter ribbon preparatory to inserting a new one—he had gone the maximum number of miles on *that* tape. He threw out his worn carbon sheets, and saw to it that a sufficient amount of paper was at hand. He then covered his typewriter with a cover to protect it from the dust. These preparations for the morning finished, he got into bed and drew the side-curtains. Almost as soon as his head touched the pillow, he slept.

His sleep was untroubled by dreams, and it seemed to him that he had closed his eyes for only a moment when he was aroused suddenly by a touch as of a soft brush being drawn across his face. He sat up and looked about him.

His side-curtains were still drawn, admitting no light. They seemed perfectly still. "Pshaw!" he exclaimed aloud, "I must have been dreaming." And he sought once more to embrace the elusive Morpheus. Finally, as he was just starting to doze off, he had the same sensation; this time he parted the curtains and peered into the room. At first he saw nothing, but the moon cast a little more light through the clouds, and gave to the room a dim duskiness. Casting its beams into the room through two windows, the moon made two hazy patches on the floor. By the light, the Author could see nothing which might have been the cause of his disturbance. He walked over to look out the window. The moon, as if to frustrate his desires, hid behind a huge bank of snowy clouds at his approach.

The Author went back to bed. A third time he was awakened. This time he sat up in bed and addressed the void around him. "Who's there?" he inquired.

"Can't you see me?" came a voice out of the darkness.

"Another American, at least," thought the Author, "answering one question with another." To his surprise, the voice answered his unuttered thought.

"Wrong again," said the voice, "we spirits have no nationality; when in America, I speak American—or English, as the case may be."

"Wrong *again*? I didn't say anything before that."

"Oh, yes, you did. You said, 'Pshaw, I must have been dreaming.' And you weren't."

"Are you a ghost?" asked the Author.

"Yes, the ghost of a world-wide celebrity."

"You must be invisible, then, if what I have heard of ghosts is true. But, then, I don't believe in ghosts."

"I am not invisible, and whether you believe in ghosts or not, I am one."

"But I didn't see anyone round when I just got up," objected the Author.

"Well, I'm not as *round* as I'm usually painted, if you will excuse the pun," said the spirit, "and besides, I was over in the corner out of sight."

"Were you hiding there? If so, why?"

"Yes, and because."

"Because what?"

"Because I seem to have a propensity for joking."

"I wonder who he is," thought the Author.

"I am one whose existence you doubt," came the answer to his thought.

"Who said I don't believe your existence, except inasmuch as you are a ghost? Who are you?"

"Open the curtain and take a look. Then your questions will answer themselves."

The Author opened the curtain and peered out. There, standing between him and the window, was a rather stout person, with white whiskers, a soiled red suit adorned with fur which was worn in spots. On his head was a red cap with a tassel. But the most amazing thing, in the Author's opinion, was the fact that, although his visitor should be blocking his view of the window, he could see the window right through him.

The Author looked at this apparition for fully a minute, dazed. Was it really the jolly looking fellow of the picture post cards who was thus confronting him? Did he *really* exist? Or was it but a phantom creation of his own imagination?

The transparent trespasser interrupted his thoughts. "I see you do not recognise me. Well, I am a real, dead, fog and mist spirit. I am, I may say with as much modesty as possible, considering the circumstances, the most popular spirit there is at this time of year."

"Not—?"

"Yes."

"But you look so thin—comparatively, I mean, and tired looking. And those clothes—"

"Thin and tired, from late hours this past week. Transparent, from having died so long ago, and consequently being only a shade. You should see some of the newer shades… As to my clothes, these," indicating his costume, "are my working togs."

"But—"

"I came here with a twofold purpose in mind. To convince you of my existence, and to deliver a story."

"A story?"

"Yes. For you to have published under your name. That is what kept me working late nights recently. You see, I have been so very busy this time of year, that I haven't had much time to write. I have been working on this story ever since I gave Dickens the idea for his 'Christmas Carol.'"

"What! You gave Dickens—?"

"Why certainly! All the really great Christmas stories that have been written since the time of Noah—"

"But Noah was long before—"

"Don't interrupt your elders, it isn't polite. Now, where was I?… Yes, all the Christmas stories ever written were inspired by me; the greatest, directly, and the others were copied from those. And poems—"

"I didn't know you were an author, much less a poet!" exclaimed the Author.

"It isn't generally known, but I was the poet who invented the pterodactyl meter," said the bewhiskered myth.

"Why, Santa Claus, I never believed it of you."

Santa sighed. "Well, I suppose I don't look it, but I have written some real poetry in my time." Then he resumed after a pause, "But to go on with my story. I have always wanted to see my masterpiece in print. Since I didn't start to write it until I had died, it was difficult to find a publisher who would undertake to print a story by a spirit. And then, too, my other work takes up so much of my time, I haven't much time left in which to write. You see, I get the first part written, and when I am on the last part, the fashions on earth are changed. So I have to rewrite the first part. I knew you were in need of a story, and I hastened to polish this up, and bring it all up to date, in time for you to send it to the publisher. In order to convince you of my existence, I needed some material proof. This is furnished by the story which shall remain your property when I have disappeared."

"But," said the Author, as Santa proffered a sheaf of gelatinous-looking hand-written sheets to him, "that would be plagiarism."

"Well, if you try to publish it under *my* name, the public would aver that you wrote it yourself anyway, or that you were crazy altogether. Under your own name— Why that's no worse than Dickens did, using my idea for a story."

"But you see," argued the Author, "he clothed the plot in his own words. Every author has his own style, besides, and the story would be instantly recognised as the work of another."

"No, indeed. You see, another reason I am giving *you* this story is that you write in almost exactly my style, so the difference will not be noticed."

"Well, I suppose it's all right to do it to help out the editor; but remember, I do not give my approval. I wouldn't do it to benefit myself, but I am expected to fill the space."

"I'm glad you're taking a sensible view of it at last… By the way, you write under a pseudonym, don't you?"

"Yes, but what difference does that make?"

"Well, you see, you are not offering stories under your own name, so the public knows only the *nom de plume*."

"True, my stories are all published under the name of *George G. George*."

"There! You see, to the public, George G. George may be a man or a woman."

"Yes."

"Or it may be more than one author. Thus, after the Christmas issue, George G. George shall be two people—you and I."

"In that case, I give my hearty approval. But does the story come up to my standard?"

"Does it? And how! Why, it far surpasses anything you ever wrote. I have been working on it three times as long as you've been on earth, and then some. That story alone will make George G. George go down in history as a great author."

"Then I'll mail it at once."

"No; you must type it first. It is written by hand."

The Author examined the manuscript. The room was very dimly lighted by the moon, but the letters seemed to glow so that he could read it distinctly.

"I'll type it at once," he announced. "Won't you be seated while I copy it?"

"Thanks. Would you mind returning the original when you have finished with it?"

"Of course not. Would you rather have a carbon copy?"

The vague visitor smiled. "I believe you threw away the old carbon paper tonight, or rather last night. Have you any more?"

The Author looked in his desk. "I guess I haven't any left at that. I sha'n't need a carbon copy for myself, as I shall keep a copy of the Christmas Number for my files."

The Author did not turn on the electric light, because Santa said that he would have to leave if strong light were to shine upon him. "I'm only a spirit you know. And the manuscript would likewise become invisible."

The Author began to click away at the story. He became so interested that the faster he read, the faster he typed, and soon he was at the end of the story. "That," he said, his eye gleaming with pride for a fellow-author, "is the best story I have ever read—and that's going some. The best part of it is that it's as modern as my latest, and more than twice as interesting."

Santa seemed to beam all over. "Thank you. I thought you'd like it. And now I must be going. It's almost daylight."

The Author returned the gelatinous manuscript with fervent thanks. "Won't you come to see me once in a while, now that I believe you exist?"

"Thanks, I will. And I shall wake you the same way as I did this time—by letting my hirsute facial adornment oscillate gently above your somnolent countenance, as they sometimes say in books." With this, he was gone; melted into the atmosphere, it seemed. The Author went to the window and stood gazing out. It was the grey dawn of a cold winter's morning. Outside, the snow was falling, and the earth was already covered with a thin sheet of glistening whiteness.

The Author counted the typewritten papers in his hand. There were sixteen—just the number he had promised! He folded the story, and placed it in an envelope, which he addressed and left on his desk.

He was soon back in bed, with no story to trouble him for a while. He dozed off…

The next morning when he awoke, he had almost forgotten the incidents of the previous night and the early part of the morning, and with great difficulty recalled them. The plot of the story he could not remember. In fact, he remembered nothing of the story save that it was the most excellent Christmas story he had ever read.

"I wonder if it was all a dream," he mused. "If so, there will be no envelope on my desk." But there was. He mailed it as soon as possible. "It will be great to read something I've submitted, and not remember what it is until I see it in print. I suppose I shall easily recall it as soon as I see it though."

The next day a letter came from the editor. It ran—

"… and I have decided that it is about time to get to work. You have three days in which to write a Christmas story, or to be dropped from our staff. I refuse to stand any of your nonsense in such a crucial time.

"However, your extremely silly practical joke will be forgiven, if you have a good story by the end of the week. Please do not keep me in suspense any longer…"

The Author read it through, and hastily dispatched a telegram to inquire what was wrong with the story he sent, or whether it had been received; and what was the practical joke referred to.

"Did he discover that I didn't write the story," he questioned himself, "and if so, how?"

The reply arrived before noon.

"We received the sixteen pages, but they were all blank."

The Author stared at the yellow slip. Sixteen blank pages! He rushed over to his typewriter and removed the cover which was supposed to protect it from dust. Then, for the first time since the evening of Santa's arrival, he discovered there was no ribbon to imprint the letters on the paper.

He sat dejectedly on the side of his bed. "I guess there isn't anything to do now but make a clean breast of the affair, and take the consequences."

That afternoon was spent in carefully typing a letter to the editor, explaining his part in the so-called practical joke, and, where it was possible, laying most of the blame on poor Old Nick—pardon me, St. Nicholas.

"As an explanation," the editor replied, "your letter was a total failure. As a piece of fiction, it is the best Christmas story you have ever written, and as such, has the place of honour in this issue. It was not quite sixteen pages, but we can fill the rest of the magazine with poetry about Christmas and mistletoe. The public always falls for that."

SHADOWS OF EVIL
OR, THE FATAL DREAM

Anonymous

First published in The New Monthly Magazine, *volume 148, 1871*

While I haven't been able to decode the story's author, the editor of *The New Monthly Magazine*, William Francis Ainsworth, was a surgeon, distinguished geologist, traveller and cousin of the novelist William Harrison Ainsworth. He founded the West London Hospital and was the Honorary Treasurer of it until his death.

"Shadows of Evil" is a suitably macabre tale on which to end things and I hope that you get through it *relatively* unscathed. I also hope you are around to read this book with your loved ones *next* Christmas (I'm foreshadowing the story here). This tale has never been reprinted since 1871.

"Oh! grandmamma, do tell us a story—a nice, horrible Christmas ghost story."

So pleaded little Alice, putting up a bright-eyed, saucy, rosy little face to my old, wrinkled, faded one, and her request was instantly followed up by a chorus of:

"Oh, yes! Do, please do! How delightful!" from all the young folks now fast leaving their different occupations, and gathering round their granny by the fire.

It was a pretty sight, and one that made my old heart glad, to see the eager, flushed faces upturned towards mine in wondering expectation, the firelight glimmering and playing on the little golden heads and parted rosy lips. And my thoughts went back to other Christmas nights, long, long past, when my hair was as bright, and my eyes as young and happy, as those of my little grandchildren sitting here at my feet.

Retrospection is, I think, always more or less sad, and I felt my eyes growing dim and wet, when little Alice again impatiently demanded a ghost story, and brought me back from the past to the present with a start—from the past, peopled with so many dear dead ghosts, to this present Christmas night, bright with the glowing firelight, and merry with the laughing childish voices. I recollected a strange weird story that had had great fascination for me when I was a girl. This story I had found in an old manuscript, a sort of diary belonging to my father. It had been written by an aunt of his, to whom the tale had been related by one of the actors in it. I had kept this manuscript by me; so, being the only ghost-story I could think of, I sent one of the children for it, and determined to read them that. As for its truth I certainly cannot vouch; but that consideration, I thought, was not very likely to trouble the heads of my little grandchildren.

MY GREAT-AUNT'S STORY

I haven't slept for three nights and days now, and begin to feel fairly worn out. A lady—a dear friend of ours—is dying; the doctor says there is no hope of recovery, and the end must be very near. How solemnly beautiful she looks! Lying there so still and white, the long black lashes drooping over the wasted cheeks, and the thick, white hair thrown back over the pillow from the low, broad brow. Sitting here in my chair by the bedside, and looking at her lying there so calm and motionless, death seems to have lost all his terrors, to be rather some loving holy angel than the awful ruthless tyrant he is so often depicted. As I watch her my thoughts involuntarily go back to the time when we first met her, six years ago. Since then she has lived entirely with us, nominally in the capacity of governess to my two little children, though she has been far too much of an invalid ever to do very much.

Six years ago! It seems a long time, and yet, though the subject has been tacitly ignored during all that time, the story she told me then, comes back as vividly and clearly to my mind as when I first heard it. A strange eerie story it was, too; and as I feel I require a strong mental effort to keep me awake, I think I will employ the chilly, still hours of the night, in setting it down as well as I remember in her own words.

Six years ago my husband and I were taking a little holiday on the Continent, and, in the course of our travels, we stayed some time at an hotel in Antwerp. One morning I chanced to be in the coffee-room, in common with several other people who were breakfasting. I was reading the newspaper, and was holding it up so as to effectually hide my face. When I looked up, I noticed that a lady in deep mourning had entered. She was sitting still, bending forward, with her chin resting on her hand, apparently lost in deep thought. Her features were small and regular, her eyes were large and dark, and had a peculiarly startled, mournful expression. She was so pale as to be almost ghastly, and, though she did not look much above forty, her hair was white as snow. I was looking at her, wondering who she was, when she suddenly lifted her head and fixed her large, wild eyes on my face. She gazed at me for a minute or so, when, to my amazement, her expression changed from listless apathy to intense horror. Her features worked convulsively, her whole frame trembled, and she turned from white to livid. She staggered to her feet, and, trembling in every limb, advanced a few paces, cried in an unnatural, subdued scream, pointing at me:

"She—she—the murderess! The fiend—the fiend!" And, uttering a gasping cry, fell heavily to the ground.

She was carried upstairs, and a doctor sent for, but for two nights and days all efforts were powerless to arouse her from a state of insensibility, and when she did awake she was in a raging fever. It may be imagined that her illness caused no slight sensation in the hotel, and in spite of my assertion that I had never seen her before, I thought I was looked on with some suspicion and rather avoided; but this may have been only my fancy—my husband said it was.

At any rate, we were so much interested in the strange lady that we determined to stay in Antwerp until she was on a fair road to recovery. I tried to be of service in nursing and waiting on her, but was obliged to give it up; for as soon as she saw me at her bedside, though delirious, and recognising no one, she sprang up, shrieked out something about daughter, murder, and fiend, and fell back in a fit. Her illness was a dangerous and tedious one, but at last she was well enough to be moved to the sofa in her sitting-room. That same day she sent a message, saying she wished to see me. Now I didn't much like the idea of going alone, for, in the first place, I was fearful of making her worse again, and, in the second, I was rather afraid of her; for on the two occasions when we had met, her expression as well as her wild words had been so full of a strange hatred, that I thought she might try to do me a mischief.

However, I am easily persuaded, and I consented to go under my husband's escort. She was lying on the sofa, her chin resting on her hand, in the old position. When we entered, the strange expression I had noticed before again crossed her features, now fearfully lined and pallid, and we could see that she had great difficulty in commanding herself. Before I had half crossed the room, she almost screamed to me to come no nearer, and then, in an agitated voice, she put me through a perfect catechism as to who I was, my name, my age, where I lived, etc., becoming calmer and more composed as we proceeded. Among other things, she asked me to remove the hair from my forehead, and when I had done so she looked very much relieved. Presently she called me to sit by her on the sofa, and then, turning to us, she said:

"I feel that I owe you an explanation of my conduct, which must have appeared to you both strange and impertinent, and in a few days, when I hope to be stronger, I shall be quite ready to give you that explanation."

Then turning to me, and handing me a miniature which she took from her neck, she asked:

"Did you ever see any one like that?"

When I had looked I quite started, for it was the portrait of a girl exactly like myself. I feel this strange likeness a great drawback to describing her, as I am thus forced to describe myself as well—perhaps at the risk of being thought vain—but, *qu'importe?* Her skin was a clear olive, and quite colourless. Her hair was of a dark chestnut brown, very long and thick; her eyebrows were straight and black, as were her lashes. A straight, short nose, a full, small mouth, oval face, and great black eyes, which had a timid, scared look, completed the picture. When I returned the miniature, she said, in a low voice:

"That was my daughter!"

At her request we passed a portion of each day with her, in order, as she said, to get quite accustomed to me, and in a short time we became mutually attached. It was not till a few weeks later that she told us the story, as far as I can remember as follows:

*

Five years ago my husband died, and I and my daughter Pauline were left alone and friendless in the world. We had no near relations, and were all in all to each other. We were neither rich nor poor, but managed to live very comfortably, though very quietly, in a small house in London. Pauline was nineteen years of age, and was engaged to a young barrister—a Mr. Lawrence, to whom she was shortly going to be married. It was some few months after my dear husband's death that the awful curse that blighted, and eventually destroyed, her young life first began. She declared that, whenever she looked in a glass, she saw by the side of her own another face, the facsimile of her own. At first, thinking she couldn't be in earnest, we laughed, and joked her about it; but we were soon convinced of the reality of her own belief in it, for she got depressed and nervous, and at last so ill, that we became alarmed, and took her to a physician, who couldn't in the least understand her case, but thought her nerves must be out of order, and treated her accordingly, but without the slightest result. It was about this time that Pauline received an invitation from an old maiden aunt of my husband's to spend a month or two with her in Scotland. Glad of an opportunity of giving her change of air and scene, we readily consented to her going. She stayed away three months, and, when she returned, brought with her the tidings of her aunt's death, which had taken place very suddenly after a few days' illness. She seemed very glad to come home, and said she had been very dull and lonely in Scotland, never having seen anybody but her aunt and her two servants. On my asking her whether she were still annoyed by seeing double in a glass, she told me no—but said, that since she had been away she had been equally troubled in another way. I asked her in what way, and she told me that she constantly dreamt the same dream over and over again. It was a connected story, and took an entire week to complete, always being taken up where it was broken off the previous night; then she had one night's respite, and then came the same six nights' dream all over again. As she seemed very much agitated, I asked her if the dream were disagreeable?

"To me it is, very," she said, "and yet when you have heard it you will think me, perhaps, very foolish for minding it at all. I dreamt that one night my aunt and I were startled by a loud knocking at the gate, the cause of which proved to be a stranger who had lost his way, and asked shelter for himself and horse. Next morning I saw that he was a tall, fair man, with waving golden hair, and deep blue eyes that had an odd sneering look in them, and seemed to have the faculty of seeing right through you, and reading your thoughts. He was extremely handsome, and the delicacy of his complexion gave him almost an effeminate look. He exercised a strange power over those around him; everyone felt constrained and uncomfortable in his presence. He rarely spoke, and, when he did, it was in deep, measured, passionless tones, that sounded like the voice of a dead man. He continued staying with us, making himself quite at home, week after week, and while my aunt secretly resented this, she seemed utterly unable even to hint to him on the propriety of his going. Even the servants stood in awe of him, and obeyed him as their master, while over me his influence was almost boundless; he had but to express a wish, or look at me with his strange eyes, and I felt compelled to obey him. From the first I had disliked him, but now I positively hated him; but it was a hate mixed with fear. One day I was sitting by the little river that ran through my aunt's grounds, thinking that I would endure it no longer, but would return home, when, on looking up, I saw my tormentor, Mr. Mandeville, slowly coming towards me with his usual sneering smile playing on his lips and in his eyes. My first impulse was to fly, but he had seen me, and evidently wished to speak to me, and what he wished to do that I knew he would do. So I waited, and when he reached me he flung himself on the grass by my side, looked at me attentively for a minute or two in a way that made me shudder, and then said:

'"Good morning, Pauline; I have come here on purpose to talk to you.'

"I started; how dared he, a stranger, address me with such familiarity.

"'Sir,' I began, indignantly.

"'Ah!' he interrupted, with a low, musical, unmirthful laugh, 'I see you don't like being called Pauline? Well, it does not much matter, as I shall soon possess the right of calling you by whatever name I please.'

"I felt so astonished that I could do nothing but look an inquiry, to which, after gazing at me coldly and insolently, he presently replied:

"'You must be aware that *you* are the cause of my protracted stay in this place. At first I was simply struck by your great beauty. Then I grew interested in you—then I loved you.' He stopped, looked at me, and gave the same low musical laugh as before. 'You must have known I loved you.'

"And with that he tried to take my hand.

"'No! no!' I cried, snatching it away and shrinking back in terror.

"'Pauline,' he said, gently, but firmly, drawing me towards him, 'you will marry me, you *must* be my wife—say you will.'

"But I only answered with a sob. Then, taking me in his arms with an iron strength that defeated all my efforts at resistance, and utterly subdued me, he fixed his deep blue eyes on mine with an intensity I cannot describe, asking me at intervals if I would marry him. At first my answer was always 'No;' but after a time, under the influence of this strange mesmerism, I began to experience a new sensation of calm and happiness, and even love for this man. I felt that some power quite independent of myself was forcing me to do as he wished; but utterly unable to resist it. I actually promised to marry him whenever and as soon as he liked. Then he told me that, thinking I should consent, he had prepared everything, including the license and the witnesses, so that the marriage could take place at once. I seemed to be listening to him in a dream, and, scarcely had he finished speaking, when I fell fast asleep in his arms. When I recovered consciousness, I found myself in a little country church, which I knew to be about thirteen miles from my aunt's house; a clergyman and two other men who were present were strangers to me. And here the ceremony was performed, and I returned home the lawful wedded wife of a man who was almost a stranger to me, and whom, until today, I had detested. The marriage was kept a profound secret, and our life went on much as before, only that my husband's influence over me increased, and I gradually left off caring for him, and began to hate him even more than I had done before. We constantly quarrelled now—I was always trying to resist his authority, which I felt was becoming intolerable—and, in hopes of causing a separation or a divorce, I never let pass an opportunity of provoking, and even insulting him. Well, things went on like this for about two months, when one day during a quarrel, when I was in a great passion, I lost all control of myself, and struck him in the face.

"'So, Pauline,' he said, with an odious laugh, 'you have decided that it is to be war. Neither man nor woman has ever struck me before, and never shall again. I am sorry you have forced me to this.'

"So saying, he took hold of my hands and struck me a violent blow on the left temple. I fell sick and faint to the ground. He took me up in his arms, carried me to my own room, and bathed and bound my bleeding temple. I was ill for several weeks after that, and he tended and waited on me with the tenderest care possible. But I determined, in spite of his kindness, that as soon as I was well I would stop no longer with him; and accordingly, I had not been downstairs a week, when I left him and Scotland, and came to London home again."

And this was Pauline's dream. It certainly was a very remarkable one; but, however, I represented to her that after all it was only a dream, the repetition of which was probably caused by its having impressed her very much at first, and her nerves being in a very excitable state. I told her that I had often heard of dreams which were continued from night to night, and were quite as sensible and connected as hers, and had yet meant nothing, and had had no result whatever.

But this did not satisfy Pauline, for she declared that she knew the Philip Mandeville of her dream was really alive somewhere, and that some day he would come and claim her. Her marriage with Edward Lawrence was now at hand, and whether it was that she was so busy with her preparations I don't know, but whatever the cause, her troublesome dream quite ceased, and indeed she seemed to forget all about it. At last the wedding-day arrived. They were married very quietly, and went to spend a three weeks' holiday in Italy. They had taken a pretty little house close to mine, and I had got everything very nice and comfortable by the time they returned. Pauline was looking very well and happy—much better than when she went away—and was never troubled now with unpleasant dreams. They lived very quietly and happily in their new home for nearly two years, when, in obedience to a cruel fate, one miserable night our happiness was destroyed, and all our lives were blasted for ever, and the third and last act of the awful tragedy began.

It happened one evening Edward took Pauline and I to the opera. She was in high spirits that night, and was enjoying herself thoroughly—as, indeed, were we all. In the interlude before the last act, she took up the opera-glasses and began examining the people in the boxes, when suddenly she dropped the glasses, turned very white, and uttered a sort of moan.

"What is it, darling?" I asked.

She didn't answer, but turning to Edward, caught hold of his arm almost fiercely, and said, in a harsh whisper:

"Let us go home, let us go home this instant."

Surprised and rather alarmed, we got up and followed Pauline, who was already nearly at the door, and we had scarcely joined her in the entrance-hall when she fainted. The next morning she said she felt much better, but her face belied her, for she looked very ill and pale. When we were alone I asked her what had upset her so at the opera; and she told me, with a terrified look, that she had seen her dream husband, and that he had seen and recognised her. Of course I thought this was all nonsense, and only an accidental resemblance to an imaginary face, but there was no convincing Pauline that it was so, and she insisted on leaving London directly, and spending some time in the country. We were away about a month, and when we returned home late one evening, the servant told us that a gentleman had called, and was then waiting for us in the drawing-room. We asked his name, but he had given none, saying only that he was very well known to Pauline. On hearing this Pauline turned very pale, and trembled so violently that she had to lean against the wall for support.

"Edward," she moaned, "don't go, don't go; I don't know him, and I cannot see him."

But Edward, looking very stern and angry, said he must understand why she was so agitated at the presence of an utter stranger, and told her he insisted on her going. In reply, Pauline burst into tears, and implored him not to force her, on which Edward took hold of her arm and almost dragged her upstairs to the drawing-room. When we entered, a gentleman rose and advanced towards us, and I saw with a feeling of surprise and even terror, that in appearance he exactly resembled the description of the man of Pauline's almost forgotten dream. He advanced with a smile to Pauline, who was very pale, but quite calm now, took her hands in his, kissed her, saying, in a low voice:

"I have found you at last, my darling. I have come to take you home."

Pauline was quite passive, and spoke not a word; and, indeed, for a few moments we all seemed to be under a spell. Edward was the first to recover, and advancing to his wife, pulled her roughly from the stranger's grasp, saying, or rather screaming, for he was in an awful passion:

"Who are you that you dare to treat my wife thus?"

The gentleman appeared much surprised, looked first at Pauline, then at Edward, and then said, calmly:

"Who am I? My name is Philip Mandeville, and that lady is my wife."

"Your wife!"

"Yes, my wife; if you require proof, I can give it you."

He handed us what proved to be a certificate of marriage between himself, Philip Mandeville, and Pauline Rivers, properly registered, signed, and witnessed. We were stupefied, Edward even more so than I, as he had never even heard of the dream. I glanced at Pauline. She was standing motionless, white as death, but looking more asleep than awake, without any expression whatever on her face. I thought, could she have deceived me, had she really enacted what she had described to me as only a dream? Had she really married and fled from this man, and been base enough to marry another? This terrible thought made me turn faint and dizzy for a moment, and I was obliged to accept of a chair brought me by Mr. Mandeville. But after reflecting a few minutes, and remembering how good and true Pauline had been all her life, and that her visit to her aunt was the only time she had ever been separated from me, I came to the conclusion that she was the innocent died some months previously. She was very old and feeble; so old that her persistence in declaring that no stranger had ever visited her mistress at that or any other time, weighed very little in our favour, though our counsel made the most of it, and was eventually thrown entirely on one side. Our chance would, I think, have been greater if Pauline had not disclosed her dream, which was only treated as a silly fabrication.

Under the conviction that Philip Mandeville and his witnesses really believed that Pauline was his wife, we offered large rewards for the discovery of a woman resembling her, feeling certain that somewhere or other there must be such a woman. But it was all in vain. No such person could be found, and at last Edward wholly and openly doubted the truth of Pauline's story. But it was not so with me; no amount of evidence against her could shake my faith in her. And was I not right? For who in the whole world was so competent to judge of her guilt or innocence as I, who had known her all her life? But, nevertheless, this constant disappointment, and, still more, Edward's conviction of his wife's falseness, made us sadly disheartened. But, as a drowning man will catch at a straw, so I suddenly remembered that both in the dream and in our prosecutor's story he had struck her a severe blow on the temple. Ought there not to be a scar? This question was put to Mr. Mandeville, and he admitted having struck her, adding, with his mocking smile, that he had no doubt that she still bore traces of the scar. He seemed excessively surprised to find that there was no appearance of any scar whatever, but neither he nor the jury would believe that there never had been any, and in the end the verdict was given in favour of Mr. Mandeville, and Pauline was pronounced guilty of bigamy, we having to pay all costs. It is impossible to describe the misery we experienced when it was thus determined, for to Pauline I had always spoken as hopefully as I could of the truth being sure to prevail at last; so it was a still greater blow to her than to me. Her greatest grief was caused by Edward's never having come near us since the trial. With some difficulty we found out his address, for he was still in London, and Pauline wrote to him, imploring him to come and see her once more, if only to tell her he believed her. The next day he came to see us, but it was only to bid her farewell for ever, and to tell her that he never, never could forgive her.

He said that he was going to start for Australia that night. It was all in vain that Pauline wept and clung to him, going on her knees to him to implore him to take her with him; he only put her from him harshly and coldly. But he was so changed in appearance and voice, and looked so ill and broken-hearted, that even I, who saw him treat my poor child so, had not the heart to reproach him. That night he sailed, as he intended, and from that day to this he has been lost to us.

All these terrible events were too much for Pauline's health to withstand, and she had a dangerous attack of brain fever, from which she was never expected to recover. However, youth is strong and elastic, and after a weary two months, which nearly pulled me down, she was pronounced entirely out of danger. But never after that was she anything but a mere shadow of her former self. The beauty of feature was still hers, but she had lost for ever in this world the beauty of freshness and youth. Her great dark eyes, larger than ever now, seen in contrast with her thin, haggard face, always wore a mournful, startled, terrified expression.

Mr. Mandeville, who had constantly called during her illness, was now oftener at our house than ever, and nothing I could say or do could prevent him. He told Pauline that he was very anxious that they should renew their relations as husband and wife, but that he should never compel her against her wish I asked him how he could be so mean-spirited as to wish to live with a woman whom he must believe to have been false to him, and who he knew did not love him. He answered, with a laugh, that he loved her so much that he could forgive her anything, even the loss of her beauty.

For some considerable time Pauline was resolute in her determination to have nothing whatever to do with him; but gradually, to my dismay, this man seemed to be gaining a strange influence over her. She always knew instinctively when he was coming, and for some time previously would be very restless. She quite ceased showing any repugnance for him while he was with her, and would always show him the greatest deference, obeying his slightest word or wish, though after he had gone she would profess to hate him again as much as ever.

And so it went on, his power over her growing stronger and stronger, through, I am convinced, some horrible mesmeric influence, till one day, utterly regardless of my most earnest entreaties, she consented to become his wife.

In about a week from this time they started for the Continent, I accompanying them at Pauline's desire. For some time we travelled about, and finally we settled in a beautiful country-house near Liège. Mr. Mandeville appeared to be excessively fond of his wife, and was kindness itself to both of us, but in spite of his kindness and his attentions, I always detested him, construing them into hypocrisy and satire. Pauline, ever since we lived with him, seemed to have lost all individuality, and to have become a mere automaton. She always looked more asleep than awake, rarely spoke, always implicitly obeyed her so-called husband, passively accepted his affection, but never gave any in return, entirely lost all interest in everything, and habitually had an expression of vacancy, seeming more like a sleep-walker than a rational being. This impassiveness continued for about a year, when another change took place in her—another step nearer to the end. It was on the second anniversary of Edward's departure for Australia that she suddenly woke up as from a trance.

From that day her manner towards her husband totally changed. She no longer obeyed his every word and look; but, on the contrary, treated his wishes with open disrespect, avoided him as much as possible, repulsed his caresses, never said a civil word to him. In fact, she ceased to be the gentle being I had ever known her, and seemed to have regained more than her former hatred of him. At first he treated this open rebellion with great forbearance, never taking offence, thinking that she couldn't be well, and under this idea he even petted her more than before. But her manner towards him, instead of becoming better, became more and more insolent, and was at last so intolerable that her husband could stand it in silence no more, and the quarrels and altercations between them were frequent and violent, he never losing his temper, and always ending by subduing her with his quiet, cutting sarcasms. One day, during the course of a quarrel, Pauline said something very insulting; Philip insisted on her apologising, which she refusing to do, he commanded her to leave the room, and said he would carry her upstairs and lock her up if she refused to obey. But Pauline, who had worked herself up into a perfect frenzy of passion, without waiting for the threat to be fulfilled, went up to her husband, struck him in the face, and, without speaking a word, left the room.

Shocked, I hastened after her, and saw her distinctly entering my room. I followed her, but when I got into the room she was not there! Surprised and perplexed, I went along the passage leading to her own apartments, and, as I was looking, I saw her, as I thought, descending the stairs. I called to her, but she did not answer. I followed her downstairs, but when I got to the bottom, she was nowhere to be seen. More and more astonished and uneasy, I searched everywhere downstairs, and at last went up again, where I found Pauline lying insensible on her bed. When she recovered, I asked why she had not answered me when I called to her on the stairs. She said she had never been down at all, but had gone straight to her own room. And thus it was that the monstrous thing first appeared—for, from that day, Pauline, I, Philip, and the servants were constantly seeing another being, exactly like Pauline in face, figure, and dress, with this only difference, that this other had a fearful scar across the left temple. At first it was only seen occasionally, then more frequently, and at last continually. It haunted Pauline—wherever she went, it went—whatever she did, it did, as if in hideous mockery. Often, at dead of night, a fearful mocking, demoniac laugh would ring through the house, awakening and terrifying every one in it. We could keep no servants; one left as fast as another came, and we were shunned and avoided by everybody.

Philip had hitherto treated Pauline with great gentleness and forbearance, but now his conduct towards her underwent a great change. He neglected her utterly. He seemed to have a horror of any one seeing her— and who can wonder, attended as she always was by that fearful shadow? He kept her entirely shut up in her own apartments, allowing no one but victim of some horrible, mysterious plot, but whether devised by man or devil I knew not.

Presently, after a scene of furious altercation between the two men, Mr. Mandeville turned to Pauline, and bade her come with him, but she, suddenly acquiring speech and action, and shrinking from his touch, shrieked out:

"No, no, no! Edward! Mother! Save me!" and fell fainting into my arms.

We carried her upstairs, where I remained with her, leaving Edward to dismiss our unwelcome guest; and when I came down in the evening I heard that he had gone soon after we had left the room, saying that we should shortly hear of him again through his lawyer. And this was no empty threat, for, two days afterwards—during which time Edward had been to Scotland, and found in Goldmore church the registered entry of the marriage, and signed in Pauline's own handwriting—we received a letter from his lawyer, summoning us to appear at court. The evidence went terribly against us; Mr. Mandeville produced the witnesses and the clergyman, who all swore to Pauline as the woman at whose marriage in Goldmore church they had been present. He also gave the whole story of his acquaintance with her, which tallied with the dream in date and circumstance exactly. In fact, the evidence on his side was complete—there was not a single loophole—while we, on the contrary, had not a shred. No one but Edward and I—and even his belief was far from strong, but only born of a wild, despairing, reasonless hope—believed in Pauline's story that she had never seen, much less married, this man but in a dream, and our belief in her was less than no use. Her aunt, who could have proved that no gentleman had ever stayed with her during Pauline's residence in Scotland, was dead. Her house was situated in a wild, uninhabited part of the country, the nearest village being ten miles off. She was extremely unsocial and retiring in her habits, wanted no friends, and made none. Her entire household consisted of but herself and two servants, both of whom had lived with her parents before her, and were then extremely old. These servants were sought for, and summoned to appear at the trial, but only one answered the summons, the other having himself and me to be with her, and never allowed her to go out, except when he himself took her to walk in the gardens, which he had caused to be walled all round. He would often absent himself for weeks at a time, and when he returned would sometimes fill the house with visitors; and then for days there would be nothing but feasting, and drinking, and music, and dancing, interrupted every now and again by the terrible unearthly laugh, which would startle the guests in the midst of their feasting, and turn the women pale with fear.

At these entertainments he never permitted his wife to be present, always explaining to his guests that she was either away on a visit, or in too delicate a state of health to allow of any excitement. But his constant ill-treatment never reached actual violence—he never lost his temper even. His lips were for ever set in a mirthless stereotyped smile; his low musical voice never changed in key or intonation; yet he never let an opportunity pass of wounding my unhappy child's feelings by his quiet sneers, taunting her about her lost husband, and her awful fiend attendant. And still the dreadful double never left her, and from having at first been half frightened to death by it, she was fast becoming reconciled to its horrid presence. It used to talk to her, giving her advice, and telling her to do this or that—she always quietly obeying it.

Under its devilish influence a great change came over Pauline. Till then she had always confided everything to me, talked to and consulted me freely on every subject; but now she became sullen and moody—would go for whole days without speaking a word, and taunted and insulted her husband more than ever, the fiend always at her elbow inciting her on. And still the strange, wild cries continued night after night, and day after day, making one's blood run cold.

Sometimes I tried to speak to Pauline of the mysterious shadow that haunted her; but she would never allow me to say anything on the subject, saying it was no business of mine—it did me no harm. At last, one awful night, I was awakened by the sound of a shot, followed by a yell, so fiendish, so discordant, and so triumphant, that I shuddered to the very marrow.

Hurriedly throwing something over me, I rushed to my daughter's room, whence the sound proceeded, and was there met by a sight so ghastly and horrible, that I staggered back almost fainting against the wall. On the bed lay Philip Mandeville, in a pool of his own blood, dead—Pauline, a pistol in her hand, was lying beside him insensible—and over them both was her semblance standing out dark and distinct against the brilliant moonlight that was streaming through the window, with an expression of fiendish triumph and delight on its ghastly features, the horrid scar standing out red and swollen from the livid deathlike brow. One hand was grasping Pauline by the throat as if trying to strangle her, and the other, red with blood, was waving wildly in the air. I, together with the servants who had rushed to the room, shrank back in terror.

"Mine, mine—she is mine for ever!" shrieked the fearful monster, and vanished.

Philip Mandeville was dead—murdered—and murdered by Pauline. She herself confessed to having done the deed at the instigation of the fiend. She became a prey to bitter remorse, which brought on another attack of brain fever, and within a month of her husband's death she was hopelessly insane.

The law acquitted her of the crime on the plea of insanity, and she was allowed to remain where she was under my care. She had temporary intervals of sanity, when she would implore me to save her from the fiend, who still continued to haunt her. In her ravings she would constantly call on Edward, and implore him to come to her, saying that she had avenged him. And so we dragged on six weary months; when one night—the whole of the preceding day she had been perfectly sane and rational, though very weak and ill—I was awakened by the same fiendish yell as before, and found my dear child lying beside me, quite dead, with a knife buried in her heart, and the demon bending exultingly over her.

Having finished the last words, I laid aside my pen and went to the bedside to see if Mrs. Rivers still slept. Bending over her I gently kissed her pallid brow, and started back to find it cold as ice.

Yes, she was indeed at rest now, for, even as I was writing, her sorely tried spirit had bade farewell to its earthly home, and was winging its happy way to rejoin her poor murdered child in a brighter, purer world than ours.

And here my aunt's manuscript ended. I closed the faded, yellow leaves, laid aside my spectacles, and drew my chair closer to the fire, and for a few minutes no one spoke.

It made me smile to see the little round faces looking so very grave, so prematurely wise.

"Is it true, grandmamma?" at last asks little Alice, looking up with her great, wide blue eyes, in a whispered voice, as if timid of breaking the silence.

"I cannot tell you, my child," I answered, smoothing the bright soft curls; "but true or not, you may be sure Pauline is happy now."

"But the demon claimed her for ever, granny," the child continued, in a low, awed tone.

"Then take my word for it, my dear, that the fiend overstated his power; for, however deep the mystery, and however great the suffering, all God's creatures are certain to be good and happy *at last*. And now don't you think we had better ring for supper?" I went on, kissing her soft red lips. "What say you, little folks all—wouldn't you like to renew your acquaintance with the Christmas pudding?"

"Oh, yes—let us have supper," chimed in a chorus of small voices; and, under the influence of this new idea, the spell was broken—they seemed entirely to forget the story I had just read, and chattered, and played, and laughed as merrily as ever.

At last supper was over, and that period arrived when even plum-pudding ceased to charm, and at length all the sleepy little heads were softly nestled to rest, where everything was forgotten in sweet dreamless sleep. But I sat up long by the glowing firelight, thinking of dear old friends and sweet familiar faces—now long since dead and gone—and wondering if I should ever see another Christmas night on earth.

ACKNOWLEDGEMENTS

This is the fifth hardback I've published with the British Library, and I have so much fun digging around, trying to find lost, rare and unusual stories to put in what I hope are eclectic, fun and joyous volumes. However, my editor who first commissioned me, Jonny Davidson, has left his permanent role at the British Library. Jonny, thank you so much for giving me the chance to join the British Library family and being with me through some incredible books, and also for your unwavering support when I had to go for a pretty serious heart procedure in 2024. I'm honoured to call you a friend, and this book is dedicated to you. Your time, effort and love that's gone into collecting this trove of supernatural writing is so much bigger than us and will outlive us. It's bloody marvellous. You should be so very proud of what you've achieved. I'm very proud of you.

To Cerys at British Library Publishing, who keeps me sane and on the straight and narrow: thank you, you're a dear friend. To Gary Wigglesworth for sending me books. I love you!

To Mike Ashley, as always, for his research skills and advice.

To family Mains who know the signs a major deadline is coming up and just let me get on with it.

To you, dear reader! Look at the book you've bought or have been gifted! Isn't it lush? Take it next to the Christmas tree, let the foil of this book come alive under the fairy lights. If you're a new reader or have been with me from the start, thank you. I don't take my role in your life as Storyfinder General for granted, and I'm looking forward to the macabre journeys we'll discover together with my future books!

JM

PS: Those who want to explore the televisual aspect of ghost stories at Christmas would do well to pre-order the estimable Jon Dear's forthcoming book *No Digging: The Story of the BBC Ghost Stories for Christmas* (Headpress, 2026). It's going to make for such a great Christmas present next year.

JOHNNY MAINS is an eminent anthologist renowned for finding "lost" works of fiction. His latest books have been *His Beautiful Hands: The Short Stories of Oscar Cook* (Ramble House, 2025), *The Dead of Summer: Strange Tales of May Eve & Midsummer* (British Library, 2025), *At the Change of the Moon* by Bernard C. Blake (Mislaid Books, 2025) and *The Devil's Cauldron: A Story for Christmas* by J. W. Nicholas (Mislaid Books, 2025).